KU-781-267

CONTENTS

The Triumph of the Scarlet Pimpernel

by Baroness Orczy

CORONET BOOKS
Hodder and Stoughton

This edition published 1998 by Hodder & Stoughton
A division of Hodder Headline PLC

A Coronet paperback

The right of Baroness Orczy to be identified as the Author of
the Work has been asserted in accordance with the
Copyright, Designs and Patents Act 1988.

10 9 8 7 6 5 4 3

British Library Cataloguing in Publication data

A CIP catalogue record for this title
is available from the British Library

ISBN 0 340 73945 2

Printed and bound in Great Britain by
Clays Ltd, St Ives plc

Hodder and Stoughton
A division of Hodder Headline PLC
338 Euston Road
London NW1 3BH

CHAPTER 1

'The Everlasting Stars Look Down, Like Glistening Eyes Bright with Immortal Pity, Over the Lot of Man'

I

Nearly five years have gone by!

Five years, since the charred ruins of grim Bastille – stone image of Absolutism and of Autocracy – set the seal of victory upon the expression of a people's will and marked the beginning of that marvellous era of Liberty and of Fraternity which has led us step by step from the dethronement of a King, through the martyrdom of countless innocents, to the tyranny of an oligarchy more arbitrary, more relentless, above all more cruel, than any that the dictators of Rome or Stamboul ever dreamed of in their wildest thirst for power. An era that sees a populace always clamouring for the Millennium, which ranting demagogues have never ceased to promise: a Millennium to be achieved alternatively through the extermination of Aristocracy, of Titles, of Riches, and the abrogation of Priesthood: through dethroned royalty and desecrated altars, through an army without leadership, or an Assembly without power.

They have never ceased to prate, these frothy rhetoricians! And the people went on, vaguely believing that one day, soon, that Millennium would surely come, after seas of blood had purged the soil of France from the last vestige of bygone oppression, and after her sons and daughters had been massacred in their thousands and their tens of thousands, until their headless bodies had built up a veritable scaling ladder for the tottering feet of lustful climbers, and these in their turn had perished to make way for other ranters, other speechmakers, a new Demosthenes or long-tongued Cicero.

Inevitably these too perished, one by one, irrespective of their virtues or their vices, their errors or their ideals. They slew and were slain in their turn. They struck blindly, like raging beasts, most of them for fear lest they too should be struck by beasts more furious than they. All have perished; but not before their iniquities have for ever sullied what might have been the most glorious page in the history of France – her fight for Liberty. Because of these monsters – and of a truth there were only a few – the fight, itself sublime in its ideals, noble in its conception, has become abhorrent to the rest of mankind.

But they, arraigned at the bar of history, what have they to say, what to show as evidence of their patriotism, the purity of their intentions?

On this day of April, 1794, year II of the New Calendar, eight thousand men, women, and not a few children, are crowding the prisons of Paris to overflowing. Four thousand heads have fallen under the guillotine in the past three months. All the great names of France, her noblesse, her magistracy, her clergy, members of past Parliaments, shining lights in the sciences, the arts, the Universities, men of substance, poets, brain-workers, have been torn from their homes, their churches or their places of refuge, dragged before a travesty of justice, judged, condemned and slaughtered; not singly, not individually, but in batches – whole families, complete hierarchies, entire households: one lot for the crime of being rich, another for being nobly born; some because of their religion, others because of professed free-thought. One man for devotion to his friend, another for perfidy; one for having spoken, another for having held his tongue, and another for no crime at all – just because of his family connexions, his profession, or his ancestry.

For months it had been the innocents; but since then it has also been the assassins. And the populace, still awaiting the Millennium, clamour for more victims and for more – for the aristocrat and for the sans-culotte, and howl with execration impartially at both.

II

But through this mad orgy of murder and of hatred, one man survives, stands apart indeed, wielding a power which the whole pack of infuriated wolves thirsting for his blood are too cowardly to challenge. The Girondists and the Extremists have fallen. Hébert, the idol of the mob, Danton its hero and its mouthpiece, have been hurled form their throne, sent to the scaffold along with ci-devant nobles, aristocrats, royalists and traitors. But this one man remains, calm in the midst of every storm, adored, almost deified, by a few, dreaded by all, sphinx-like, invulnerable, sinister – Robespierre!

Robespierre at this time was at the height of his popularity and of his power. The two great Committees of Public Safety and of General Security were swayed by his desires, the Clubs worshipped him, the Convention was packed with obedient slaves to his every word. The Dantonists, cowed into submission by the bold coup which had sent their leader, their hero, their idol, to the guillotine, were like a tree that has been struck at the root.

Robespierre was in truth absolute master of France. The man who had dared to drag his only rival down to the scaffold was beyond the reach of any attack. By this final act of unparalleled despotism he had revealed the secrets of his soul, shown himself to be rapacious as well as self-seeking. Something of his aloofness, of his incorruptibility, had vanished, yielding to that ever-present and towering ambition which hitherto none had dared to suspect. But ambition is the one vice to which the generality of mankind will always accord homage, and Robespierre, by gaining the victory over his one rival, had virtually begun to rule, whilst his colleagues in the Convention, in the Clubs and in the Committees, had tacitly agreed to obey. The tyrant out of his vaulting ambition had brought forth the slaves.

Faint-hearted and servile, they brooded over their wrongs, gazed with smouldering wrath on Danton's vacant seat in the Convention, which no one cared to fill. But they did not murmur, hardly dared to plot, and gave assent to every decree, every measure, every suggestion promulgated by the dictator who held their lives in the hollow of his thin white hand; who with a word, a gesture, could send his enemy, his detractor, a mere critic of his actions, to the guillotine.

CHAPTER 2

Feet of Clay

I

On this 26th day of April, 1794, three women and one man were assembled in a small, closely curtained room on the top floor of a house in the Rue de la Planchette, which is situated in a remote and dreary quarter of Paris. The man sat upon a chair which was raised on a dais. He was neatly, indeed immaculately, dressed, in dark cloth coat and tan breeches, with clean linen at throat and wrists, white stockings and buckled shoes. His own hair was concealed under a mouse-coloured wig. He sat quite still, with one leg crossed over the other, and his thin, bony hands were clasped in front of him.

Behind the dais there was a heavy curtain which stretched right across the room, and in front of it, at opposite corners, two young girls, clad in grey, clinging draperies, sat upon their heels, with the palms of their hands resting flat upon their thighs. Their hair hung loose down their backs, their chins were uplifted, their eyes fixed, their bodies rigid in an attitude of contemplation. In the centre of the room a woman stood, gazing upwards at the ceiling, her arms folded across her breast. Her grey hair, lank and unruly, was partially hidden by an ample floating veil of an indefinite shade of grey, and from her meagre shoulders and arms, her garment – it was hardly a gown – descended in straight, heavy, shapeless folds. In front of her was a small table, on it a large crystal globe, which rested on a stand of black wood, exquisitely carved and inlaid with mother-of-pearl, and beside it a small metal box.

Immediately above the old woman's head an oil lamp shed a feeble and lurid light upon the scene. Against the wall half a dozen chairs, on the floor a threadbare carpet, and in one corner a broken-down chiffonier represented the sum total of the furniture in the stuffy little room. The curtains in front of the window, as well as the portières which masked both the doors, were heavy and thick, excluding all light and most of the outside air.

The old woman, with eyes fixed upon the ceiling, spoke in a dull, even monotone.

'Citizen Robespierre, who is the Chosen of the Most High, hath deigned to enter the humble abode of his servant,' she said. 'What is his pleasure today?'

'The shade of Danton pursues me,' Robespierre replied, and his voice too sounded toneless, as if muffled by the heavily weighted atmosphere. 'Can you not lay him to rest?'

The woman stretched out her arms.

'Blood!' she exclaimed in a weird, cadaverous wail. 'Blood around thee and blood at they feet! But not upon thy head, O Chosen of the Almighty! Thy decrees are those of the Most High! Thy hand wields His avenging Sword! I see thee walking upon a sea of blood, yet thy feet are as white as lilies and thy garments are spotless as the driven snow. Avaunt,' she cried in sepulchral tones, 'ye spirits of evil! Avaunt, ye vampires and ghouls! and venture not with your noxious breath to disturb the serenity of our Morning Star!'

The girls in front of the dais raised their arms above their heads and echoed the old soothsayer's wails.

'Avaunt!' they cried solemnly. 'Avaunt!'

Now from a distant corner of the room, a small figure detached itself out of the murky shadows. It was the figure of a young negro, clad in white from head to foot. In the semi-darkness the draperies which he wore were alone visible, and the whites of his eyes. Thus he seemed to be walking without any feet, to have eyes without any face, and to be carrying a heavy vessel without using any hands. His appearance indeed was so startling and so unearthly that the man upon the dais could not suppress an exclamation of terror. Whereupon a wide row of dazzlingly white teeth showed somewhere between the folds of the spectral draperies, and further enhanced the spook-like appearance of the blackamoor. He carried a deep bowl fashioned of chased copper, which he placed upon the table in front of the old woman, immediately behind the crystal globe and the small metal box. The seer then opened the box, took out a pinch of something brown and powdery, and holding it between finger and thumb, she said solemnly:

'From out the heart of France rises the incense of faith, of hope, and of love!' and she dropped the powder into the bowl. 'May it prove acceptable to him who is her chosen Lord!'

A bluish flame shot up from out the depth of the vessel, shed for the space of a second or two its ghostly light upon the gaunt features of the old hag, the squat and grinning face of the negro, and toyed with will-o'-the-wisp-like fitfulness with the surrounding gloom. A sweet-scented smoke rose upwards to the ceiling. Then the flame died down again, making the crimson darkness around appear by contrast more lurid and more mysterious than before.

Robespierre had not moved. He accepted the tangible

incense, took a deep breath, as if to fill his entire being with its heady fumes, just as he was always ready to accept the fulsome adulation of his devotees and of his sycophants.

The old charlatan then repeated her incantations. Once more she took powder from the box, threw some of it into the vessel, and spoke in a sepulchral voice:

'From out the heart of those who worship thee rises the incense of their praise!'

A delicate white flame rose immediately out of the vessel. It shed a momentary, unearthly brightness around, then as speedily vanished again. And for the third time the witch spoke the mystic words:

'From out the heart of an entire nation rises the incense of perfect joy in thy triumph over thine enemies!'

This time, however, the magic powder did not act quite so rapidly as it had done on the two previous occasions. For a few seconds the vessel remained dark and unresponsive, nothing came to dispel the surrounding gloom. Even the light of the oil lamp overhead appeared suddenly to grow dim. At any rate, so it seemed to the autocrat who sat clutching the arms of his chair, his narrow eyes fixed upon the sybil, who in her turn was gazing on the metal vessel as if she would extort some cabalistic mystery from its depth.

All at once a bright red flame shot out of the bowl. The old witch bending over her cauldron looked as if she were smeared with blood, her eyes appeared bloodshot, her long hooked nose cast a huge black shadow over her mouth, distorting the face into a hideous, cadaverous grin. From her throat issued strange sounds like those of an animal in the throes of pain.

'Red! Red!' she lamented, and gradually as the flame subsided and finally flickered out altogether, her words became more distinct. She raised the crystal globe and gazed fixedly into it. 'Always red,' she went on slowly.

'Thrice yesterday did I cast the spell in the name of Our Chosen . . . thrice did the spirits cloak their identity in a blood-red flame . . . red . . . danger of death through that which is red . . .'

'A truce on riddles, Mother!' Robespierre exclaimed at last impatiently, and descended hastily from the dais. He approached the old necromancer, seized her by the arm, thrust his head in front of hers in an endeavour to see something which apparently was revealed to her in the crystal globe. 'What is it you see in there?' he queried harshly.

But she pushed him aside, gazed with rapt intentness into the globe.

'Red!' she murmured. 'Scarlet . . . aye, scarlet! And now it takes shape . . . Scarlet . . . and it obscures the Chosen One . . . the shape becomes more clear . . . the Chosen One appears more dim . . .'

Then she gave a piercing shriek.

'Beware! . . . beware! . . . that which is Scarlet is shaped like a flower . . . five petals, I see them distinctly . . . and the Chosen One I see no more . . .'

'Malediction!' the man exclaimed. 'What foolery is this?'

'No foolery,' the old charlatan resumed in a dull monotone. 'Thou didst consult the oracle, oh thou, who art the Chosen of the people of France! and the oracle has spoken. Beware of a scarlet flower! From that which is scarlet comes danger of death for thee!'

Whereat Robespierre tried to laugh.

'Some one has filled thy head, Mother,' he said in a voice which he vainly tried to steady, 'with tales of the mysterious Englishman who goes by the name of the Scarlet Pimpernel—'

'Thy mortal enemy, O Messenger of the Most High!' the old blasphemer broke in solemnly. 'In far-off fogbound England he hath sworn thy death. Beware—'

'If that is the only danger which threatens me—' the other began, striving to speak carelessly.

'The only one, and the greatest one,' the hag went on insistently. 'Despise it not because it seems small and remote.'

'I do not despise it; neither do I magnify it. A gnat is a nuisance, but not a danger.'

'A gnat may wield a poisoned dart. The spirits have spoken. Heed their warning, O Chosen of the People! Destroy the Englishman ere he destroy thee!'

'Pardi!' Robespierre retorted, and despite the stuffiness of the room he gave a shiver as if he felt cold. 'Since thou dost commune with the spirits, find out from them how I can accomplish that.'

The woman once more raised the crystal globe to the level of her breast. With her elbows stretched out and her draperies falling straight all around her, she gazed into it for a while in silence. Then she began to murmur.

'I see the Scarlet Flower quite plainly . . . a small Scarlet Flower. . . . And I see the great Light which is like an aureole, the Light of the Chosen One. It is of dazzling brightness – but over it the Scarlet Flower casts a Stygian shadow.'

'Ask them,' Robespierre broke in peremptorily, 'ask thy spirits how best I can overcome mine enemy.'

'I see something,' the witch went on in an even monotone, still gazing into the crystal globe, 'white and rose and tender . . . is it a woman . . . ?'

'A woman?'

'She is tall, and she is beautiful . . . a stranger in the land . . . with eyes dark as the night and tresses black as the raven's wing . . . Yes, it is a woman . . . She stands between the Light and that blood-red flower. She takes the flower in her hand . . . she fondles it, raises it to her lips . . . Ah!' and the old seer gave a loud cry of triumph. 'She tosses it mangled and bleeding into the consuming Light . . . And now it lies faded, torn, crushed, and the Light grows in radiance.'

'But the woman? Who is she?' the man broke in impatiently. 'What is her name?'

'The spirits speak no names,' the seer replied. 'Any woman would gladly be thy handmaid, O Elect of France! The spirits have spoken,' she concluded solemnly. 'Salvation will come to thee by the hand of a woman.'

'And mine enemy?' he insisted. 'Which of us two is in danger of death now – now that I am warned – which of us two? – mine English enemy, or I?'

Nothing loth, the old hag was ready to continue her sortilege. Robespierre hung breathless upon her lips. His whole personality seemed transformed. He appeared eager, fearful, credulous – a different man to the cold, calculating despot who sent thousands to their death with his measured oratory, the mere power of his presence. Indeed, history has sought in vain for the probable motive which drove this cynical tyrant into consulting this pitiable charlatan. That Catherine Théot had certain psychic powers has never been gainsaid, and it was only to be expected that in the great upheaval of this awful Revolution, men and women should turn to the mystic and the supernatural as to a solace and respite from the fathomless misery of their daily lives.

Catherine Théot was one of many: for the nonce, one of the most noteworthy in Paris. She believed herself to be endowed with the gift of prophecy, and her fetish was Robespierre. In this at least she was genuine. She believed him to be a new Messiah, the Elect of God. Nay! she loudly proclaimed him as such, and one of her earliest neophytes, an ex-Carthusian monk named Gerle, who sat in the Convention next to the great man, had whispered in the latter's ear the insidious flattery which had gradually led his footsteps to the witch's lair.

Whether his own vanity – which was without limit and probably without parallel – caused him to believe in his own heaven-sent mission, or whether he only desired to strengthen his own popularity by endowing it with supernatural prestige, is a matter of conjecture. Certain it is that he did lend himself to Catherine Théot's cabalistic practices and that he allowed himself to be flattered and worshipped by the numerous neophytes who flocked to this new temple of magic, either from mystical fervour or merely to serve their own ends by fawning on the most dreaded man in France.

II

Catherine Théot had remained rigidly still, in rapt contemplation. It seemed as if she pondered over the Chosen One's last peremptory demand.

'Which of us two,' he had queried, in a dry, hard voice, 'is in danger of death now – now that I am warned – mine English enemy, or I?'

The next moment, as if moved by inspiration, she took another pinch of powder out of the metal box. The nigger's bright black eyes followed her every movement, as did the dictator's half-contemptuous gaze. The girls had begun to intone a monotonous chant. As the seer dropped the powder into the metal bowl, a highly scented smoke shot upwards and the interior of the vessel was suffused with a golden glow.

The dictator of France felt a strange exultation running through him, as with deep breaths he inhaled the potent fumes. It seemed to him as if his body had suddenly become etherealized, as if he were in truth the Chosen of the Most High as well as the idol of France. Thus disembodied, he felt in himself boundless strength: the power to rise triumphant over all his enemies, whoever they might be. There was a mighty buzzing in his ears like the reverberation of thousands of trumpets and drums ringing and beating in unison to his exaltation and to his might. His eyes appeared to see the whole of the people of France, clad in white robes, with ropes round their necks, and bowing as slaves to the ground before him. He was riding on a cloud. His throne was of gold. In his hand he had a sceptre of flame, and beneath his feet lay, crushed and mangled, a huge scarlet flower. The sybil's voice reached his ears as if through a supernal trumpet:

'Thus lie for ever crushed at the feet of the Chosen One, those who have dared to defy his power!'

Greater and greater became his exultation. He felt himself uplifted high, high above the clouds, until he could see the world as a mere crystal ball at his feet. His head had touched the portals of heaven; his eyes gazed upon his own majesty, which was second only to that of God. An eternity went by. He was immortal.

Then suddenly, through all the mystic music, there came a sound, so strange and yet so human, that the almighty dictator's wandering spirit was in an instant hurled back to earth, brought down with a mighty jerk which left him giddy, sick, with throat dry and burning eyes.

And yet that sound had been harmless enough: just a peal of laughter, merry and inane – nothing more. It came faintly echoing from beyond the heavy portière. Yet it had unnerved the most ruthless despot in France. He looked about him, scared and mystified. Nothing had been changed since he had gone wandering into Elysian fields. He was still in a stuffy, curtained room; there was the dais on which he had sat; the two women still chanted their weird lament; and there was the old necromancer in her shapeless, colourless robe, coolly setting down the crystal globe upon its carved stand. There was the blacka-moor, grinning and mischievous, the metal vessel, the oil lamp, the threadbare carpet. What of all this had been a dream?

'What was that?' Robespierre murmured at last.

The old woman looked up.

'What was what, O Chosen One?' she asked.

'I heard a sound—' he mumbled. 'A laugh . . . Is anyone else in the room?'

'People are waiting in the antechamber,' she replied carelessly, 'until it is the pleasure of the Chosen One to go. As a rule they wait patiently, and in silence. But one of them may have laughed.' Then, as he made no fur-ther comment but still stood there silent, as if irresolute, she queried with a great show of deference: 'What is thy next pleasure, O thou who art beloved of the people of France?'

'Nothing!' he murmured. 'I'll go now. Do not,' he added peremptorily, 'let anyone know that I have been here.'

'Only those who idolize thee—' she began.

'I know – I know,' he broke in more gently, for the fulsome adulation soothed his exacerbated nerves. 'But I have many enemies . . . and thou too art watched with malevolent eyes . . . Let not our enemies make capital of our intercourse.'

'I swear to thee, O Mighty Lord, that thy servant obeys thy behests in all things.'

'That is well,' he retorted drily. 'But thy adepts are wont to talk too much. I'll not have my name bandied about for the glorification of thy necromancy.'

'Thy name is sacred to thy servants,' she insisted with ponderous solemnity. 'As sacred as is thy person. Thou art the regenerator of the true faith, the Elect of the First Cause, the high priest of a new religion. We are but thy servants, thy handmaids, thy worshippers.'

All this charlatanism was precious incense to the limitless vanity of the despot. His impatience vanished, as did his momentary terror. He became kind, urbane, condescending. At the last, the old hag almost prostrated herself before him, and clasping her wrinkled hands together, she said in tones of reverential entreaty:

'In the name of thyself, of France, of the entire world, I adjure thee to lend ear to what the spirits have revealed this day. Beware the danger that comes to thee from the scarlet flower. Set thy almighty mind to compass its destruction. Do not disdain a woman's help, since the spirits have proclaimed that through a woman thou shalt be saved. Remember! Remember!' she adjured him with evergrowing earnestness. 'Once before, the world was saved through a woman. A woman crushed the serpent beneath her foot. Let a woman now crush that scarlet flower beneath hers. Remember!'

She actually kissed his feet; and he, blinded by self-conceit to the folly of this fetishism and the ridicule of his own acceptance of it, raised his hand above her head as if in the act of pronouncing a benediction.

Then without another word he turned to go. The young negro brought him his hat and cloak. The latter he wrapped closely round his shoulders, his hat he pulled down well over his eyes. Thus muffled and, he hoped, unrecognizable, he passed with a firm tread out of the room.

III

For awhile the old witch waited, straining her ears to catch the last sound of those retreating footsteps; then, with a curt word and an impatient clapping of her hands, she dismissed her attendants, the negro as well as her neophytes. These young women at her word lost quickly enough their air of rapt mysticism, became very human indeed, stretched out their limbs, yawned lustily, and with none too graceful movements uncurled themselves and struggled to their feet. Chattering and laughing like so many magpies let out of a cage, they soon disappeared through the door in the rear.

Again the old woman waited silent and motionless until that merry sound too gradually subsided. Then she went across the room to the dais, and drew aside the curtain which hung behind it.

'Citizen Chauvelin!' she called peremptorily.

A small figure of a man stepped out from the gloom. He was dressed in black, his hair, of a nondescript blond shade and his crumpled linen alone told light in the general sombreness of his appearance.

'Well?' he retorted drily.

'Are you satisfied?' the old woman went on with eager impatience.

'You heard what I said?'

'Yes, I heard,' he replied. 'Think you he will act on it?'

'I am certain of it.'

'But why not have named Theresia Cabarrus? Then, at least, I would have been sure—'

'He might have recoiled at an actual name,' the woman replied, 'suspected me of connivance. The Chosen of the people of France is shrewd as well as distrustful. And I have my reputation to consider. But, remember what I said: "tall, dark, beautiful, a stranger in this land!" So, if indeed you require the help of the Spaniard—'

'Indeed I do!' he rejoined earnestly. And, as if speaking to his own inward self, 'Theresia Cabarrus is the only woman I know who can really help me.'

'But you cannot force her consent, citizen Chauvelin,' the sybil insisted.

The eyes of citizen Chauvelin lit up suddenly with a flash of that old fire of long ago, when he was powerful enough to compel the consent or the co-operation of any man, woman or child on whom he had deigned to cast an appraising glance. But the flash was only momentary. The next second he had once more resumed his unobtrusive, even humble, attitude.

'My friends, who are few,' he said, with a quick sign of impatience; 'and mine enemies, who are without number, will readily share your conviction, Mother, that citizen Chauvelin can compel no one to do his bidding these days. Least of all the affianced wife of powerful Tallien.'

'Well, then,' the sybil argued, 'how think you that—'

'I only hope, Mother,' Chauvelin broke in suavely, 'that after your séance today, citizen Robespierre himself will see to it that Theresia Cabarrus gives me the help I need.'

Catherine Théot shrugged her shoulders.

'Oh!' she said drily, 'the Cabarrus knows no law save that of her caprice. And as Tallien's fiancée she is almost immune.'

'Almost, but not quite! Tallien is powerful, but so was Danton.'

'But Tallien is prudent, which Danton was not.'

'Tallien is also a coward; and easily led like a lamb, with a halter. He came back from Bordeaux tied to the apron-strings of the fair Spaniard. He should have spread fire and terror in the region; but at her bidding he dispensed justice and even mercy instead. A little more airing of his moderate views, a few more acts of unpatriotic clemency, and powerful Tallien himself may become "suspect".'

'And you think that, when he is,' the old woman rejoined with grim sarcasm, 'you will hold his fair betrothed in the hollow of your hand?'

'Certainly!' he assented, and with an acid smile fell to contemplating his thin, talon-like palms. 'Since Robespierre, counselled by Mother Théot, will himself have placed her there.'

Whereupon Catherine Théot ceased to argue, since the other appeared so sure of himself. Once more she shrugged her shoulders.

'Well, then, if you are satisfied . . .' she said.

'I am. Quite,' he replied, and at once plunged his hand in the breast-pocket of his coat. He had caught the look of avarice and of greed which had glittered in the old hag's eyes. From his pocket he drew a bundle of notes, for which Catherine immediately stretched out a grasping hand. But before giving her the money, he added a stern warning.

'Silence, remember! And, above all, discretion!'

'You may rely on me, citizen,' the sybil riposted quietly. 'I am not likely to blab.'

Then as Chauvelin, without another word, had turned unceremoniously to go, she placed a bony hand upon his arm.

'And I can rely on you, citizen,' she insisted firmly, 'that when the Scarlet Pimpernel is duly captured . . .'

'There will be ten thousand livres for you,' he broke in impatiently, 'if my scheme with Theresia Cabarrus is successful. I never go back on my word.'

'And I'll not go back on mine,' she concluded drily. 'We are dependent on one another, citizen Chauvelin. You want to capture the English spy, and I want ten thousand livres, so that I may retire from active life and quietly cultivate a plot of cabbages somewhere in the sunshine. So you may leave the matter to me, my friend. I'll not allow the great Robespierre to rest till he has compelled Theresia Cabarrus to do your bidding. Then you may use her as you think best. That gang of English spies must be found, and crushed. We cannot have the Chosen of the Most High threatened by such vermin. Ten thousand livres, you say?' the sybil went on, and once again, as in the presence of the dictator, a mystic exultation appeared to possess her soul. Gone was the glitter of avarice from her eyes; her wizened face seemed transfigured, her shrunken form to gain in stature. 'Nay! I would serve you on my knees and accord you worship, if you avert the scarlet danger that hovers over the head of the Beloved of France!'

CHAPTER 3

The Fellowship of Grief

I

In the antechamber of Catherine Théot's abode of mysteries some two hours later, half a dozen persons were sitting. The room was long, narrow and bare, its walls dank and colourless, and save for the rough wooden benches on which these persons sat, was void of any furniture.

These persons who sat or sprawled upon the benches did not speak to one another. They appeared to be waiting. One or two of them were seemingly asleep; others, from time to time, would rouse themselves from their apathy, look with dim, inquiring eyes in the direction of a heavy portière which hung in front of a door near the far end of the room, and would strain their ears to listen. This occurred every time that a cry, or a moan, or a sob came from behind the portière. When this subsided again all those in the bare waiting-room resumed their patient, lethargic attitude, and a silence – weird and absolute – reigned once more over them all. Now and then somebody would sigh, and at one time one of the sleepers snored.

Far away a church clock struck six.

II

A few minutes later, the portière was lifted, and a girl came into the room. She held a shawl, very much the worse for wear, tightly wrapped around her meagre shoulders, and from beneath her rough woollen skirt her small feet appeared, clad in well-worn shoes and darned worsted stockings. Her hair, which was fair and soft, was partially hidden under a white muslin cap, and as she walked with a brisk step across the room, she looked neither to right nor left, appeared to move as in a dream. And her large grey eyes were brimming over with tears.

Neither her rapid passage across the room nor her exit through a door immediately opposite the window created the slightest stir amongst those who were waiting. Only one of the men, a huge, ungainly giant, whose long limbs appeared to stretch half-across the bare wooden floor, looked up lazily as she passed.

After the girl had gone, silence once more fell on the small assembly. A few minutes went by, then the door behind the portière was opened and a cadaverous voice spoke the word, 'Enter!'

There was a faint stir among those who waited. A woman rose from her seat, said dully: 'My turn, I think?' and, gliding across the room like some bodiless spectre, she presently vanished behind the portière.

'Are you going to the Fraternal Supper tonight, citizen Langlois?' the giant said, after the woman had gone. His tone was rasping and harsh and his voice came with a wheeze and an obviously painful effort from his broad, doubled-up chest.

'Not I!' Langlois replied. 'I must speak with Mother Théot. My wife made me promise. She is too ill to come herself, and the poor unfortunate believes in the Théot's incantations.'

'Come out and get some fresh air, then,' the other rejoined. 'It is stifling in here!'

It was indeed stuffy in the dark, smoke-laden room. The man put his bony hand up to his chest, as if to quell a spasm of pain. A horrible, rasping cough shook his big body and brought a sweat to his brow. Langlois, a wizened little figure of a man, who looked himself as if he had one foot in the grave, waited patiently until the spasm was over, then, with the indifference peculiar to these turbulent times, he said lightly:

'I would just as soon sit here as wear out shoe-leather on the cobblestones of this God-forsaken hole. And I don't want to miss my turn with Mother Théot.'

'You'll have another four hours mayhap to wait in this filthy atmosphere.'

'What an aristo you are, citizen Rateau!' the other retorted drily. 'Always talking about atmosphere!'

'So would you, if you had only one lung wherewith to inhale this filth,' growled the giant through a wheeze.

'Then don't wait for me, my friend,' Langlois concluded with a careless shrug of his narrow shoulders. 'And, if you don't mind missing your turn . . .'

'I do not,' was Rateau's curt reply. 'I would as soon be last as not. But I'll come back presently. I am the third from now. If I'm not back you can have my turn, and I'll follow you in. But I can't—'

His next words were smothered in a terrible fit of coughing, as he struggled to his feet. Langlois swore at him for making such a noise, and the women, roused from their somnolence, sighed with impatience or resignation. But all those who remained seated on the benches watched with a kind of dull curiosity the ungainly figure of the asthmatic giant as he made his way across the room and anon went out through the door.

The women once more settled themselves against the dank walls, with feet stretched out before them and arms folded over their breasts, and in that highly uncomfortable position prepared once more to go to sleep.

Langlois buried his hands in the pockets of his breeches, spat contentedly upon the floor, and continued to wait.

III

In the meanwhile, the girl who, with tear-filled eyes, had come out of the inner mysterious room in Mother Théot's apartments, had, after a slow descent down the interminable stone stairs, at last reached the open air.

The Rue de la Planchette is only a street in name, for the houses in it are few and far between. One side of it is taken up for the major portion of its length by the dry moat which at this point forms the boundary of the Arsenal and of the military ground around the Bastille. The house wherein lodged Mother Théot is one of a small group situated behind the Bastille, the grim ruins of which can be distinctly seen from the upper windows. Immediately facing those houses is the Porte St Antoine, through which the wayfarer in this remote quarter of Paris has to pass in order to reach the more populous parts of the great city. This is just a lonely and squalid backwater, broken up by undeveloped land and timber yards. One end of the street abuts on the river, the other becomes merged in the equally remote suburb of Popincourt.

But, for the girl who had just come out of the heavy,

fetid atmosphere of Mother Théot's lodgings, the air which reached her nostrils as she came out of the wicket gate, was positive manna to her lungs. She stood for awhile quite still, drinking in the balmy spring air, then walked deliberately in the direction of the Porte St Antoine.

She was very tired, for she had come to the Rue de la Planchette on foot all the way from the small apartment in the St Germain quarter, where she lodged with her mother and sister and a young brother; she had become weary and jaded by sitting for hours on a hard wooden bench, waiting her turn to speak with Mother Théot, and then standing for what seemed an eternity of time in the presence of the soothsayer, who had further harassed her nerves by weird prophecies and mystic incantations.

But for the nonce weariness was forgotten. Régine de Serval was going to meet the man she loved, at a trysting place which they had marked as their own: the porch of the church of Petit St Antoine, a secluded spot where neither prying eyes could see them nor ears listen to what they had to say. A spot which to poor little Régine was the very threshold of Paradise, for here she had Bertrand all to herself, undisturbed by the prattle of Joséphine or Jacques or the querulous complaints of maman, cooped up in that miserable apartment in the old St Germain quarter of the city.

So she walked briskly and without hesitation. Bertrand had agreed to meet her at five o'clock. It was now close on half-past six.

Régine had crossed the Rue des Balais, and the church porch of Petit St Antoine was but a few paces farther on, when she became conscious of heavy, dragging footsteps some little way behind her. Immediately afterwards, the distressing sound of a racking cough reached her ears, followed by heartrending groans as of a human creature in grievous bodily pain. The girl, not in the least frightened, instinctively turned to look, and was moved to pity on seeing a man leaning against the wall of a house, in a state bordering on collapse, his hands convulsively grasping his chest, which appeared literally torn by a violent fit of coughing. Forgetting her own troubles, as well as the joy which awaited her so close at hand, Régine unhesitatingly recrossed the road, approached the sufferer, and in a gentle voice asked him if she could be of any assistance to him in his distress.

'A little water,' he gasped, 'for mercy's sake!'

She had stepped boldly through the wicket-gate of the nearest porte-cochère, and finding her way to the lodge of the concierge, she asked for a drop of water for a passer-by who was in pain. A jug of water was at once handed to her by a sympathetic concierge, and with it she went back to complete her simple act of mercy.

For a moment she was puzzled, not seeing the poor vagabond there, where she had left him, half-swooning against the wall. But soon she spied him, in the very act of turning under the little church porch of Petit St Antoine, the hallowed spot of her frequent meetings with Bertrand.

IV

He seemed to have crawled there for shelter, and there he collapsed upon the wooden bench, in the most remote angle of the porch. Of Bertrand there was not a sign.

Régine was soon by the side of the unfortunate. She held up the jug of water to his quaking lips, and he drank eagerly. After that he felt better, muttered vague words of thanks. But he seemed so weak, despite his stature, which appeared immense in this narrow enclosure, that she did not like to leave him. She sat down beside him, suddenly conscious of fatigue. He seemed harmless enough, and after awhile began to tell her of his trouble. This awful asthma he had contracted in the campaign against the English in Holland. He had but lately been discharged out of the army as totally unfit, and as he had no money wherewith to pay a doctor, he would no doubt have been dead by now but that a comrade had spoken to him of Mother Théot, a marvellous sorceress, who knew the art of drugs and simples, and could cure all ailments of the body by the mere laying on of hands.

'Ah, yes,' the girl sighed involuntarily, 'of the body!'

Through the very act of sitting still, a deadly lassitude had crept into her limbs. She was thankful not to move, to say little, and to listen with half an ear to the vagabond's jeremiads. Anyhow, she was sure that Bertrand would no longer be waiting. He was ever impatient if he thought that she failed him in anything, and it was she who had appointed five o'clock for their meeting. Even now the church clock way above the porch was striking half-past six. And the asthmatic giant went glibly on. He had partially recovered his breath.

'Aye!' he was saying, in response to her lament, 'and of the mind, too. I had a comrade whose sweetheart was false to him while he was fighting for his country. Mother Théot gave him a potion which he administered to the faithless one, and she returned to him as full of ardour as ever before.'

'I have no faith in potions,' the girl said, and shook her head sadly the while tears once more gathered in her eyes.

'No more have I,' the giant assented carelessly. 'But if my sweetheart was false to me I know what I would do.'

This he said in so droll a fashion, and the whole idea

of this ugly, ungainly creature having a sweetheart was so comical, that despite her will, the ghost of a smile crept round the young girl's sensitive mouth.

'What would you do, citizen?' she queried gently.

'Just take her away, out of reach of temptation,' he replied sententiously. 'I should say, "This must stop," and "You come away with me, ma mie!"'

'Ah!' she retorted impulsively, 'it is easy to talk. A man can do so much. What can a woman do?'

She checked herself abruptly, ashamed of having said so much. In these days of countless spies, of innumerable confidence tricks set to catch the unwary, it was more than foolhardy to speak of one's private affairs to any stranger, let alone to an out-at-elbows vagabond who was just the sort of refuse of humanity who would earn a precarious livelihood by the sale of information, true or false, wormed out of some innocent fellow-creature. Hardly, then, were the words out of her mouth than the girl repented of her folly, turned quick, frightened eyes on the abject creature beside her.

But he appeared not to have heard. A wheezy cough came out of his bony chest. Nor did he meet her terrified gaze.

'What did you say, citoyenne?' he muttered fretfully. 'Are you dreaming? . . . or what? . . .'

'Yes – yes!' she murmured vaguely, her heart still beating with that sudden fright. 'I must have been dreaming . . . But you . . . you are better—?'

'Better? Perhaps,' he replied, with a hoarse laugh. 'I might even be able to crawl home.'

'Do you live very far?' she asked.

'No. Just by the Rue de l'Anier.'

He made no attempt to thank her for her gentle ministration, and she thought how ungainly he looked – almost repellent – sprawling right across the porch, with his long legs stretched out before him and his hands buried in the pockets of his breeches. Nevertheless, he looked so helpless and so pitiable that the girl's kind heart was again stirred with compassion, and when presently he struggled with difficulty to his feet, she said impulsively:

'The Rue de l'Anier is on my way. If you will wait, I'll return the jug to the kind concierge who let me have it and I'll walk with you. You really ought not to be about the street alone.'

'Oh, I am better now,' he muttered, in the same ungracious way. 'You had best leave me alone. I am not a suitable gallant for a pretty wench like you.'

But already the girl had tripped away with the jug, and returned two minutes later to find that the curious creature had already started on his way and was fifty yards and more farther up the street by now. She shrugged her shoulders, feeling mortified at his ingratitude, and not a little ashamed that she had forced her compassion where it was so obviously unwelcome.

CHAPTER 4

One Dram of Joy Must Have a Pound of Care

I

She stood for a moment, gazing mechanically on the retreating figure of the asthmatic giant. The next moment she heard her name spoken, and turned quickly with a little cry of joy.

'Régine!'

A young man was hurrying towards her, was soon by her side and took her hand.

'I have been waiting,' he said reproachfully, 'for more than an hour.'

In the twilight his face appeared pinched and pale, with dark, deep-sunken eyes that told of a troubled soul and a consuming, inward fire. He wore cloth clothes that were very much the worse for wear, and boots that were down at heel.

'I am sorry, Bertrand,' the girl said simply. 'But I had to wait such a long time at Mother Théot's, and—'

'But what were you doing now?' he queried with an impatient frown. 'I saw you from a distance. You came out of yonder house, and then stood here like one bewildered. You did not hear when first I called.'

'I have had quite a funny adventure,' Régine explained;

31

'and I am very tired. Sit down with me, Bertrand, for a moment. I'll tell you all about it.'

'It is too late—' he began, and the frown of impatience deepened upon his brow. He tried to protest, but Régine did look very tired. Already, without waiting for his consent, she had turned into the little porch, and Bertrand perforce had to follow her.

The shades of evening now were fast gathering in, and the lengthened shadows stretched out away, right across the street. The last rays of the sinking sun still tinged the roofs and chimney pots opposite with a crimson hue. But here, in the hallowed little trysting place, the kingdom of night had already established its sway. The darkness lent an air of solitude and of security to this tiny refuge, and Régine drew a happy little sigh as she walked deliberately to its farthermost recess and sat down on the wooden bench in its extreme and darkest angle.

Behind her, the heavy oaken door of the church was closed. The church itself, owing to the contumaciousness of its parish priest, had been desecrated by the ruthless hands of the Terrorists and left derelict, to fall into decay. The stone walls themselves appeared cut off from the world, as if ostracised. But between them Régine felt safe, and when Bertrand Moncrif somewhat reluctantly sat down beside her, she also felt almost happy.

'It is very late,' he murmured once more, ungraciously.

She was leaning her head against the wall, looked so pale, with eyes closed and bloodless lips, that the young man's heart was suddenly filled with compunction.

'You are not ill, Régine?' he asked, more gently.

'No,' she replied, and smiled bravely up at him. 'Only very tired and a little dizzy. The atmosphere in Catherine Théot's rooms was stifling, and then when I came out—'

He took her hand, obviously making an effort to be

patient and to be kind; and she, not noticing the effort or his absorption, began to tell him about her little adventure with the asthmatic giant.

'Such a droll creature,' she explained. 'He would have frightened me but for that awful, churchyard cough.'

'And Mother Théot, what had she to say?'

Régine gave a shudder.

'She foretells danger for us all,' she said.

'The old charlatan!' he retorted with a shrug of the shoulders. 'As if everyone was not in danger these days!'

'She gave me a powder,' Régine went on simply, 'which she thinks will calm Joséphine's nerves.'

'And that is folly,' he broke in harshly. 'We do not want Joséphine's nerves to be calmed.'

But at his words, which in truth sounded almost cruel, Régine roused herself with a sudden air of authority.

'Bertrand,' she said firmly, 'you are doing a great wrong by dragging the child into your schemes. Joséphine is too young to be used as a tool by a pack of thoughtless enthusiasts.'

A bitter, scornful laugh from Bertrand broke in on her vehemence.

'Thoughtless enthusiasts!' he exclaimed roughly. 'Is that how you call us, Régine? My God! where is your loyalty, your devotion? Have you no faith, no aspirations? Do you no longer worship God or reverence your King?'

'In heaven's name, Bertrand, take care!' she whispered hoarsely, looked about her as if the stone walls of the porch had ears and eyes fixed upon the man she loved.

'Take care!' he rejoined bitterly. 'Yes! that is your creed now. Caution! Circumspection! You fear—'

'For you,' she broke in reproachfully; 'for Joséphine; for maman; for Jacques – not for myself, God knows!'

'We must all take risks, Régine,' he retorted more

composedly. 'We must all risk our miserable lives in order to end this awful, revolting tyranny. The despotism of a bloodthirsty autocrat has made of the people of France a people of slaves, cringing, fearful, abject – swayed by his word, too cowardly now to rebel.'

'And what are you? My God!' she cried passionately. 'You and your friends, my poor young sister, my foolish little brother? What are you, that you think you can stem the torrent of this stupendous Revolution? How think you that your feeble voices will be heard above the roar of a whole nation in the throes of misery and of shame?'

'It is the still small voice,' Bertrand replied, in the tone of a visionary, who sees mysteries and who dreams dreams, 'that is heard by its persistence even above the fury of thousands in full cry. Do we not call our organisation "the Fatalists"? Our aim is to take every opportunity by quick, short speeches, by mixing with the crowd and putting in a word here and there, to make propaganda against the fiend Robespierre. The populace are like sheep; they'll follow a lead. One day, one of us will find the word and speak it at the right time, and the people will follow us and turn against that execrable monster and hurl him from his throne, down into Gehenna.'

He spoke below his breath, in a hoarse whisper which even she had to strain her ears to hear.

'I know, I know, Bertrand,' she rejoined, and her tiny hand stole out in a pathetic endeavour to capture his. 'Your aims are splendid. You are wonderful, all of you. Who am I, that I should even with a word or a prayer, try to dissuade you to do what you think is right? But Joséphine is so young, so hot-headed! What help can she give you? She is only seventeen. And Jacques! He is just an irresponsible boy! Think, Bertrand, think! If anything were to happen to these children, it would kill maman!'

He gave a shrug of the shoulders and smothered a weary sigh.

'You and I will never understand one another, Régine,' he began; then added quickly, 'over these matters,' because, following on his cruel words, he had heard the tiny cry of pain, so like that of a wounded bird, which much against her will had escaped her lips. 'You do not understand,' he went on, more quietly, 'that in a great cause the sufferings of individuals are naught beside the glorious achievement that is in view.'

'The sufferings of individuals,' she murmured, with a pathetic little sigh. 'In truth 'tis but little heed you pay, Bertrand, to my sufferings these days.' She paused awhile, then added under her breath: 'Since first you met Theresia Cabarrus, three months ago, you have eyes and ears only for her.'

'It is useless, Régine——' he began.

'I know,' she broke in quietly. 'Theresia Cabarrus is beautiful; she has charm, wit, power – all things which I do not possess.'

'She has fearlessness and a heart of gold,' Bertrand rejoined and, probably despite himself, a sudden warmth crept into his voice. 'Do you not know of the marvellous influence which she exercised over that fiend Tallien, down in Bordeaux? He went there filled with a veritable tiger's fury, ready for a wholesale butchery of all the royalists, the aristocrats, the bourgeois, over there – all those, in fact, whom he chose to believe were conspiring against this hideous Revolution. Well! under Theresia's influence he actually modified his views and became so lenient that he was recalled. You know, or should know, Régine,' the young man added in a tone of bitter reproach, 'that Theresia is as good as she is beautiful.'

'I do know that, Bertrand,' the girl rejoined with an effort. 'Only—'

'Only what?' he queried roughly.

'I do not trust her . . . that is all.' Then, as he made no attempt at concealing his scorn and his impatience, she went on in a tone which was much harsher, more uncompromising than the one she had adopted hitherto: 'Your infatuation blinds you, Bertrand, or you – an enthusiastic royalist, an ardent loyalist – would not place your trust in an avowed Republican. Theresia Cabarrus may be kind-hearted – I don't deny it. She may have done and she may be all that you say; but she stands for the negation of every one of your ideals, for the destruction of what you exalt, the glorification of the principles of this execrable Revolution.'

'Jealousy blinds you, Régine,' he retorted moodily.

'No, it is not jealousy, Bertrand – not common, vulgar jealousy – that prompts me to warn you, before it is too late. Remember,' she added solemnly, 'that you have not only yourself to think of, but that you are accountable to God and to me for the innocent lives of Joséphine and of Jacques. By confiding in that Spanish woman—'

'Now you are insulting her,' he broke in mercilessly. 'Making her out to be a spy.'

'What else is she?' the girl riposted vehemently. 'You know that she is affianced to Tallien, whose influence and whose cruelty are second only to those of Robespierre. You know it, Bertrand!' she insisted, seeing that at last she had silenced him and that he sat beside her, sullen and obstinate. 'You know it, even though you choose to close your eyes and ears to what is common knowledge.'

There was silence after that for a while in the narrow porch, where two hearts once united were filled now with bitterness, one against the other. The girl shivered as with cold and drew her tattered shawl more closely round her shoulders. She was vainly trying to swallow her tears. Goaded into saying more than she had ever meant to, she felt the finality of what she had said. Something had finally snapped just now: something that could never in after years be put together again. The boy and girl love which had survived the past two years of trouble and of stress, lay wounded unto death, bleeding at the foot of the shrine of a man's infatuation and a woman's vanity. How impossible this would have seemed but a brief while ago!

Through the darkness, swift visions of past happy times came fleeting before the girl's tear-dimmed gaze: visions of walks in the woods round Auteuil, of drifting down-stream in a boat on the Seine on hot August days – aye! even of danger shared and perilous moments passed together, hand in hand, with bated breath, in darkened rooms, with curtains drawn and ears straining to hear the distant cannonade, the shouts of an infuriated populace or the rattle of death carts upon the cobblestones. Swift visions of past sorrows and past joys! An immense self-pity filled the girl's heart to bursting. An insistent sob that would not be suppressed rose to her throat.

'Oh, Mother of God, have mercy!' she murmured through her tears.

Bertrand, shamed and confused, his heart stirred by the misery of this girl whom he had so dearly loved, his nerves strained beyond endurance through the many mad schemes which his enthusiasm was for ever evolving, felt like a creature on the rack, torn between compunction and remorse on the one hand and irresistible passion on the other.

'Régine,' he pleaded, 'forgive me! I am a brute, I know. Oh, my dear,' he added pitiably, 'if you would only understand . . .'

At once her tender, womanly sentiment was to the fore, sweeping pride and just resentment out of the way. Hers was one of those motherly natures that are always more ready to comfort than to chide. Already she had swallowed her tears, and now that with a wearied gesture he had buried his face in his hands, she put her arm around his neck, pillowed his head against her breast.

'I do understand, Bertrand,' she said gently. 'And you must never ask my forgiveness, for you and I have loved one another too well to bear anger or grudge one toward the other. There!' she said, and rose to her feet, and seemed by that sudden act to gather up all the moral strength of which she stood in such sore need. 'It is getting late, and maman will be anxious. Another time we must have a more quiet talk about our future. But,' she added, with renewed seriousness, 'if I concede you Theresia Cabarrus without another murmur, you must give me back Joséphine and Jacques. If – if I – am to lose you – I could not bear to lose them as well. They are so young . . .'

'Who talks of losing them?' he broke in, once more impatient, enthusiastic. 'And what have I to do with it all? Joséphine and Jacques are members of the Club. They may be young, but they are old enough to know the value of an oath. They are pledged just like I am, just like we all are. I could not, even if I would, make them false to their oath.' Then, as she made no reply, he leaned over to her, took her hands in his, tried to read her inscrutable face through the shadows of night. He thought that he read obstinacy in her rigid attitude, the unresponsive placidity of her hands. 'You would not have them false to their oath?' he insisted.

She made no reply to that, only queried dully:

'What are you going to do tonight?'

'Tonight,' he said with passionate earnestness, his eyes glowing with the fervid ardour of self-immolation, 'we are going to let hell loose around the name of Robespierre.'

'Where?'

'At the open-air supper in the Rue St Honoré. Joséphine and Jacques will be there.'

She nodded mechanically, quietly disengaged her hands from his feverish grasp.

'I know,' she said quietly. 'They told me they were going. I have no influence to stop them.'

'You will be there, too?' he asked.

'Of course. So will poor maman,' she replied simply.

'This may be the turning point, Régine,' he said with passionate earnestness, 'in the history of France!'

'Perhaps!'

'Think of it, Régine! Your sister, your young brother! Their name may go down to posterity as the saviours of France!'

'The saviours of France!' she murmured vaguely.

'One word has swayed a multitude before now. It may do so again . . . tonight!'

'Yes,' she said. 'And those poor children believe in the power of their oratory.'

'Do not you?'

'I only remember that you, Bertrand, have probably spoken of your plan to Theresia Cabarrus, that the place will be swarming with the spies of Robespierre, and that you and the children will be recognised, seized, dragged into prison, then to the guillotine! My God!' she added, in a pitiful murmur. 'And I am powerless to do anything but look on like an insentient log, whilst you run your rash heads into a noose, and then follow you all to death, whilst maman is left alone to perish in misery and in want.'

'A pessimist again, Régine!' he said with a forced laugh, and in his turn rose to his feet. ''Tis little we have accomplished this evening,' he added bitterly, 'by talking.'

She said nothing more. An icy chill had hold of her heart. Not only of her heart, but of her brain and her whole being. Strive as she might, she could not enter into

Bertrand's schemes, and as his whole entity was wrapped up in them she felt estranged from him, out of touch, shut out from his heart. Unspeakable bitterness filled her soul. She hated Theresia Cabarrus, who had enslaved Bertrand's fancy, and above all she mistrusted her. At this moment she would gladly have given her life to get Bertrand away from the influence of that woman and away from that madcap association which called itself 'the Fatalists,' and into which he had dragged both Joséphine and Jacques.

Silently she preceded him out of the little church porch, the habitual trysting place, where at one time she had spent so many happy hours. Just before she turned off into the street, she looked back, as if through the impenetrable darkness which enveloped it now she would conjure up, just once more, those happy images of the past. But the darkness made no response to the mute cry of her fancy, and with a last sigh of intense bitterness, she followed Bertrand down the street.

II

Less than five minutes after Bertrand and Régine had left the porch of Petit St Antoine, the heavy oak door of the church was cautiously opened. It moved noiselessly upon its hinges, and presently through the aperture the figure of a man emerged, hardly discernible in the gloom. He slipped through the door into the porch, then closed the former noiselessly behind him.

A moment or two later his huge, bulky figure was lumbering up the Rue St Antoine, in the direction of the Arsenal, his down-at-heel shoes making a dull clip-clop on the cobblestones. There were but very few passers-by at this hour, and the man went along with his peculiar shuffling gait until he reached the Porte St Antoine. The city gates were still open at this hour, for it was only a little while ago that the many church clocks of the quartier had struck eight, nor did the sergeant at the gate pay much heed to the beggarly caitiff who went by; only he and the half-dozen men of the National Guard who were in charge of the gate, did remark that the belated wayfarer appeared to be in distress with a terrible asthmatic cough which caused one of the men to say with grim facetiousness:

'Pardi! but here's a man who will not give maman guillotine any trouble!'

They all noticed, moreover, that after the asthmatic giant had passed through the city gate, he had turned his shuffling footsteps in the direction of the Rue de la Planchette.

CHAPTER 5

Rascality Rejoices

I

The Fraternal Suppers were a great success. They were the invention of Robespierre, and the unusual warmth of these early spring evenings lent the support of their balmy atmosphere to the scheme.

Whole Paris is out in the streets on these mild April nights. Families out on a holiday, after the daily spectacle of the death-cart taking the enemies of the people, the conspirators against their liberty, to the guillotine.

And maman brings a basket filled with whatever scanty provisions she can save from the maximum per day allowed for the provisioning of her family. Beside her, papa comes along, dragging his youngest by the hand – the latter no longer chubby and rosy, as were his prototypes in the days gone by, because food is scarce and dear, and milk unobtainable; but looking a man for all that, though bare-footed and bare-kneed, with the red cap upon his lank, unwashed locks, and hugging against his meagre chest a tiny toy guillotine, the latest popular fancy.

The Rue St Honoré is a typical example of what goes on all over the city. Though it is very narrow and there-fore peculiarly inconvenient for the holding of outdoor entertainments, the Fraternal Suppers there are extensively patronized, because the street itself is consecrated as holding the house wherein lives Robespierre.

Here, as elsewhere, huge braziers are lit at intervals, so that materfamilias may cook the few herrings she has brought with her if she be so minded, and all down the narrow street tables are set, innocent of cloths or even of that cleanliness which is next to the equally neglected virtue of godliness. But the tables have an air of cheeriness nevertheless, with resin torches, tallow candles, or old stable lanthorns set here and there, the flames flickering in the gentle breeze, adding picturesqueness to the scene which might otherwise have seemed sordid, with those pewter mugs and tin plates, the horn-handled knives and iron spoons.

A motley throng, in truth! The workers of Paris, its proletariat, all conscripted servants of the State – slaves, we might call them, though they deem themselves free men – all driven into hard manual labour, partly by starvation and wholly by the decree of the Committees, who decide how and when and in what form the nation requires the arms or hands – not the brains, mind you! – of its citizens. For brains the nation has no use, only in the heads of those who sit in Convention or on Committees. 'The State hath no use for science,' was grimly said to Lavoisier, the great chemist, when he begged for a few days' surcease from death in order to complete some important experiments.

But coal-heavers are useful citizens of the State; so are smiths and armourers and gunmakers, and those who can sew and knit stockings, do anything in fact to clothe and feed the national army, the defenders of the sacred soil of France. For them, for these workers – the honest, the industrious, the sober – are the Fraternal Suppers invented; but not for them only. There are the 'tricotteuses,' sexless hags, who, by order of the State, sit at the foot of the scaffold surrounded by their families and their children and knit, and knit, the while they jeer – still by order of the State – at the condemned – old men, young women, children even, as they walk up to the guillotine. There are the 'insulteuses publiques,' public insulters, women mostly – save the mark! – paid to howl and blaspheme as the death-carts rattle by. There are the 'tappe-durs,' the hit-hards, who, armed with weighted sticks, form the bodyguard around the sacred person of Robespierre. Then, the members of the Société Révolutionnaire, recruited from the refuse of misery and of degradation of this great city; and – oh, the horror of it all! – the 'Enfants Rouges,' the red children, who cry 'Death' and 'à la lanterne' with the best of them – precocious little offsprings of the new Republic. For them, too, are Fraternal Suppers established: for all the riff-raff, all the sweepings of abject humanity. For they too must be amused and entertained, lest they sit in clusters and talk themselves into the belief that they are more wretched, more indigent, more abased, than they were in the days of monarchial oppression.

II

And so, on these balmy evenings of mid-April, family parties are gathered in the open air, around meagre suppers that are 'fraternal' by order of the State.

There is even laughter around the festive boards, fun and frolic. Jokes are cracked, mostly of a grim order. There is intoxication in the air: spring has got into the heads of the young. And there is even kissing under the shadows, love-making, sentiment; and here and there perhaps a shred of real happiness.

The provisions are scanty. Every family brings its own. Two or three herrings, sprinkled with shredded onions and wetted with a little vinegar, or else a few boiled prunes or a pottage of lentils and beans.

'Can you spare some of that bread, citizen?'

'Aye! if I can have a bite of your cheese.'

They are fraternal suppers! Do not, in the name of Liberty and Equality, let us forget that. And the whole of it was Robespierre's idea. He conceived and carried it through, commanded the voices in the Convention that voted the money required for the tables, the benches, the tallow candles. He lives close by, in this very street, humbly, quietly, like a true son of the people, sharing house and board with citizen Duplay, the cabinet-maker, and with his family.

A great man, Robespierre! The only man! Men speak of him with bated breath, young girls with glowing eyes. He is the fetish, the idol, the demigod. No benefactor of mankind, no saint, no hero-martyr was ever worshipped more devotedly than this death-dealing monster by his votaries. Even the shade of Danton is reviled in order to exalt the virtues of his successful rival.

'Danton was gorged with riches: his pockets full, his stomach satisfied! But look at Robespierre!'

'Almost a wraith! – so thin, so white!'

'An ascetic!'

'Consumed by the fire of his own patriotism.'

'His eloquence!'

'His selflessness!'

'You have heard him speak, citizen?'

A girl, still in her 'teens, her elbows resting on the table, her hands supporting her rounded chin, asks the question with bated breath. Her large grey eyes, hollow and glowing, are fixed upon her vis-à-vis, a tall, ungainly creature, who sprawls over the table, vainly trying to dispose of his long limbs in a manner comfortable to himself.

His hair is lank and matted with grease, his face covered in coal-dust; a sennight's growth of beard, stubbly and dusty, accentuates the squareness of his jaw even whilst it fails to conceal altogether the cruel, sarcastic curves of his mouth. But for the moment, in the rapt eyes of the young enthusiast, he is a prophet, a seer, a human marvel: he has heard Robespierre speak.

'Was it in the Club, citizen Rateau?' another woman asks – a young matron with a poor little starveling at her breast.

The man gives a loud guffaw.

'In the Club?' he says with a curse, and spits in a convenient direction to show his contempt for that or any other institution. 'I don't belong to any Club. There's no money in my pocket. And the Jacobins and the Cordeliers like to see a man with a decent coat on his back.'

His guffaw broke in a rasping cough which seemed to tear his broad chest to ribbons. His neighbours alongside the table, the young enthusiast opposite, the comely matron, paid no heed to him – waited indifferently until the clumsy lout had regained his breath. Only when he once more stretched out his long limbs, raised his head and looked about him, panting and blear-eyed, did the girl insist quietly:

'But you have heard *Him* speak!'

'Aye!' the ruffian replied drily. 'I did.'

'When?'

'Night before last. Tenez! He was stepping out of citizen Duplay's house yonder. He saw me leaning against the wall close by. I was tired, half asleep, what? He spoke to me and asked me where I lived.'

'Where you lived?' the girl echoed, disappointed.

'And where did you say you lived, citizen?' the young matron went on, in her calm, matter-of-fact tone.

'I live far from here, the other side of the water. Not in an aristocratic quarter like this one – what?'

'You told *Him* that you lived there?' the girl still insisted. Any scrap or crumb of information even remotely connected with her idol was manna to her body and balm to her soul.

'Yes, I did,' citizen Rateau assented.

'Then,' the girl resumed earnestly, 'solace and comfort will come to you very soon, citizen. He never forgets. His eyes are upon you. He knows your distress and that you are poor and weary. Leave it to him, citizen Rateau. He will know how and when to help.'

'He will know, more like,' here broke in a harsh voice, vibrating with excitement, 'how and when to lay his talons on an obscure and helpless citizen whenever his Batches for the guillotine are insufficient to satisfy his lust!'

A dull murmur greeted this tirade. Only those who sat close by the speaker knew which he was, for the lights were scanty and burnt dim in the open air. The others only heard – received this arrow-shot aimed at their idol – with for the most part a kind of dull resentment. The women were more loudly indignant. One or two young devotees gave a shrill cry or so of passionate indignation.

'Shame! Treason!'

'Guillotine, forsooth! The enemies of the people all deserve the guillotine!'

And the enemies of the people were those who dared raise their voice against their Chosen, their Fetish, the great, incomprehensible Mystery.

Citizen Rateau was once more rendered helpless by a tearing fit of coughing.

But from afar, down the street, there came one or two assenting cries.

'Well spoken, young man! As for me, I never trusted that blood-hound!'

And a woman's voice added shrilly: 'His hands reek of blood. A butcher, I call him!'

'And a tyrant!' assented the original spokesman. 'His aim is a dictatorship, with his minions hanging around him like abject slaves. Why not Versailles, then? How are we better off now than in the days of kingship? Then, at least, the streets of Paris did not stink of blood. Then, at least—'

But the speaker got no farther. A hard crust of very dry, black bread, aimed by a sure hand, caught him full in the face, whilst a hoarse voice shouted lustily:

'Hey there, citizen! If thou'lt not hold the tongue 'tis thy neck that will be reeking with blood o'er soon, I'll warrant!'

'Well said, citizen Rateau!' put in another, speaking with his mouth full, but with splendid conviction. 'Every word uttered by that jackanapes yonder reeks of treason!'

'Shame!' came from every side.

'Where are the agents of the Committee of Public Safety? Men have been thrown into prison for less than this.'

'Denounce him!'

'Take him to the nearest Section!'

'Ere he wreaks mischief more lasting than words!' cried a woman, who tried as she spoke to give to her utterance its full, sinister meaning.

'Shame! Treason!' came soon from every side. Voices were raised all down the length of the tables – shrill, full-throated, even dull and indifferent. Some really felt indignation – burning, ferocious indignation; others only made a noise for the sheer pleasure of it, and because the past five years had turned cries of 'Treason!' and of 'Shame!'

into a habit. Not that they knew what the disturbance was about. The street was long and narrow, and the cries came some way from where they were sitting; but when cries of 'Treason!' flew through the air these days, 'twas best to join in, lest those cries turned against one, and the next stage in the proceedings became the approach of an Agent of the Sûreté, the nearest prison, and the inevitable guillotine.

So every one cried 'Shame!' and 'Treason!' whilst those who had first dared to raise their voices against the popular demagogue drew together into a closer batch, trying no doubt to gather courage through one another's proximity. Eager, excited, a small compact group of two men – one a mere boy – and three women, it almost seemed as if they were suffering from some temporary hallucination. How else would five isolated persons – three of them in their first youth – have dared to brave a multitude?

In truth Bertrand Moncrif, face to face as he believed with martyrdom, was like one transfigured. Always endowed with good looks, he appeared like a veritable young prophet, haranguing the multitude and foretelling its doom.

Beside him Régine, motionless and white as a wraith, appeared alive only by her eyes, which were fixed on her beloved. In the hulking giant with the asthmatic cough she had recognised the man to whom she had ministered earlier in the day. Somehow, his presence here and now seemed to her sinister and threatening. It seemed as if all day he had been dogging her footsteps: first at the soothsayer's, then he surely must have followed her down the street. Then he had inspired her with pity; now his hideous face, his grimy hands, that croaking voice and churchyard cough, filled her with nameless terror.

He appeared to her excited fancy like a veritable spectre of death, hovering over Bertrand and over those she loved. With one arm she tried to press her brother Jacques to her breast, to quench his eagerness and silence his foolhardy tongue. But he, like a fierce, impatient young animal, fought to free himself from her loving embrace, shouted approval to Bertrand's oratory, played his part of young propagandist, heedless of Régine's warnings and of his mother's tears. Next to Régine, her sister Joséphine – a girl not out of her 'teens, with all the eagerness and exaggeration of extreme youth, was shouting quite as loudly as her brother Jacques, clapping her small hands together, turning glowing, defying, arrogant eyes on the crowd of great unwashed whom she hoped to sway with her ardour and her eloquence.

'Shame on us all!' she cried with passionate vehemence. 'Shame on us French women and French men, that we should be the abject slaves of such a bloodthirsty tyrant!'

Her mother, pale-faced, delicate, had obviously long since given up all hope of controlling this unruly little crowd. Her wan face only expressed despair – despair that was absolutely final – and the resignation of silent self-immolation, content to suffer beside those she loved, only praying to be allowed to share their martyrdom, even though she had no part in their enthusiasm.

Bertrand, Joséphine and Jacques had all the ardour of martyrdom. Régine and her mother all its resignation.

III

The Fraternal Supper threatened to end in a free fight, wherein the only salvation for the young fire-eaters would lie in a swift taking to their heels. And even then the chances would be hopelessly against them. Spies of the Convention, spies of the Committees, spies of Robespierre himself, swarmed all over the place. They were marked men and women, those five. It was useless to appear defiant and high-minded and patriotic. Even Danton had gone to the guillotine for less.

'Shame! Treason!'

The balmy air of mid-April seemed to echo the sinister words. But Bertrand appeared unconscious of all danger. Nay! it almost seemed as if he courted it.

'Shame on you all!' he called out loudly, and his fresh, sonorous voice rang out above the tumult and the hoarse murmurings. 'Shame on the people of France for bowing their necks to such monstrous tyranny. Citizens of Paris, think on it! Is not Liberty a mockery now? Do you call your bodies your own? They are but food for cannon at the bidding of the Convention. Your families? You are parted from those you love. Your wife? You are torn from her embrace. Your children? They are taken from you for the service of the State. And by whose orders? Tell me that! By whose orders, I say?'

He was lashing himself into a veritable fury of self-sacrifice, stood up beside the table and with a gesture even bade Joséphine and Jacques be still.

This of course was the end – this folly, this mad, senseless, useless folly! Already through the gloom she could see as in a horrible vision all those she cared for dragged before a tribunal that knew of no mercy; she could hear the death-carts rattling along the cobblestones, she could see the hideous arms of the guillotine, ready to receive this unique, this beloved, this precious prey. She could feel Joséphine's arms clinging pitiably to her for courage; she could see Jacques' defiant young face, glorying in martyrdom; she could see maman, drooping like a faded flower, bereft of what was life to her – the nearness of her children. She could see Bertrand, turning with a dying look of love, not to her but to the beautiful Spaniard who had captured his fancy and then sold him without compunction to the spies of Robespierre and of her own party.

IV

But for the fact that this was a 'Fraternal Supper,' that people had come out here with their families, their young children, to eat and to make merry and to forget all their troubles as well as the pall of crime that hung over the entire city, I doubt not but what the young Hotspur and his crowd of rashlings would ere now have been torn from their seats, trampled under foot, at best been dragged to the nearest Commissary, as the asthmatic citizen Rateau had already threatened. Even as it was, the temper of many a paterfamilias was sorely tried by this insistence, this wilful twisting of the tigers' tails. And the women were on the verge of reprisals. As for Rateau, he just seemed to gather his huge limbs together, uttered an impatient oath and an angry: 'By all the cats and dogs that render this world hideous with their howls, I have had about enough of this screeching oratory.' Then he threw one long leg over the bench on which he had been sitting, and in an instant was lost in the gloom, only to reappear in the dim light a few seconds later, this time on the farther side of the table, immediately behind the young rhetorician, his ugly, begrimed face with its grinning, toothless mouth and his broad, bent shoulders towering above the other's slender figure.

'Knock him down, citizen!' a young woman cried excitedly. 'Hit him in the face! Silence his abominable tongue!'

But Bertrand was not to be silenced yet. No doubt the

fever of notoriety, of martyrdom, had got into his blood. His youth, his good looks – obvious even in the fitful light and despite his tattered clothes – were an asset in his favour, no doubt; but a man-eating tiger is apt to be indiscriminate in his appetites and will devour a child with as much gusto as a gaffer; and this youthful firebrand was teasing the man-eating tiger with reckless insistence.

'By whose orders,' he reiterated, with passionate vehemence, 'by whose orders are we, free citizens of France, dragged into this abominable slavery? Your bodies, citizens, your freedom, your wives, your children, are the slaves, the property, the toys of one man – real tyrant and traitor, the oppressor of the weak, the enemy of the people; and that man is—'

Again he was interrupted, this time more forcibly. A terrific blow on the head deprived him of speech and of sight. His senses reeled, there was a mighty buzzing in his ears, which effectually drowned the cries of execration or of approval that greeted his tirade, as well as a new and deafening tumult which filled the whole narrow street with its weird and hideous sounds.

Whence the blow had come, Bertrand had no notion. It had all been so swift. He had expected to be torn limb from limb, to be dragged to the nearest Commissariat: he courted condemnation, envisaged the guillotine; 'stead of which he was prosily knocked down by a blow which would have felled an ox.

Just for a second, his fast-fading perceptions struggled back into consciousness. He had a swift vision of a giant form towering over him, with grimy fist uplifted and toothless mouth grinning hideously and of the crowd, rising from their seats, turning their backs upon him, waving arms and caps frantically, and shouting, shouting, with vociferous lustiness. He also had an equally swift pang of remorse as the faces of his companions – of Régine and Mme. de Serval, of Joséphine and Jacques – whom he dragged with him into this mad and purposeless outburst, rose prophetically before him from out the gloom, with wide-eyed, scared faces and arms uplifted to ward off vengeful blows.

But the next moment these lightning-like visions faded into complete oblivion. He felt something hard and heavy hitting him in the back. All the lights, the faces, the out-stretched hands, danced wildly before his eyes, and he sank like a log on the greasy pavement, dragging pewter plates, mugs and bottles down with him in his fall.

CHAPTER 6

One Crowded Hour of Glorious Life

I

And all the while, the people were shouting:

'Le voilà!'

'Robespierre!'

The Fraternal Supper was interrupted. Men and women pushed and jostled and screamed, the while a small, spare figure in dark cloth coat and immaculate breeches, with smooth brown hair and pale, ascetic face, stood for a moment under the lintel of a gaping porte-cochère. He had two friends with him; handsome, enthusiastic St Just, and Couthon, delicate, half-paralysed, wheeled about in a chair, with one foot in the grave, whose devotion to the tyrant was partly made up of ambition, and wholly of genuine admiration.

At the uproarious cheering which greeted his appearance, Robespierre advanced into the open, whilst a sudden swift light of triumph darted from his narrow, pale eyes.

'And you still hesitate!' St Just whispered excitedly in his ear. 'Why, you hold the people absolutely in the hollow of your hand!'

'Have patience, friend!' Couthon remonstrated quietly. 'Robespierre's hour is about to strike. To hasten it now, might be courting disaster.'

Robespierre walked a few steps down the street, keeping close to the houses on his left; his two friends, St Just and Couthon in his carrying chair, were immediately behind him, and between these three and the mob, the 'tappe-durs', striding two abreast, formed a solid phalanx.

Then, all of a sudden, the great man came to a halt, faced the crowd, and with an impressive gesture imposed silence and attention. His bodyguard cleared a space for him and he stood in the midst of them, with the light of a resin torch striking full upon his spare figure and bringing into bold relief that thin face so full of sinister expression, the cruel mouth and the coldly glittering eyes. He was looking straight across the table, on which the débris of Fraternal Suppers lay in unsavoury confusion.

On the other side of the table, Mme. de Serval with her three children sat, or rather crouched, closely huddled against one another. Joséphine was clinging to her mother, Jacques to Régine. Gone was the eagerness out of their attitude now, gone the enthusiasm that had reviled the bloodthirsty tyrant in the teeth of a threatening crowd. It seemed as if, with that terrific blow dealt by a giant hand to Bertrand who was their leader in this mad adventure, the awesome fear of death had descended upon their souls. The two young faces as well as that of Mme. de Serval appeared distorted and haggard, whilst Régine's eyes, dilated with terror, strove to meet Robespierre's steady gaze, which was charged with sinister mockery.

And for one short interval of time the crowd was silent; and the everlasting stars looked down from above on the doings of men. To these trembling, terrified young creatures, suddenly possessed with youth's passionate desire to live, with a passionate horror of death, these few seconds of tense silence must have seemed like an eternity of suffering. Then Robespierre's thin face lighted up in a portentous smile – a

smile that caused those pale cheeks younder to take on a
still more ashen hue.

'And where is our eloquent orator of a while ago?' the
great man asked quietly. 'I heard my name, for I sat at my
window looking with joy on the fraternization of the people
of France. I caught sight of the speaker, and came down to
hear more clearly what he had to say. But where is he?'

His pale eyes wandered slowly along the crowd; and
such was the power exercised by this extraordinary man,
so great the terror that he inspired, that every one there
– men, women and children, workers and vagabonds –
turned their eyes away, dared not meet his glance lest in
it they read an accusation or a threat.

Indeed, no one dared to speak. The young rhetorician had
disappeared, and every one trembled lest they should be
implicated in his escape. He had evidently got away under
cover of the confusion and the noise. But his companions
were still there – four of them; the woman and the boy
and the two girls, crouching like frightened beasts before
the obvious fury, the certain vengeance of the people. The
murmurs were ominous. 'Death! Guillotine! Traitors!' were
words easily distinguishable in the confused babbling of the
sullen crowd.

Robespierre's cruel, appraising glance rested on those
four pathetic forms, so helpless, so desperate, so terrified.

'Citizens,' he said coldly, 'did you not hear me ask where
your eloquent companion is at this moment?'

Régine alone knew that he lay like a log under the table,
close to her feet. She had seen him fall, struck by that
awful blow from a brutal fist; but at the ominous query
she instinctively pressed her trembling lips close together,
whilst Joséphine and Jacques clung to her with the strength
of despair.

'Do not parley with the rabble, citizen,' St Just whispered

eagerly. 'This is a grand moment for you. Let the people of their own accord condemn those who dared to defame you.'

And even Couthon, the prudent, added sententiously:

'Such an opportunity may never occur again.'

The people, in truth, were over-ready to take vengeance into their own hands.

'À la lanterne, les aristos!'

Gaunt, bedraggled forms leaned across the table, shook begrimed fists in the direction of the four crouching figures. With the blind instinct of trapped beasts, they retreated into the shadows step by step, as those threatening fists appeared to draw closer, clutching at the nearest table and dragging it with them, in an altogether futile attempt at a barricade.

Behind them there was nothing but the row of houses, no means of escape even if their trembling knees had not refused them service; whilst vaguely, through their terror, they were conscious of the proximity of that awful asthmatic creature with the wheezy cough and the hideous, toothless mouth. At times he seemed so close that they shut their eyes, almost feeling his grimy hands around their throat, his huge, hairy arms dragging them down to death.

It all happened in the space of a very few minutes, far fewer even than it would take completely to visualise the picture. Robespierre, like an avenging wraith, theatrical yet impassive, standing in the light of a huge resin torch, which threw alternate lights and shadows, grotesque and weird, upon his meagre figure, now elongating the thin, straight nose, now widening the narrow mouth, misshaping the figure till it appeared like some fantastic ghoul-form from the nether world. Behind him, his two friends were lost in the gloom, as were now Mme. de Serval and her children. They were ensconced against a heavy porte-cochère, a rickety table alone standing between them and the mob, who were ready to drag them to the nearest lanthorn and immolate them before the eyes of their outraged idol.

'Leave the traitors alone!' Robespierre commanded. 'Justice will deal with them as they deserve.'

'À la lanterne!' the people – more especially the women – demanded insistently.

Robespierre turned to one of his 'tappe-durs.'

'Take the aristos to the nearest Commissariat,' he said. 'I'll have no bloodshed to mar our Fraternal Supper.'

'The Commissariat, forsooth!' a raucous voice positively bellowed. 'Who is going to stand between us and our vengeance? Robespierre has been outraged by this rabble. Let them perish in sight of all!'

How it all happened after that, none who were there could in truth have told you. The darkness, the flickering lights, the glow of the braziers, which made the inky blackness around more pronounced, made everything indistinguishable to ordinary human sight. Certain it is that citizen Rateau – who had constituted himself the spokesman of the mob – was at one time seen towering behind the four unfortunates with his huge arms stretched out, his head thrown back, his mouth wide open, screaming abuse and vituperation, demanding the people's right to take the law into its own sovereign hands.

At that moment the light of the nearest resin torch threw his hulking person into bold relief against a heavy porte-cochère which was immediately behind him. The mob acclaimed him, cheered him to the echoes, agreed with him that summary justice in such a case was alone satisfying. The next instant a puff of wind blew the flame of the torch in a contrary direction, and darkness suddenly enveloped the ranting colossus and the cowering prey all ready to his hand.

'Rateau!' shouted some one.

'Hey, there! citizen Rateau! Where art thou?' came soon from every side.

No answer came from the spot where Rateau had last been seen, and it seemed as if just then a strong current of air had slammed a heavy door to somewhere in the gloom. Citizen Rateau had disappeared, and the four traitors along with him.

It took a few seconds of valuable time ere the mob suspected that it was being robbed of its prey. Then a huge upheaval occurred, a motion of the human mass densely packed in the Rue St Honoré, that was not unlike the rush of water through a narrow gorge.

'Rateau!' People were yelling the name from end to end of the street.

II

Superstition, which was rampant in these days of carnage and of crime, had possession of many a craven soul. Rateau had vanished. It seemed as if the Evil One, whose name had been so freely invoked during the course of the Fraternal Supper, had in very truth spirited Rateau away.

Robespierre himself had not altogether realised what had happened. In his innermost heart he had already yielded to his friends' suggestion, and was willing to let mob-law run its course. As St Just had said: what a triumph for himself if his detractors were lynched by the mob! When Rateau towered above the four unfortunates, hurling vituperation above their heads, the tyrant smiled, well satisfied; and when the giant thus incontinently vanished, Robespierre for a moment or two remained complacent and content.

Then the whole crowd oscillated in the direction of the mysterious porte-cochère. Those who were in the front ranks threw themselves against the heavy panels, whilst those in the rear pushed with all their might. But the porte-cochères of old Paris are heavily constructed. Woodwork that had resisted the passage of centuries withheld the onslaught of a pack of half-starved caitiffs. But only for a while.

The mob, fearing that it was getting foiled, broke into a howl of execration, and Robespierre, his face more drawn and grey than before, turned to his companions, trying to read their thoughts.

'If it should be—' St Just murmured, yet dared not put his surmise into words.

Nor had he time to do so, or Robespierre the leisure to visualise his own fears. Already the massive oak panels were yielding to persistent efforts. The mighty woodwork began to crack under the pressure of this living battering-ram; when suddenly the howls of those who were in the rear turned to a wild cry of delight. Those who were pushing against the porte-cochère paused in their task. All necks were suddenly craned upwards. The weird lights of torches and the glow of braziers glinted on gaunt necks and upturned chins, turned heads and faces into phantasmagoric, unearthly shapes.

Robespierre and his two companions instinctively looked up too. There, some few mètres lower down the street, on the third-floor balcony of a neighbouring house, the figure of Rateau had just appeared. The window immediately behind him was wide open and the room beyond was flooded with light, so that his huge person appeared distinctly silhouetted – a black and gargantuan mass – against the vivid and glowing background. His head was bare, his lank hair fluttered in the breeze, his huge chest was bare and his ragged shirt hung in tatters from his brawny arms. Flung across his left shoulder, he held an inanimate female form, whilst with his right hand he dragged another through the open window in his wake. Just below him, a huge brazier was shedding its crimson glow.

The sight of him – gaunt, weird, a veritable tower of protean revenge – paralysed the most ebullient, silenced every clamour. For the space of two seconds only did he stand there, in full view of the crowd, in full view of the almighty tyrant whose defamation he had sworn to avenge. Then he cried in stentorian tones:

'Thus perish all conspirators against the liberty of the people, all traitors to its cause, by the hands of the people and for the glory of their chosen!'

And, with a mighty twist of his huge body, he picked up the inanimate form that lay lifeless at his feet. For a moment he held the two in his arms, high above the iron railing of the balcony; for a moment those two lifeless, shapeless forms hung in the darkness in mid-air, whilst an entire crowd of fanatics held their breath and waited, awed and palpitating, only to break out into frantic cheering as the giant hurled the two lifeless bodies down, straight into the glowing brazier.

'Two more to follow!' he shouted lustily.

There was pushing and jostling and cheering. Women screamed, men blasphemed and children cried. Shouts of 'Vive Rateau!' mingled with those of 'Vive Robespierre!' A circle was formed, hands holding hands, and a wild sara-band danced around the glowing brazier. And this mad orgy of enthusiasm lasted for full three minutes, until the foremost among those who, awestruck and horrified, had approached the brazier in order to see the final agony of the abominable traitor, burst out with a prolonged 'Malediction!'

Beyond that exclamation, they were speechless – pointed with trembling hands at the shapeless bundles on which the dull fire of the braziers had not yet obtained a purchase.

The bundles were shapeless indeed. Rags hastily tied together to represent human forms; but rags only! No female traitors, no aristos beneath! The people had been fooled, hideously fooled by a traitor all the more execrable, as he had seemed one of themselves.

'Malediction! Death to the traitor!'

Aye, death indeed! The giant, whoever he might be, would have to bear a charmed life if he were to escape the maddened fury of a foiled populace.

But Rateau had disappeared. It all seemed like a dream, a nightmare. Had Rateau really existed, or was he a wraith, sent to tease and to scare those honest patriots who were out for liberty and for fraternity? Many there were who would have liked to hold on to that theory – men and women whose souls, warped and starved by the excesses and the miseries of the past five years, clung to any superstition, any so-called supernatural revelations, that failed to replace the old religion that had been banished from their hearts.

But in this case not even superstition could be allowed free play. Rateau had vanished, it is true. The house from whence he had thus mocked and flouted the people was searched through and through by a mob who found nothing but bare boards and naked walls, empty rooms and disused cupboards on which to wreak its fury.

But down there, lying on the top of the brazier, were those two bundles of rags slowly being consumed by the smouldering embers, silent proofs of the existence of that hulking creature whose size and power had, with that swiftness peculiar to human conceptions, already become legendary.

And in a third-floor room, a lamp that had recently been extinguished, a coil of rope, more rags, male and female

clothes, a pair of boots, a battered hat, were mute witnesses
to the swift passage of the mysterious giant with the wheezy
cough – the trickster who had fooled a crowd and thrown
the great Robespierre himself into ridicule.

CHAPTER 7

Two Interludes

I

Two hours later the Rue St Honoré had resumed its habitual graveyard-like stillness.

Here, as in other quarters of Paris, the fraternal suppers had come to an end; and perspiring matrons, dragging weary children at their skirts, wended their way homewards, whilst their men went to consummate the evening's entertainment at one of the numerous clubs or cabarets where the marvellous doings in the Rue St Honoré could be comfortably lived over again or retailed to those, less fortunate, who had not been there to see.

In the early morning the 'nettoyeurs publiques' would be coming along, to clear away the débris of the festivites and to gather up the tables and benches which were the property of the several Municipal sections, and put them away for the next occasion.

But these 'nettoyeurs' were not here yet.

And so the streets were entirely deserted, save here and there for the swift passage of a furtive form, hugging the walls, with hands in pockets and crimson cap pulled over the eyes, anxious only to escape the vigilance of the night-watchman, swift of foot and silent of tread; and anon, in the Rue St Honoré itself, when even these nightbirds had ceased to flutter, the noiseless movement of a dark and mysterious form that stirred cautiously upon the greasy cobblestones. More silent, more furtive than any hunted beast creeping out of its lair, this mysterious form emerged from under one of the tables that was standing nearly opposite the house where Robespierre lived and close to the one where the superhuman colossus had wrought his magic trick.

It was Bertrand Moncrif. No longer a fiery Demosthenes now, but a hunted, terror-filled human creature, whom a stunning blow from a giant fist had rendered senseless, even whilst it saved him from the consequences of his own folly. His senses still reeling, his limbs cramped and aching, he had lain stark and still under the table just where he had fallen, not sufficiently conscious to realise what was happening beyond his very limited range of vision or to marvel what was the ultimate fate of his companions.

His only instinct throughout this comatose condition was the blind one of self-preservation. Feeling rather than hearing the tumult around him, he had gathered his limbs close together, lain as still as a mouse, crouching within himself in the shelter of the table above. It was only when the silence around had lasted an eternity of time that he ventured out of his hiding-place. With utmost caution, hardly daring to breathe, he crept on hands and knees and looked about him, up and down the street. There was no one about. The night fortunately was moonless and dark; nature had put herself on the side of those who wished to pass unperceived.

Bertrand struggled to his feet, smothering a cry of pain. His head ached furiously, his knees shook under him; but he managed to crawl as far as the nearest house, and rested for awhile against its wall. The fresh air did him good.

He ventured to look fearfully up and down the street. Tables scattered pell-mell, the unsavoury remnants of fraternal suppers, a couple of smouldering braziers, collectively met his gaze. And, at one point, sprawling across a table, with head lost between outstretched arms, a figure, apparently asleep, perhaps dead.

Bertrand, now nothing but a bundle of nerves, could hardly suppress a cry of terror. It seemed to him as if his life depended on whether that sprawling figure was alive or dead. But he dared not approach in order to make sure. For awhile he waited, sinking more and more deeply into the shadows, watching that motionless form on which his life depended.

The figure did not move, and gradually Bertrand nerved himself up to confidence and then to action. He buried his head in the folds of his coat-collar and his hands in the pockets of his breeches, and with silent, stealthy footsteps he started to make his way down the street. At first he looked back once or twice at the immobile figure sprawling across the table. It had not moved, still appeared as if it might be dead. Then Bertrand took to his heels and, no longer looking either behind him or to the right or left, with elbows pressed close to his side, he started to run in the direction of the Tuileries.

A minute later, the motionless figure came back to life, rose quickly and with swift, noiseless tread, started to run in the same direction.

II

In the cabarets throughout the city, the chief topic of conversation was the mysterious event of the Rue St Honoré. Those who had seen it all had marvellous tales to tell of the hero of the adventure.

'The man was eight or else nine feet high; his arms reached right across the street from house to house. Flames spurted out of his mouth when he coughed. He had horns on his head; cloven feet; a forked tail!'

These were but a few of the asseverations which rendered the person of the fictitious citizen Rateau a legendary one in the eyes of those who had witnessed his amazing prowess. Those who had not been thus favoured listened wide-eyed and open-mouthed.

But all agreed that the mysterious giant was in truth none other than the far-famed Englishman – that spook, that abominable trickster, that devil incarnate, known to the Committees as the Scarlet Pimpernel.

'But how could it be the Englishman?' was suddenly put forward by citizen Hottot, the picturesque landlord of the Cabaret de la Liberté, a well-known rendezvous close to the Carrousel. 'How could it be the Englishman who played you that trick, seeing that you all say it was citizen Rateau who . . . The devil take it all!' he added, and scratched his bald head with savage vigour, which he always did whene'er he felt sorely perplexed. 'A man can't be two at one and the same time; nor two men become one. Nor . . . Name of a name of a dog!' concluded the worthy citizen, puffing and blowing in the maze of his own puzzlement like an old walrus that is floundering in the water.

'It was the Englishman, I tell thee!' one of his customers asserted indignantly. 'Ask anyone who saw him! Ask the tappe-durs! Ask Robespierre himself! *He* saw him, and turned as grey as – as putty, I tell thee!' he concluded, with more conviction than eloquence.

'And *I* tell thee,' broke in citizen Sical, the butcher – he with the bullet-head and bull-neck and a fist that could in truth have felled an ox; 'I tell thee that it was citizen Rateau. Don't I know citizen Rateau?' he added, and brought that heavy fist of his down upon the upturned cask on which stood pewter mugs and bottles of eau de vie, and glared aggressively round upon the assembly.

One man alone was bold enough to take up the challenge – a wizened little fellow, a printer by trade, with skin of the texture of grained oak and a few unruly curls that tumbled over one another above a highly polished forehead.

'And I tell thee, citizen Sical,' he said with firm decision; 'I tell thee and those who aver, as thou dost, that citizen Rateau had anything to do with those monkey-tricks, that ye lie. Yes!' he reiterated emphatically, and paying no heed to the glowering looks and blasphemies of Sical and his friends. 'Yes, ye lie! Not consciously, I grant you: but you lie nevertheless. Because all the while that ye were supping at the expense of the State in the open, and had your gizzards stirred by the juggling devices of some unknown mountebank, citizen Rateau was lying comfortably drunk and snoring lustily in the antechamber of Mother Théot, the soothsayer, right at the other end of Paris!'

'How do you know that, citizen Langlois?' queried the host with icy reproval, for butcher Sical was his best customer, and Sical did not like being contradicted. But little Langlois with the shiny forehead and tiny, beady, humorous eyes, continued unperturbed.

'Pardi!' he said gaily, 'because I was at Mother Théot's myself, and saw him there.'

Sical, and those who had fought against the Scarlet Pimpernel theory, were too staggered to speak. They continued to imbibe citizen Hottot's eau de vie in sullen brooding. The idea of the legendary Englishman, which had so unexpectedly been strengthened by citizen Langlois' statement concerning Rateau, was repugnant to their common sense. Superstition was all very well for women and weaklings like Langlois; but for men to be asked to accept

71

the theory that a kind of devil in human shape had so thrown dust in the eyes of a number of perfectly sober patriots that they literally could not believe what they saw, was nothing short of an insult.

And they had *seen* Rateau at the fraternal supper, had talked with him, until the moment when . . . Then who in Satan's name had they been talking with?

'Here, Langlois! Tell us—'

And Langlois, who had become the hero of the hour, told all he knew, and told it, we are told, a dozen times and more. How he had gone to Mother Théot's at about four o'clock in the afternoon, and had sat patiently waiting beside his friend Rateau, who wheezed and snored alternately for a couple of hours. How, at six o'clock or a little after, Rateau went out because – the aristo, forsooth! – had found the atmosphere filthy in Mother Théot's antechamber – no doubt he went to get another drink.

'At about half-past seven,' the little printer went on glibly, 'my turn came to speak with the old witch. When I came out it was long past eight o'clock and quite dark. I saw Rateau sprawling upon a bench, half asleep. I tried to speak with him, but he only grunted. However, I went out then to get a bit of supper at one of the open-air places, and at ten o'clock I was once more past Mother Théot's place. One or two people were coming out of the house. They were all grumbling because they had been told to go. Rateau was one who was for making a disturbance, but I took him by the arm. We went down the street together, and parted company in the Rue de l'Anier, where he lodges. And here I am!' concluded Langlois, and turned triumphantly to challenge the gaze of every one of the sceptics around him.

There was not a single doubtful point in his narrative, and though he was questioned – aye! and severely cross-questioned, too – he never once swerved from his narrative or in any manner did he contradict himself. Later on it transpired that there were others who had been in Mother Théot's antechamber that day. They too subsequently corroborated all that the little printer had said. One of them was the wife of Sical's own brother; and there were others. So, what would you?

'Name of a name of a dog, then, who was it who spirited the aristos away?'

CHAPTER 8

The Beautiful Spaniard

I

In the Rue Villedot, which is in the Louvre quarter of Paris, there is a house, stone built and five-storied, with grey shutters to all the windows and balconies of wrought iron – a house exactly similar to hundreds and thousands of others in every quarter of Paris. During the day the small wicket in the huge porte-cochère is usually kept open; it allows a peep into a short dark passage, and beyond it to the lodge of the concierge.

On the left of the entrance passage and opposite the lodge of the concierge there is a tall glass door, and beyond it the vestibule and primary staircase, which gives access to the principal apartments – those that look out upon the street and are altogether more luxurious and more airy than those which give upon the courtyard. To the latter two back stairways give access. They are at the far corners of the courtyard; both are pitch dark and reek of stuffiness and evil smells. The apartments which they serve, especially those on the lower floors, are dependent for light and air on what modicum of these gifts of heaven comes down the shaft into the quadrangle.

After dark, of course, porte-cochère and wicket are both closed, and if a belated lodger or visitor desires to enter the house, he must ring the bell and the concierge in his lodge will pull a communicating cord that will unlatch the wicket. It is up to the belated visitor or lodger to close the wicket after him, and he is bound by law to give his name, together with the number of the apartment to which he is going, in to the concierge as he goes past the lodge. The concierge, on the other hand, will take a look at him so that he may identify him should trouble or police inquiry arise.

On this night of April, somewhere near midnight, there was a ring at the outer door. Citizen Leblanc, the concierge, roused from his first sleep, pulled the communicating cord. A young man, hatless and in torn coat and muddy boots and breeches, slipped in through the wicket and hurried past the lodge, giving only one name, but that in a clear voice, as he passed:

'Citoyenne Cabarrus.'

The concierge turned over in his bed and grunted, half asleep. His duty clearly was to run after the visitor, who had failed to give his own name; but to begin with, the worthy concierge was very tired; and then the name which the belated caller had given was one requiring special consideration.

The citoyenne Cabarrus was young and well favoured, and even in these troublous days, youth and beauty demanded certain privileges which no patriotic concierge could refuse to grant. Moreover, the aforesaid lady had visitors at all hours of the day and late into the night – visitors for the most part with whom it was not well to interfere. Citizen Tallien, the popular Representative in the Convention was, as every one knew, her ardent adorer. 'Twas said by all and sundry that since the days when he met the fair Cabarrus in Bordeaux and she exercised such a mellowing influence upon his bloodthirsty patriotism, he had no thought save to win her regard.

But he was not the only one who came to the dreary old apartment in the Rue Villedot, with a view to worshipping at the Queen of Beauty's shrine. Citizen Leblanc had seen many a great Representative of the People pass by his lodge since the beautiful Theresia came to dwell here. And if he became very confidential and his interlocutor very insistent, he would throw out a hint that the greatest man in France today was a not infrequent visitor in the house.

Obviously, therefore, it was best not to pry too closely into secrets, the keeping of which might prove uncomfortable for one's peace of mind. And citizen Leblanc, tossing restlessly in his sleep, dreamed of the fair Cabarrus and wished himself in the place of those who were privileged to pay their court to her.

II

And so the belated visitor was able to make his way across the courtyard and up the dark back stairs unmolested. But even this reassuring fact failed to give him confidence. He hurried on with the swift and stealthy footstep which had become habitual to him, glancing over his shoulder from time to time, wide-eyed and with ears alert, and heart quivering with apprehension.

Up the dark and narrow staircase he hurried, dizzy and sick, his head reeling in the dank atmosphere, his shaking hands seeking the support of the walls as he climbed wearily up to the third floor. Here he almost measured his length upon the landing, tottered up again and came down sprawling on his knees against one of the doors – the one

which had the number 22 painted upon it. For the moment
it seemed as if he would once more fall into a swoon. Terror
and relief were playing havoc with his whirling brain. He
had not sufficient strength to stretch out an arm in order to
ring the bell, but only beat feebly against the panel of the
door with his moist palm.

A moment later the door was opened, and the unfortunate
fell forward into the vestibule at the feet of a tall apparition
clad in white and holding a small table lamp above her
head. The apparition gave a little scream which was entirely
human and wholly feminine, hastily put down the lamp
on a small console close by, and by retreating forcefully
farther into the vestibule, dragged the half-animate form
of the young man along too; for he was now clinging to
a handful of white skirt with the strength of despair.

'I am lost, Theresia!' he moaned pitiably. 'Hide me, for
God's sake! . . . only for tonight!'

Theresia Cabarrus was frowning now, looked more perplexed than kindly, and certainly made no attempt to raise
the crouching figure from the ground. Anon she called
loudly: 'Pepita!' and whilst waiting for an answer to this
call, she remained quite still, and the frown of puzzlement
on her face yielded to one of fear. The young man, obviously
only half-conscious, continued to moan and to implore.

The next moment an old woman came from somewhere
out of the darkness, threw up her hands at sight of that
grovelling figure on the floor, and would no doubt have
broken out in loud lament but that her young mistress
ordered her at once to close the door.

'Then help the citoyen Moncrif to a sofa in my room,'
the beautiful Theresia went on peremptorily. 'Give him a
restorative and see above all to it that he hold his tongue!'

With a quick imperious jerk she freed herself from the
convulsive grasp of the young man, and walking quickly

across the small vestibule, she went through a door at the
end of it that had been left ajar, leaving the unfortunate
Moncrif to the ministrations of Pepita.

III

Theresia Cabarrus was, in this year 1794, in her twenty-
fourth year, and perhaps in the zenith of her beauty and
in the plenitude of that power which had subjugated so
many men. In what that power consisted the historian has
vainly tried to guess; for it was not her beauty only that
brought so many to her feet. In the small oval face, the
pointed chin, the full, sensuous lips, so typically Spanish,
we look in vain for traces of that beauty which we are
told surpassed that of other women of her time; whilst in
the dark, velvety eyes, more tender than spiritual, and in
the narrow arched brows, we fail to find an expression
of that *esprit* which had moulded Tallien to her will and
even brought Robespierre out of the shell of his asceticism
– a willing victim to her wiles.

But who would be bold enough to analyse that subtle
quality, acknowledged by all, possessed by a very few,
which is vaguely denoted by the word 'charm'? Theresia
Cabarrus must have possessed it to a marvellous degree
– that, and an utter callousness for the feelings of her
victims, which would leave her mind cool and keen to
pursue her own ends, whilst theirs was thrown into that
maze of jealousy and of passion wherein prudence flies
to the winds and the fever of self-immolation gets into
the blood.

At this moment, in the sparsely furnished room of her

dingy apartment, she looked like an angry goddess. Her figure, which undeniably was superb, was drawn to its full height, its splendid proportions accentuated by the clinging folds of her modish gown – a marvel of artistic scantiness, which only half concealed the perfectly modelled bust, and left the rounded thigh, in its skin-tight, flesh-coloured undergarment, unblushingly exposed. Her blue-black hair was dressed in the new fashion, copied from ancient Greece and snooded by a glittering antique fillet; and her small bare feet were encased in satin sandals. Truly a lovely woman, but for that air of cold displeasure coupled with fear, which marred the harmony of the dainty, child-like features.

After awhile Pepita came back.

'Well?' queried Theresia impatiently.

'Poor M. Bertrand is very ill,' the old Spanish woman replied. 'He has fever, the poor cabbage. Bed is the only place for him . . .'

'He cannot stay here, as thou well knowest, Pepita,' the imperious beauty retorted drily. 'Thy head and mine are in danger every moment that he spends under this roof.'

'But thou couldst not turn a sick man out into the streets in the middle of the night.'

'Why not?' Theresia riposted coldly.

'Because he would die on thy doorstep,' was old Pepita's muttered reply.

Theresia shrugged her shoulders.

'He dies if he goes,' she said slowly, 'and we die if he stays. Tell him to go, Pepita, ere citizen Tallien comes.'

'It is late,' she protested. 'Citizen Tallien will not come tonight.'

'Not only he,' Theresia rejoined coldly, 'but – but – the other – Thou knowest well, Pepita – those two arranged to meet here in my lodgings tonight.'

'But not at this hour!'

'After the sitting of the Convention.'

'It is nearly midnight. They'll not come,' the old woman persisted obstinately.

'They arranged to meet here, to talk over certain matters which interest their party,' citoyenne Cabarrus went on, equally firmly. 'They'll not fail. So tell citizen Moncrif to go, Pepita. He endangers my life by staying here.'

'Then do the dirty work thyself,' the old woman muttered sullenly. 'I'll not be a party to cold-blooded murder.'

'Well, since citizen Moncrif's life is more valuable to thee than mine—' Theresia began, but got no farther.

Bertrand Moncrif, very pale, still looking scared and wild, had quietly entered the room.

'You wish me to go, Theresia,' he said simply. 'You did not think surely that I would do anything that might endanger your safety. My God!' he added with passionate vehemence, 'Do you not know that I would at any time lay down my life for yours?'

'Of course, of course, Bertrand,' she said a little impatiently, though obviously trying to be kind. 'But I do entreat you not to go into heroics at this hour, and not to put on tragic airs. You must see that for yourself as well as for me it would be fatal if you were found here, and—'

'And I am going, Theresia,' he broke in seriously. 'I ought never to have come. I was a fool, as usual!' he added with bitterness. 'But after that awful fracas I was dazed and hardly knew what I was doing.'

The frown of vexation reappeared upon the woman's fair, smooth brow.

'The fracas?' she asked quickly. 'What fracas?'

'In the Rue St Honoré. I thought you knew.'

'No. I know nothing,' she retorted, and her voice now was trenchant and hard. 'What happened?'

'They were deifying that brute Robespierre—'

'Silence!' she broke in harshly. 'Name no names.'

'They were deifying a bloodthirsty tyrant, and I—'

'And you rose from your seat,' she broke in again, and this time with a laugh that was cruel in its biting irony: 'and lashed yourself into a fury of eloquent vituperation. Oh, I know! I know!' she went on excitedly. 'You and your Fatalists, or whatever you call yourselves! And that rage for martyrdom! . . . Senseless, stupid and selfish! Oh, my God! *how* selfish! And then you came here to drag me down with you into an abyss of misery, along with you to the guillotine . . . to . . .'

It seemed as if she were choking, and her small white hands, with a gruesome and pathetic gesture, went up to her neck, smoothed it and fondled it, as if to shield it from that awful fate.

Bertrand tried to pacify her. It was he who was the more calm of the two now. It seemed as if *her* danger had brought him back to full consciousness. He forgot his own danger, the threat of death which lay in wait for him, probably on the very threshold of this house. He was a marked man now; martyrdom had ceased to be a dream: it had become a grim reality. But of this he did not think. Theresia was in danger, compromised by his own callous selfishness. His mind was full of her; and Régine, the true and loyal friend, the beloved of past happier years, had no place in his thoughts beside the exquisite enchantress, whose very nearness was paradise.

'I am going,' he said earnestly. 'Theresia, my beloved, try to forgive me. I was a fool – a criminal fool! But lately – since I thought that you – you did not really care; that all my hopes of future happiness were naught but senseless dreams; since then I seem to have lost my head – I don't know *what* I am doing! . . . And so—'

He got no farther. Ashamed of his own weakness, he was

too proud to let her see that she made him suffer. For the moment, he only bent the knee and kissed the hem of her diaphanous gown. He looked so handsome then, despite his bedraggled, woebegone appearance – so young, so ardent, that Theresia's egotistical heart was touched, as it had always been when the incense of his perfect love rose to her sophisticated nostrils. She put out her hand and brushed with a gentle, almost maternal, gesture the matted brown hair from his brow.

'Dear Bertrand,' she murmured vaguely. 'What a foolish boy to think that I do not care!'

Already he had been brought back to his senses. The imminence of her danger lent him the courage which he had been lacking, and unhesitatingly now he jumped to his feet and turned to go. But she, quick in the transition of her moods, had already seized him by the arm.

'No, no!' she murmured in a hoarse whisper. 'Don't go just yet . . . not before Pepita has seen if the stairs are clear.'

Her small hand held him as in a vice, whilst Pepita, obedient and silent, was shuffling across the vestibule in order to execute her mistress's commands. But, even so, Bertrand struggled to get away. An epitome of their whole life, this struggle between them! – he trying to free himself from those insidious bonds that held him one moment and loosed him the next; that numbed him to all that he was wont to hold sacred and dear – his love for Régine, his loyalty, his honour. An epitome of her character and his: he, weak and yielding, ever a ready martyr thirsting for self-immolation; and she, just a bundle of feminine caprice, swayed by sentiment one moment and by considerations of ambition or of personal safety the next.

'You must wait, Bertrand,' she urged insistently. 'Citizen Tallien may be on the stairs – he or – or the other. If they saw you! . . . My God!'

'They would conclude that you had turned me out of doors,' he riposted simply. 'Which would, in effect, be the truth. I entreat you to let me go!' he added earnestly.

The old woman's footsteps were heard hurrying back. Bertrand struggled to free himself – did in truth succeed; and Theresia smothered a desperate cry of warning as he strode rapidly through the door and across the vestibule only to be met here by Pepita, who pushed him with all her might incontinently back.

Theresia held her tiny handkerchief to her mouth to deaden the scream that forced itself to her lips. She had followed Bertrand out of the salon, and now stood in the doorway, a living statue of fear.

'Citizen Tallien,' Pepita had murmured hurriedly. 'He is on the landing. Come this way.'

She dragged Bertrand by the arm, not waiting for orders from her mistress this time, along a narrow dark passage, which at its extreme end gave access to a tiny kitchen. Into this she pushed him and locked the door upon him.

'Name of a name!' she muttered as she shuffled back to the vestibule. 'If they should find him here!'

Citoyenne Cabarrus had not moved. Her eyes, dilated with terror, mutely questioned the old woman as the latter made ready to admit the visitor. Pepita gave reply as best she could, by silent gestures, indicating the passage and the action of turning a key in the lock. Her wrinkled old lips hardly stirred, and then only in order to murmur quickly and with a sudden assumption of authority:

'Self-possession, my cabbage, or you'll endanger yourself and us all!'

Theresia pulled herself together. Obviously the old woman's warning was not to be ignored, nor had it been given a moment too soon. Outside, the visitor had renewed his impatient rat-tat against the door. The eyes of mistress and maid met for one brief second. Theresia was rapidly regaining her presence of mind; whereupon Pepita smoothed out her apron, readjusted her cap, and went to open the door, even whilst Theresia said in a firm voice, loudly enough for the new visitor to hear:

'One of my guests, at last! Open quickly, Pepita!'

CHAPTER 9

A Hideous, Fearful Hour

I

A young man – tall, spare, with sallow skin and shifty, restless eyes – pushed unceremoniously past the old servant, threw his hat and cane down on the nearest chair, and hurrying across the vestibule, entered the salon where the beautiful Spaniard, a picture of serene indifference, sat ready to receive him.

She had chosen for the setting of this scene a small settee covered in old rose brocade. On this she half sat, half reclined, with an open book in her hand, her elbow resting on the frame of the settee, her cheek leaning against her hand. Immediately behind her, the light from an oil lamp tempered by a shade of rose-coloured silk, outlined with a brilliant, glowing pencil the contour of her small head, one exquisite shoulder, and the mass of her raven hair, whilst it accentuated the cool half-tones on her diaphanous gown, on the round bare arms and bust, the tiny sandalled feet and cross-gartered legs.

A picture in truth to dazzle the eyes of any man! Tallien should have been at her feet in an instant. The fact that he paused in the doorway bore witness to the unruly thoughts that ran riot in his brain.

'Ah, citizen Tallien!' the fair Theresia exclaimed with a perfect assumption of sang-froid. 'You are the first to arrive, and are indeed welcome; for I was nearly swooning with ennui. Well!' she added, with a provocative smile, and extended a gracious arm in his direction. 'Are you not going to kiss my hand?'

'I heard a voice,' was all the response which he gave to this seductive invitation. 'A man's voice. Whose was it?'

'A man's voice?' she riposted with a perfect air of aston-ishment. 'You are crazy, mon ami; or else are crediting my faithful Pepita with a virile bass, which in truth she doth not possess!'

'Whose voice was it?' Tallien reiterated, making an effort to speak calmly, even though he was manifestly shaking with choler.

Whereupon the fair Theresia, no longer gracious or arch, looked him up and down as if he were no better than a lackey.

'Ah, ça!' she rejoined coldly. 'Are you perchance trying to cross-question me? By what right, I pray you, citizen Tallien, do you assume this hectoring tone in my presence? I am not yet your wife, remember; and 'tis not you, I imagine, who are the dictator of France.'

'Do not tease me, Theresia!' the man interposed hoarsely. 'Bertrand Moncrif is here.'

For the space of a second, or perhaps less, Theresia gave no reply to the taunt. Her quick, alert brain had already faced possibilities, and she was far too clever a woman to take the risks which a complete evasion of the truth would have entailed at this moment. She did not, in effect, know whether Tallien was speaking from positive information given to him by spies, or merely from conjecture born of jealousy. Moreover, another would be here presently – another, whose spies were credited with omniscience, and whom she might not succeed in dominating with a smile or a frown, as she could the lovesick Tallien. Therefore, after that one brief instant's reflection she decided to temporise, to shelter behind a halftruth, and replied, with a quick glance from under her long lashes:

'I am not teasing you, citizen. Bertrand came here for shelter awhile ago.'

Tallien drew a quick sigh of satisfaction, and she went on carelessly:

'But, obviously, I could not keep him here. He seemed hurt and frightened . . . He has been gone this past halfhour.'

For a moment it seemed as if the man, in face of this obvious lie, would flare out into a hot retort; but Theresia's luminous eyes subdued him, and before the cool contempt expressed by those exquisite lips, he felt all his blustering courage oozing away.

'The man is an abominable and an avowed traitor,' he said sullenly. 'Only two hours ago—'

'I know,' she broke in coldly. 'He vilified Robespierre. A dangerous thing to do. Bertrand was ever a fool, and he lost his head.'

'He will lose it more effectually tomorrow.'

'You mean that you would denounce him?'

'That I *will* denounce him. I would have done so tonight, before coming here, only – only—'

'Only what?'

'I was afraid he might be here.'

Theresia broke into a ringing if somewhat artificial peal of laughter.

'I must thank you, citizen, for this consideration of my feelings. It was, in truth, thoughtful of you to think of sparing me a scandal. But, since Bertrand is *not* here—'

'I know where he lodges. He'll not escape, citoyenne. My word on it!'

In answer to his last threatening words, the lovely Theresia rejoined, more seriously:

'So as to make sure I do not escape either!' And a flash of withering anger shot from her dark eyes on the unromantic figure of her adorer. 'Or you, mon ami! You are determined that Mme. Roland's fate shall overtake me, eh? And no doubt you will be thrilled to the marrow when you see my head fall into your precious salad-bowl. Will yours follow mine, think you? Or will you prefer to emulate citizen Roland's more romantic ending?'

Even while she spoke, Tallien had been unable to repress a shudder.

'Theresia, in heaven's name—!' he murmured.

'Bah, mon ami! There is no longer a heaven these days. You and your party have carefully abolished the Hereafter. So, after you and I have taken our walk up the steps of the scaffold—'

'Theresia!'

'Eh, what?' she went on coolly. 'Is that not perchance what you have in contemplation? Moncrif, you say, is an avowed traitor. Has openly vilified and insulted your demi-god. He has been seen coming to my apartments. Good! I tell you that he is no longer here. But let that pass. He is denounced. Good! Sent to the guillotine. Good again! And Theresia Cabarrus in whose house he tried to seek refuge, much against her will, goes to the guillotine in his company. The prospect may please you, mon ami, because for the moment you are suffering from a senseless attack of jealousy. But I confess that it does not appeal to me.'

The man was silent now; awed against his will. His curiously restless eyes swept over the graceful apparition before him. Insane jealousy was fighting a grim fight in his heart with terror for his beloved. Her argument was a sound one. Even he was bound to admit that. Powerful though he was in the Convention, his influence was as nothing compared with that of Robespierre. And he knew his redoubtable colleague well enough that an insult such as Moncrif had put upon him in the Rue St Honoré this night would never be forgiven, neither in the young hot-head himself nor in any of his friends, adherents, or mere pitying sympathisers.

Theresia Cabarrus was clever enough and quick enough to see that she had gained one point.

'Come and kiss my hand,' she said, with a little sigh of satisfaction.

This time the man obeyed, without an instant's hesitation. Already he was down on his knees, repentant and humiliated. She gave him her small, sandalled foot to kiss. After that, Tallien became abject.

'You know that I would die for you, Theresia!' he murmured passionately.

For the second time tonight, Theresia passed her cool white hand over the bent head of an ardent worshipper, whilst her lips murmured vaguely:

'Foolish! Oh, how foolish! Why do men torture themselves, I wonder, with senseless jealousy?'

Instinctively she turned her small head in the direction of the passage and the little kitchen, where Bertrand Moncrif had found temporary and precarious shelter. Self-pity and a kind of fierce helplessness not untinged with remorse made her eyes appear resentful and hard.

There, in the stuffy little kitchen at the end of the dark, dank passage, love in its pure sense, happiness, brief perhaps but unalloyed, and certainly obscure, lay in wait for her. Here, at her feet, was security in the present turmoil, power, and a fitting background for her beauty and her talents. She did not want to lose Bertrand; indeed, she did not intend to lose him. She sighed a little regretfully as she thought of his good looks, his enthusiasm, his selfless ardour. Then she looked down once more on the narrow shoulders, the lank, colourless hair, the bony hands of the erstwhile lawyer's clerk to whom she had already promised marriage and she shuddered a little when she remembered that those same hands into which she had promised to place her own and which now grasped hers in passionate adoration had, of a certainty, signed the order for those execrable massacres which had for ever sullied the early days of the Revolution. For a moment – a brief one, in truth – she marvelled if union with such a man was not too heavy a price to pay for immunity and for power.

But the hesitancy only lasted a few seconds. The next, she had thrown back her head as if in defiance of the whisperings of conscience and of heart. She need not lose her youthful lover after all. He was satisfied with so little! A few kind words here, an occasional kiss, a promise or two, and he would always remain her willing slave.

It were foolish indeed, and far, far too late, to give way to sentiment at this hour, when Tallien's influence in the Convention was second only to that of Robespierre, whilst Bertrand Moncrif was a fugitive, a suspect, a poor miserable fanatic, whose hot-headedness was for ever landing him from one dangerous situation into another.

So, after indulging in the faintest little sigh of yearning for the might-have-been, she met her latest adorer's worshipping glance with a coquettish air of womanly submission, which completed his subjugation, and said lightly:

'And now give me my orders for tonight, mon ami.'

She settled herself down more comfortably upon the settee, and graciously allowed him to sit on a low chair beside her.

II

The turbulent little incident was closed. Theresia had her way, and poor, harassed Tallien succeeded in shutting away in the innermost recesses of his heart the pangs of jealousy which still tortured him. His goddess now was all smiles, and the subtle flattery implied by her preference for him above his many rivals warmed his atrophied heart and soothed his boundless vanity.

III

'Give me my orders for tonight,' the lovely woman had said to her future lord. And he – a bundle of vanity and egoism – was flattered and soothed by this submission, though he knew in his heart of hearts that it was only pretence.

'You will help me, Theresia?' he pleaded.

She nodded, and asked coldly: 'How?'

'You know that Robespierre suspects me,' he went on, and instinctively, at the mere breathing of that awe-inspiring name his voice sank lower to a murmur. 'Ever since I came back from Bordeaux.'

'I know. Your leniency there is attributed to me.'

'It was your influence, Theresia—' he began.

'That turned you,' she broke in coldly, 'from a blood-stained beast into a right-minded justiciary. Do you regret it?'

'No, no!' he protested; 'since it gained me your love.'

'Could I love a beast of prey?' she retorted. 'But if you do not regret, you are certainly afraid.'

'Robespierre never forgives,' he rejoined vaguely. 'And he had sent me to Bordeaux to punish, not to pardon.'

'Then you *are* afraid!' she insisted. 'Has anything happened?'

'No; only his usual hints – his vague threats. You know them.'

She nodded.

'The same,' he went on sombrely, 'that he used ere he struck Danton.'

'Danton was hot-headed. He was too proud to appeal to the populace who idolised him.'

'And I have no popularity to which I can appeal. If Robespierre strikes at me in the Convention, I am doomed—'

'Unless you strike first.'

'I have no following. We none of us have. Robespierre sways the Convention with one word.'

'You mean,' she broke in more vehemently, 'that you are all cringing cowards – the abject slaves of one man. Two hundred of you are longing for this era of bloodshed to cease; two hundred would stay the pitiless work of the guillotine – and not one is plucky enough to cry, "Halt! It is enough!"'

'The first man who cries "Halt!" is called a traitor,' Tallien retorted gloomily. 'And the guillotine will not rest until Robespierre himself has said, "It is enough!"'

'He alone knows what he wants. He alone fears no one,' she exclaimed, almost involuntarily giving grudging admiration where in truth she felt naught but loathing.

'I would not fear either, Theresia,' he protested, and there was a note of tender reproach in his voice, 'if it were not for you.'

'I know that, mon ami,' she rejoined with an impatient little sigh. 'Well, what do you want me to do?'

He leaned forward in his chair, closer to her, and did not

mark – poor fool! – that, as he drew near, she recoiled ever so slightly from him.

'There are two things,' he said insinuatingly, 'which you could do, Theresia, either of which would place Robespierre under such lasting obligation to you that he would admit us into the inner circle of his friends, trust us and confide in us as he does in St Just or Couthon.'

'Trust you, you mean. He never would trust a woman.'

'It means the same thing – security for us both.'

'Well?' she rejoined. 'What are these two things?'

'Firstly, there is Bertrand Moncrif . . . and his Fatalists—'

Her face hardened. She shook her head.

'I warned Robespierre about tonight,' she said. 'I knew that a lot of young fools meant to cause a fracas in the Rue St Honoré. But the whole thing has been a failure, and Robespierre has no use for failures.'

'It need not be a failure – even yet.'

'What do you mean?'

'Robespierre will be here directly,' he urged, in a whisper rendered hoarse with excitement. 'Bertrand Moncrif is here— Why not deliver the young traitor, and earn Robespierre's gratitude?'

'Oh!' she broke in in indignant protest. Then, as she caught the look of jealous anger which at her obvious agitation suddenly flared up in his narrow eyes again, she went on with a careless shrug of her statuesque shoulders: 'Bertrand is not here, as I told you, my friend. So these means of serving your cause are out of my reach.'

'Theresia,' he urged, 'by deceiving me—'

'By tantalising me,' she broke in harshly, 'you do yourself no good. Let us understand one another, my friend,' she went on more gently. 'You wish me to serve you by serving the dictator of France. And I tell you you'll not gain your ends by taunting me.'

'Theresia, we must make friends with Robespierre! He has the power; he rules over France. Whilst I—'

'Ah!' she retorted with vehemence. 'That is where you and your weak-kneed friends are wrong! You say that Robespierre rules France. 'Tis not true. It is not Robespierre, the man, who rules; it is his name! The name of Robespierre has become a fetish, an idolatry. Before it every head is bent and every courage cowed. It rules by the fear which it evokes and by the slavery which it compels under the perpetual threat of death. Believe me,' she insisted, ''tis not Robespierre who rules, but the guillotine which he wields! And we are all of us helpless – you and I and your friends. And all the others who long to see the end of this era of bloodshed and of revenge, we have got to do as he tells us – pile up crime upon crime, massacre upon massacre, and bear the odium of it all, while he stands aloof in darkness and in solitude, the brain that guides, whilst you and your party are only the hands that strike. Oh! the humiliation of it! And if you were but men, all of you, instead of puppets—'

'Hush, Theresia, in heaven's name!' Tallien broke in peremptorily at last. He had vainly tried to pacify her while she poured forth the vials of her resentment and her contempt. But now his ears, attuned to sensitiveness by an ever-present danger, had caught a sound which proceeded from the vestibule – a sound which made him shudder – a footstep – the opening of a door – a voice. 'Hush!' he entreated. 'Every dumb wall has ears, these days!'

'You are right, my friend,' she said under her breath. 'What do I care, after all? What do any of us care now, so long as our necks are fairly safe upon our shoulders? But I'll not sell Bertrand,' she added firmly. 'If I did it I should despise myself too much and hate you worse. So tell me quickly what else I can do to propitiate the ogre!'

'He'll tell you himself,' Tallien murmured hurriedly, as the sounds in the vestibule became more loud and distinctive. 'Here they are! And, in heaven's name, Theresia, remember that our lives are at that one man's mercy!'

CHAPTER 10

The Grim Idol That The World Adores

I

Theresia, being a woman, was necessarily the more accomplished actor. While Tallien retired into a gloomy corner of the room, vainly trying to conceal his agitation, she rose quite serene in order to greet her visitors.

Pepita had just admitted into her mistress's apartments a singular group, composed of two able-bodied men supporting a palsied one. One of the former was St Just, one of the most romantic figures of the Revolutionary period, the confidant and intimate friend of Robespierre and own cousin to Armand St Just and to the beautiful Marguerite, who had married the fastidious English milor, Sir Percy Blakeney. The other was Chauvelin, at one time one of the most influential members of the Committee of Public Safety, now little more than a hanger-on of Robespierre's party. A man of no account, to whom not even Tallien and his colleagues thought it worth while to pay their court. The palsied man was Couthon, despite his crimes an almost pathetic figure in his helplessness, after his friends had deposited him in an armchair and wrapped a rug around his knees. The carrying chair in which he spent the greater part of his life had been left down below in the concierge's lodge, and St Just and Chauvelin had carried him up the three flights of stairs to citoyenne Cabarrus's apartment.

Close behind these three men came Robespierre.

Heavens! If a thunderbolt had fallen from the skies on that night of the 26th of April, 1794, and destroyed house No. 22 in the Rue Villedot, with all those who were in it, what a torrent of blood would have been stemmed, what horrors averted, what misery forefended!

But nothing untoward happened. The four men who sat that night and well into the small hours of the morning in the dingy apartment, occupied for the present by the beautiful Cabarrus, were allowed by inscrutable Providence to discuss their nefarious designs unchecked.

In truth there was no discussion. One man dominated the small assembly, even though he sat for the most part silent and apparently self-absorbed, wrapped in that taciturnity and even occasional somnolence which seemed to have become a pose with him of late.

St Just, on the other hand – young, handsome, a brilliant talker and convinced enthusiast – was only too willing to air his compelling eloquence, was in effect the mouthpiece of the great man as he was his confidant and his right hand.

Then there was Couthon, sarcastic and contemptuous, delighting to tease Tallien and to effect a truculent manner, which brought abject flattery from the other's lips.

St Just the fiery young demagogue, and Couthon the half-paralysed enthusiast, were known to be pushing their leader toward the proclamation of a triumvirate, with Robespierre as chief dictator and themselves as his two hands; and it amused the helpless cripple to see just how far the obsequiousness of Tallien and his colleagues would go in subscribing to so monstrous a project.

As for Chauvelin, he said very little, and the defer-ence wherewith he listened to the others, the occasional unctuous words which he let fall, bore testimony to the humiliating subservience to which he had sunk.

And the beautiful Theresia, presiding over the small assembly like a goddess who listens to the prattle of men, sat for the most part quite still, on the one dainty piece of furniture of which her dingy apartment boasted. She was careful to sit so that the rosy glow of the lamp fell on her in the direction most becoming to her attitude. From time to time she threw in a word; but all the while her whole attention was concentrated on what was said.

II

St Just, now as always the mouthpiece of his friend, was the first to give a serious turn to the conversation. Compliments, flatteries, had gone their round; platitudes, grandiloquent phrases on the subject of country, intellectual revolution, liberty, purity, and so on, had been spouted with varying eloquence. The fraternal suppers had been alluded to with servile eulogy of the giant brain who had conceived the project.

Then it was that St Just broke into a euphemistic account of the disorderly scene in the Rue St Honoré.

Theresia Cabarrus, roused from her queen-like indifference, at once became interested.

'The young traitor!' she exclaimed, with a great show of indignation. 'Who was he? What was he like?'

Couthon gave quite a minute description of Bertrand, an accurate one, too. He had faced the blasphemer – thus was he called by this compact group of devotees and sycophants – for fully five minutes, and despite the flickering and deceptive light, had studied his features, distorted by fury and hate, and was quite sure that he would know them again.

Theresia listened eagerly, caught every inflection of the voices as they discussed the strange events that followed. The keenest observer there could not have detected the slightest agitation on her large, velvety eyes – not even when they met Robespierre's coldly inquiring gaze. No one – not even Tallien – could have guessed what an effort it cost her to appear unconcerned, when all the while she was straining every sense in the direction of the small kitchen at the end of the passage, where the much-discussed Bertrand was still lying concealed.

However, the certainty that Robespierre's spies and those of the Committees had apparently lost complete track of Moncrif, did much to restore her assurance, and her gaiety became after awhile somewhat more real.

At one time she turned boldly to Tallien.

'You were there, too, citizen,' she said provokingly. 'Did you not recognise any of the traitors?'

Tallien stammered out an evasive answer, implored her with a look not to taunt him and not to play like a thoughtless child within sight and hearing of man-eating tiger. Theresia's dalliance with the young and handsome Bertrand must in truth be known to Robespierre's army of spies, and he – Tallien – was not altogether convinced that the fair Spaniard, despite her assurances to the contrary, was not harbouring Moncrif in her apartment even now.

Therefore he would not meet her tantalising glance; and she, delighted to tease, threw herself with greater zest than before into the discussion, amused to see sober Tallien, whom in her innermost heart she despised, enduring tortures of apprehension.

'Ah!' she exclaimed, apparently enraptured by St Just's glowing account of the occurrence, 'what would I not give to have seen it all! In truth, we do not often get such thrilling incidents every day in this dull and dreary Paris. The death-carts with their load of simpering aristos have ceased to entertain us. But the drama in the Rue St Honoré! à la bonne heure! What a palpitating scene!'

'Especially,' added Couthon, 'the spiriting away of the company of traitors through the agency of that mysterious giant, who some aver was just a coal-heaver named Rateau, well known to half the night-birds of the city as an asthmatic reprobate; whilst others vow that he was—'

'Name him not, friend Couthon,' St Just broke in with a sarcastic chuckle. 'I pray thee, spare the feelings of citizen Chauvelin.' And his bold, provoking eyes shot a glance of cool irony on the unfortunate victim of his taunt.

Chauvelin made no retort, pressed his thin lips more tightly together as if to smother any incipient expression of the resentment which he felt. Instinctively his glance sought those of Robespierre, who sat by, still apparently disinterested and impassive, with head bent and arms crossed over his narrow chest.

'Ah, yes!' here interposed Tallien unctuously. 'Citizen Chauvelin has had one or two opportunities of measuring his prowess against that of the mysterious Englishman; but we are told that, despite his great talents, he has met with no success in that direction.'

'Do not tease our modest friend Chauvelin, I pray you, citizen,' Theresia broke in gaily. 'The Scarlet Pimpernel – that is the name of the mysterious Englishman, is it not? – is far more elusive and a thousand times more resourceful and daring than any mere man can possibly conceive. 'Tis woman's wits that will bring him to his knees one day. You may take my word for that!'

'*Your* wits, citoyenne?'

Robespierre had spoken. It was the first time, since the discussion had turned on the present subject, that he had opened his lips. All eyes were at once reverentially turned to him. His own, cold and sarcastic, were fixed upon Theresia Cabarrus.

She returned his glance with provoking coolness, shrugged her splendid shoulders, and retorted airily:

'Oh, you want a woman with some talent as a sleuth-hound – a female counterpart of citizen Chauvelin. I have no genius in that direction.'

'Why not?' Robespierre went on drily. 'You, fair citoyenne, would be well qualified to deal with the Scarlet Pimpernel, seeing that your adorer, Bertrand Moncrif, appears to be a protégé of the mysterious League.'

'Bertrand Moncrif,' she said serenely, 'is no adorer of mine. He foreswore his allegiance to me on the day that I plighted troth to citizen Tallien.'

'That is as may be,' Robespierre retorted coldly. 'But he certainly was the leader of the gang of traitors whom that meddlesome English rabble chose to snatch away tonight from the vengeance of a justly incensed populace.'

'How do you know that, citizen Robespierre?' Theresia asked. She was still maintaining an outwardly calm attitude; her voice was apparently quite steady, her glance absolutely serene. 'Why do you suppose, citizen,' she insisted, 'that Bertrand Moncrif had anything to do with the fracas tonight? Methought he had emigrated to England – or somewhere,' she added airily, 'after – after I gave him his definite congé.'

'Did you think that, citoyenne?' Robespierre rejoined with a wry smile. 'Then let me tell you that you are under a misapprehension. Moncrif, the traitor, was the leader of the gang that tried to rouse the people against me tonight. You

ask me how I know it?' he added icily. 'Well, I saw him –
that is all!'

'Ah!' exclaimed Theresia, in well-played mild astonishment. 'You saw Bertrand Moncrif, citizen? He is in Paris, then?'

'Seemingly.'

'Strange, he never came to see me!'

'Strange, indeed!'

'What does he look like? Some people have told me that he is getting fat.'

The discussion had now resolved itself into a duel between these two: the ruthless dictator, sure of his power, and the beautiful woman, conscious of hers.

Both the duellists appeared perfectly calm. Of the two, in truth, Robespierre appeared the most moved. His staccato voice, the drumming of his pointed fingers upon the arms of his chair, suggested that the banter of the beautiful Theresia was getting on his nerves. And Theresia was clever enough – above all, woman enough – to note that, since the dictator was moved, he could not be perfectly sure of his ground. He would not display this secret irritation if by a word he could confound his beautiful adversary, and openly threaten where now he only insinuated.

'He saw Bertrand in the Rue St Honoré,' was the sum total of her quick reasoning; 'but does not know that he is here. I wonder what it is he does want!' came as an afterthought.

The one that really suffered throughout, and suffered acutely, was Tallien. He would have given all that he possessed to know for a certainty that Bertrand Moncrif was no longer in the house. Surely Theresia would not be foolhardy enough to provoke the powerful dictator into one of those paroxysms of spiteful fury for which he was notorious – fury wherein he might be capable of anything – insulting his hostess, setting his spies to search her apartments for a traitor if he suspected one of lying hidden away somewhere. In truth, Tallien, trembling for his beloved, was ready to swoon. How marvellous she was! how serene!

'I entreat you, citizen Robespierre,' she said, with a pout, 'to tell me if Bertrand Moncrif has grown fat.'

'That I cannot tell you, citoyenne,' Robespierre replied curtly. 'Having recognised my enemy, I no longer paid heed to him. My attention was arrested by his rescuer—'

'That elusive Scarlet Pimpernel,' she broke in gaily. 'Unrecognisable to all save to citizen Robespierre, under the disguise of an asthmatic gossoon. Ah, would I had been there!'

'I would you had, citoyenne,' he retorted. 'You would have realised that to refuse your help to unmask an abominable spy after such an episode is tantamount to treason.'

Her gaiety dropped from her like a mantle. In a moment she was serious, puzzled. A frown appeared between her brows. Her dark eyes flashed, rapidly inquiring, suspicious, fearful, upon Robespierre.

'To refuse my help?' she asked slowly. 'My help in unmasking a spy? I do not understand.'

She looked from one man to the other. Chauvelin was the only one who would not meet her gaze. No, not the only one. Tallien, too, appeared absorbed in contemplating his finger-nails.

'Citizen Tallien,' she queried harshly. 'What does this mean?'

'It means just what I said,' Robespierre intervened coldly. 'That abominable English spy has fooled us all. You said yourself that 'tis a woman's wit that will bring that elusive adventurer to his knees one day. Why not yours?'

Theresia gave no immediate reply. She was meditating.
'I fear me, citizen Robespierre,' she said after awhile,
'that you overestimate the keenness of my wits.'

'Impossible!' he retorted drily.

And St Just, ever the echo of his friend's unspoken words,
added with a great show of gallantry:

'The citoyenne Cabarrus, even from her prison in Bordeaux,
succeeded in snaring our friend Tallien, and making him the
slave of her beauty.'

'Then why not the Scarlet Pimpernel?' was Couthon's
simple conclusion.

'The Scarlet Pimpernel!' Theresia exclaimed with a shrug
of her handsome shoulders. 'The Scarlet Pimpernel, forsooth! Why, meseems that no one knows who he is! Just
now you all affirmed that he was a coal-heaver named
Rateau. I cannot make love to a coal-heaver, can I?'

'Citizen Chauvelin knows who the Scarlet Pimpernel is,'
Couthon went on deliberately. 'He will put you on the
right track. All that we want is that he should be at
your feet. It is so easy for the citoyenne Cabarrus to
accomplish that.'

'But if you know who he is,' she urged, 'why do you
need my help?'

'Because,' St Just replied, 'the moment that he lands in
France he sheds his identity, as a man would a coat. A
coal-heaver one day; a prince of dandies the next. He
has lodgings in every quarter of Paris and quits them
at a moment's notice. He has confederates everywhere:
concierges, cabaret-keepers, soldiers, vagabonds. He has
been public letter-writer, a sergeant of the National Guard,
a rogue, a thief! 'Tis only in England that he is always the
same, and citizen Chauvelin can identify him there. 'Tis
there that you can see him, citoyenne, there that you can
spread your nets for him; from thence that you can lure

him to France in your train, like you lured citizen Tallien
to obey your every whim in Bordeaux. Once a man hath
fallen a victim to the charms of beautiful Theresia Cabarrus,'
added the young demagogue gallantly, 'she need only to
beckon and he will follow, as does citizen Tallien, as did
Bertrand Moncrif, as do many others. Bring the Scarlet
Pimpernel to your feet, here in Paris, citoyenne, and we
will do the rest.'

While his young devotee spoke thus vehemently, Robespierre had relapsed into his usual pose of affected detach-
ment. His head was bent, his arms were folded across his
chest. He appeared to be asleep. When St Just paused,
Theresia waited awhile, her dark eyes fixed on the great
man who had conceived this monstrous project. Monstrous,
because of the treachery that it demanded.

Theresia Cabarrus had in truth identified herself with
the Revolutionary government. She had promised to marry
Tallien, who outwardly at least was as bloodthirsty and
ruthless as was Robespierre himself; but she was a woman
and not a demon. She had refused to sell Bertrand Moncrif
in order to pander to Tallien's fear of Robespierre. To entice
a man – whoever he was – into making love to her, and then
to betray him to his death, was in itself an abhorrent idea.
Faced with this demand upon her on the part of the most
powerful despot in France, she hesitated, even though she
did not altogether dare to refuse. Womanlike, she tried to
temporise.

She appeared puzzled; frowned. Then asked vaguely:

'Is it then that you wish me to go to England?'

St Just nodded.

'But,' she continued, in the same indeterminate manner,
'meseems that you talk very glibly of my – what shall I say?
– my proposed dalliance with the mysterious Englishman.
Suppose he – he does not respond?'

'Impossible!' Couthon broke in quickly.

'Oh!' she protested. 'Impossible? Englishmen are known to be prudish – moral – what? And if the man is married – what then?'

'The citoyenne Cabarrus underrates her powers,' St Just riposted.

'Theresia, I entreat!' Tallien put in dolefully.

He felt that the interview, from which he had hoped so much, was proving a failure – nay, worse! For he realised that Robespierre, thwarted in this desire, would bitterly resent Theresia's positive refusal to help him.

'Eh, what?' she riposted lightly. 'And is it you, citizen Tallien, who would push me into this erotic adventure? I' faith, your trust in me is highly flattering! Have you not thought that in the process I might fall in love with the Scarlet Pimpernel myself? He is young, they say; handsome, adventurous; and I am to try and capture his fancy ... the butterfly is to dance around the flame ... no, no! I am too much afraid that I may singe my wings!'

'Does that mean,' Robespierre put in coldly, 'that you refuse us your help, citoyenne Cabarrus?'

'Yes – I refuse,' she replied calmly. 'The project does not please me, I confess—'

'Not even if we guaranteed immunity to your lover, Bertrand Moncrif?'

She gave a slight shudder.

'I have no lover, except citizen Tallien,' she said steadily, and placed her fingers, which had suddenly become ice-cold, upon the clasped hands of her future lord. Then she rose, thereby giving the signal for the breaking-up of the little party.

In truth, she knew as well as did Tallien that the meeting had been a failure. Tallien was looking sallow and terribly worried. Robespierre, taciturn and sullen, gave her one threatening glance before he took his leave.

'You know, citoyenne,' he said coldly, 'that the nation has means at its disposal for compelling its citizens to do their duty.'

'Ah, bah!' retorted the fair Spaniard, shrugging her shoulders. 'I am not a citizen of France. And even your unerring Public Prosecutor would find it difficult to frame an accusation against me.'

Again she laughed, determined to appear gay and inconsequent through it all.

'Think how the accusation would sound, citizen Robespierre!' she went on mockingly. '"The citoyenne Cabarrus, for refusing to make amorous overtures to the mysterious Englishman known as the Scarlet Pimpernel, and for refusing to administer a love-philtre to him as prepared by Mother Théot at the bidding of citizen Robespierre!" Confess! Confess!' she added, and her rippling laugh had a genuine note of merriment in it at last, 'that we none of us would survive such ridicule!'

Theresia Cabarrus was a clever woman, and by speaking the word 'ridicule,' she had touched the one weak chink in the tyrant's armour. But it is not always safe to prod a tiger, even with a child's cane, or even from behind protecting bars. Tallien knew this well enough. He was on tenterhooks, longing to see the others depart so that he might throw himself once again at Theresia's feet and implore her to obey the despot's commands.

But Theresia appeared unwilling to give him such another chance. She professed intense fatigue, bade him 'good night' with such obvious finality, that he dared not outstay his welcome. A few moments later they had all gone. Their gracious hostess accompanied them to the door, since Pepita had by this time certainly gone to bed. The little procession was formed, with St Just and Chauvelin supporting their palsied comrade, Robespierre detached and silent, and finally Tallien, whose last appealing look to his beloved would have melted a heart of stone.

CHAPTER 11

Strange Happenings

I

Now the dingy little apartment in the Rue Villedot was silent and dark. The nocturnal visitors had departed more than a quarter of an hour ago; nevertheless the beautiful hostess had not yet gone to bed. In fact, she had hardly moved since she bade final adieu to her timorous lover. The enforced gaiety of the last few moments still sat like a mask upon her face. All that she had done was to sink with a sigh of weariness upon the settee.

And there she remained, with neck craned forward, listening, straining every nerve to listen, even though the heavy, measured footsteps of the five men had long since ceased to echo up and down the stone passages and stairs. Her foot, in its quaint small sandal, beat now and then an impatient tattoo upon the threadbare carpet. Her eyes at intervals cast anxious looks upon the old-fashioned clock above the mantelpiece.

It struck half-past two. Whereupon Theresia rose and went out into the vestibule. Here a tallow candle flickered faintly in its pewter sconce and emitted an evil-smelling smoke, which rose in spirals to the blackened ceiling.

Theresia paused, glanced inquiringly down the narrow

passage which gave access to the little kitchen beyond. Between the kitchen and the corner of the vestibule where she was standing, two doors gave on the passage: her bedroom, and that of her maid Pepita. Theresia was vividly conscious of the strange silence which reigned in the whole apartment. The passage was pitch dark save at its farthest end, where a tiny ray of light found its way underneath the kitchen door.

The silence was oppressive, almost terrifying. In a hoarse, anxious voice, Theresia called:

'Pepita!'

But there came no answer. Pepita apparently had gone to bed, was fast asleep by now. But what had become of Bertrand?

Full of vague misgivings, her nerves tingling with a nameless fear, Theresia picked up the candle and tiptoed down the passage. Outside Pepita's door she paused and listened.

'Pepita!' she called; and somehow the sound of her own voice added to her terror. Strange that she should be frightened like this in her own familiar apartment, and with a faithful, sturdy maid sleeping the other side of this thin partition wall!

'Pepita!' Theresia's voice was shaking. She tried to open the door, but it was locked. Why had Pepita, contrary to her habit, locked herself in?

Theresia knocked against the door, rattled the handle in its socket, called more loudly and more insistently, 'Pepita!' and, receiving no reply, fell, half-swooning with fear, against the partition wall, whilst the candle slipped out of her trembling grasp and fell with a clatter to the ground.

She was now in complete darkness, with senses reeling and brain paralysed. How long she remained thus, in a state bordering on collapse, she did not know; probably not more than a minute or so. Consciousness returned quickly, and with it the cold sweat of an abject fear; for through this returning consciousness she had perceived a groan issuing from behind the locked door. But her knees were still shaking; she felt unable to move.

'Pepita!' she called again and once more caught the sound of a smothered groan.

Whereupon, driven into action by the obvious distress of her maid, Theresia recovered a certain measure of self-control. Pulling herself vigorously together, she began by groping for the candle which had dropped out of her hand a while ago. Even as she stooped down for this she contrived to say in a moderately clear and firm voice:

'Courage, Pepita! I'll find the light and come back.' Then she added: 'Are you able to unlock the door?'

To this, however, she received no reply save another muffled groan.

Theresia now was on her hands and knees, groping for the candlestick. Then a strange thing happened. Her hands, as they wandered vaguely along the flagged floor, encountered a small object, which proved to be a key. In an instant she was on her feet again, her fingers running over the door until they encountered the keyhole. Into this she succeeded, after further groping, in inserting the key; it fitted, and turned the lock. She pushed open the door, and remained paralysed with surprise upon the threshold.

Pepita was reclining in an arm-chair, her hands tied behind her, a woollen shawl wound loosely around her mouth. In a distant corner of the room, a small oil-lamp, turned very low, cast a glimmer of light upon the scene. For Theresia to run to the pinioned woman and undo the bonds that held her was but the work of a few seconds.

'Where is M. Bertrand?' Theresia asked repeatedly, ere she got a reply from her bewildered maid.

At last Pepita was able to speak.

'In very truth, Madame,' she said slowly, 'I do not know.'

'How do you mean, you do not know?' Theresia queried.

'Just what I say, my pigeon,' Pepita retorted with marked acerbity. 'You ask me what has happened, and I say I do not know. You want to know what has become of M. Bertrand. Then go and look for yourself. When last I saw him, he was in the kitchen, unfit to move, the poor cabbage!'

'But, Pepita,' Theresia insisted, and stamped her foot with impatience, 'you must know how you came to be sitting here, pinioned and muffled. Who did it? Who has been here? God preserve the woman, will she never speak?'

Pepita by now had fully recovered her senses. She had struggled to her feet, and went to take up the lamp, then led the way toward the door, apparently intent on finding out for herself what had become of M. Bertrand and in no way sharing her mistress's unreasoning terror. She halted on the threshold and turned to Theresia, who quite mechanically started to follow her.

'M. Bertrand was sitting in the arm-chair in the kitchen,' she said simply. 'I was arranging a cushion for his head, to make him more comfortable, when suddenly a shawl was flung over my head without the slightest warning. I had seen nothing; I had not heard the merest sound. And I had not the time to utter a scream before I was muffled up in the shawl. Then I was lifted off the ground as if I were a sack of feathers, and I just remember smelling something acrid which made my head spin round and round. But I remember nothing more after that until I heard voices in the vestibule when thy guests were going away. Then I heard thy voice and tried to make thee hear mine. And that is all!'

'When did that happen, Pepita?'

'Soon after the last of thy guests had arrived. I remember I looked at the clock. It must have been half an hour after midnight.'

While the woman spoke, Theresia had remained standing in the middle of the room, looking in the gloom like an elfin apparition, with her clinging, diaphanous draperies. A frown of deep puzzlement lay between her brows and her lips were tightly pressed together as if in wrath; but she said nothing more, and when Pepita, lamp in hand, went out of the room, she followed.

II

When, the kitchen door being opened, that room was found to be empty, Theresia was no longer surprised. Somehow she had expected this. She knew that Bertrand would be gone. The windows of the kitchen gave on the ubiquitous wrought-iron balcony, as did all the other windows of the apartment. That those windows were unfastened, had only been pushed to from the outside, appeared to her as a matter of course. It was not Bertrand who had thrown the shawl over Pepita's head; therefore some one had come in from the outside and had kidnapped Bertrand – some one who was peculiarly bold and daring. He had not come in from the balcony and through the window, because the latter had been fastened as usual by Pepita much earlier in the evening. No! He had gone that way, taking Bertrand with him; but he must have entered the place in some other mysterious manner, like a disembodied sprite bent on mischief or mystery.

Whilst Pepita fumbled and grumbled, Theresia started on a tour of inspection. Still deeply puzzled, she was no longer afraid.

Something was going on in her brain, certain theories, guesses, conjectures, which she was passionately eager to set at rest. Nor did it take her long. Candle in hand, she had gone round to explore. No sooner had she entered her own bedroom than the solution of the mystery lay revealed before her, in a shutter, forced open from the outside, a broken pane of glass which had allowed a hand to creep in and surreptitiously turn the handle of the tall French window to allow of easy ingress. It had been quickly and cleverly done; the splinters of glass had made no noise as they fell upon the carpet. But for the disappearance of Bertrand, the circumstances suggested a nimble housebreaker rather than a benevolent agency for the rescue of young rashlings in distress.

The frown of puzzlement deepened on Theresia Cabarrus's brow, and her mobile mouth with the perfectly arched if somewhat thin lips expressed a kind of feline anger, whilst the hand that held the pewter candlestick trembled perceptibly.

Pepita's astonishment expressed itself by sundry exclamations: 'Name of a name!' and 'Is it possible?'

The worthy old peasant absolutely refused to connect the departure of M. Bertrand with so obvious an attempt at housebreaking.

'M. Bertrand was determined to go, the poor cabbage!' she said decisively; 'since thou didst make him understand that his staying here was a danger to thee. He no doubt took an opportunity to slip out of the front door whilst thou wast engaged in conversation with that pack of murderers, whom may the good God punish one of these days!'

Theresia Cabarrus, wearied beyond endurance by all the events of this night, as well as by her old servant's incessant gabble, finally sent her, still muttering and grumbling, to bed.

CHAPTER 12

Chauvelin

I

Theresia had opposed a stern refusal to Pepita's request that she might put her mistress to bed before she herself went to rest. She did not want to go to bed: she wanted to think. And now that that peculiar air of mystery, that silence and semi-darkness no longer held their gruesome sway in her apartment, she did not feel afraid.

Pepita went to bed. For awhile, Theresia could hear her moving about, with ponderous, shuffling footsteps; then, presently everything was still. The clock of old St Roch struck three. Not much more than half an hour had gone by since her guests had departed. To Theresia it seemed like an infinity of time. The sense of a baffling mystery being at work around her had roused her ire and killed all latent fear.

But what was the mystery?

And was there a mystery at all? Or was Pepita's rational explanation of the occurrence of this night the right one after all?

Citoyenne Cabarrus, unable to sit still, wandered up and down the passage, in and out of the kitchen; in and out of her bedroom, and thence into the vestibule. Then back again. At one moment, when standing in the vestibule, she thought she heard some one moving on the landing outside the front door. Her heart beat a little more rapidly, but she was not afraid. She did not believe in housebreakers and she felt that Pepita, who was a very light sleeper, was well within call.

So she went to the front door and opened it. The quick cry which she gave was one of surprise rather than of fear. In her belated visitor she had recognised citizen Chauvelin; and somehow, by a vague process of reasoning, his presence just at this moment seemed quite rational – in keeping with the unsolved mystery that was so baffling to the fair Theresia.

'May I come in, citoyenne?' Chauvelin said in a whisper. 'It is late, I know; but there is urgency.'

'It *is* late,' she murmured vaguely. 'What do you want?'

'Something has happened,' he replied, still speaking below his breath. 'Something which concerns you. And, before speaking of it to citizen Robespierre—'

'Enter!' she said curtly.

He came in, and she closed the door carefully behind him. Then she led the way into the withdrawing room and turned up the wick of the lamp under its rosy shade. She sat down and motioned to him to do the same.

'What is it?' she asked.

Before replying, Chauvelin's finger and thumb – thin and pointed like the talons of a vulture – went fumbling in the pocket of his waistcoat. From it he extracted a small piece of neatly folded paper.

'When we left your apartment, citoyenne – my friend St Just and I supporting poor palsied Couthon, and Robespierre following close behind us – I spied this scrap of paper, which St Just's careless foot had just kicked to one side when he was stepping across the threshold. Some unknown hand must have insinuated it underneath the door. Now I never despise stray bits of paper. I have had so many through my hands that proved after examination to be of paramount importance. So, whilst the others were busy with their own affairs I, unseen by them, had already stooped and picked the paper up.'

He paused for a moment or two, then, satisfied that he held the beautiful woman's undivided attention, he went on in his habitual dry, urbane monotone:

'Now, though I was quite sure in my own mind, citoyenne, that this billet-doux was intended for your fair hands, I felt that, as its finder, I had some sort of lien upon it—'

'To the point, citizen, I pray you!' Theresia broke in harshly.

By way of a reply, Chauvelin slowly unfolded the note and began to read:

'"Bertrand Moncrif is a young fool, but he is too good to be the plaything of a sleek black pantheress, however beautiful she might be. So I am taking him away to England where, in the arms of his long-suffering and loyal sweetheart, he will soon forget the brief madness which so nearly landed him on the guillotine and made of him a tool to serve the selfish whims of Theresia Cabarrus."'

Theresia had listened to the brief, enigmatic epistle without displaying the slightest sign of emotion or surprise. Now, when Chauvelin had finished reading, and with his strange, dry smile handed her the tiny note, she took it and for awhile contemplated it in silence, her face perfectly placid save for a curious and ominous contraction of the brows and a screwing-up of the fine eyes, which gave her a curious, snake-like expression.

'You know, of course, citoyenne,' Chauvelin said after awhile, 'who the writer of this – shall we say? – impudent epistle happens to be?'

She nodded.

'The man,' he went on placidly, 'who goes by the name of the Scarlet Pimpernel. The impudent English adventurer whom citizen Robespierre has asked *you*, citoyenne, to lure into the net which we may spread for him.'

Still Theresia was silent. She did not look at Chauvelin, but kept her eyes fixed upon the scrap of paper, which she had folded into a long, narrow ribbon and was twining in and out between her fingers.

'A while ago, citoyenne,' Chauvelin continued, 'in this very room, you refused to lend us a helping hand.'

Still no reply from Theresia. She had just smoothed out the mysterious epistle, carefully folded it into four, and was in the act of slipping it into the bosom of her gown. Chauvelin waited quite patiently. He was accustomed to waiting, and patience was an integral part of his stock in trade. Opportunism was another.

Theresia was sitting on her favourite settee, leaning forward with her hands clasped between her knees. Her head was bent, and the tiny rose-shaped lamp failed to throw its glimmer of light upon her face. The clock on the mantelshelf behind her was ticking with insentient monotony. Anon, a distant chime struck the quarter after three. Whereupon Chauvelin rose.

'I think we understand one another, citoyenne,' he said quietly, and with a sigh of complete satisfaction. 'It is late now. At what hour may I have the privilege of seeing you alone?'

'At three in the afternoon?' she replied tonelessly, like one speaking in a dream. 'Citizen Tallien is always at the Convention then, and my door will be denied to everybody else.'

'I'll be here at three o'clock,' was Chauvelin's final word. Theresia had not moved. He made her a deep bow and went out of the room. The next moment, the opening and shutting of the outer door proclaimed that he had gone.

After that, Theresia Cabarrus went to bed.

CHAPTER 13

The Fisherman's Rest

I

And whilst the whole of Europe was in travail with the repercussion of the gigantic upheaval that was shaking France to its historic foundation, the last few years had seen but very little change in this little corner of England.

The Fisherman's Rest stood where it had done for two centuries and long before thrones had tottered and anointed heads fallen on the scaffold. The oak rafters, black with age, the monumental hearth, the tables and high-backed benches, seemed like mute testimonies to good order and to tradition, just as the shiny pewter mugs, the foaming ale, the brass that glittered like gold, bore witness to unimpaired prosperity and an even, well-regulated life.

Over in the kitchen yonder, Mistress Sally Waite, as she now was, still ruled with a firm if somewhat hasty hand. She still queened it over her father's household, presided over his kitchen, and drove the young scullery wenches to their task with her sharp tongue and an occasional slap. But *The Fisherman's Rest* could not have gone on without her. The copper saucepans would in truth not have glittered so, nor would the home-brewed ale have tasted half so luscious to Master Jellyband's faithful customers, had not Mistress Sally's strong brown hands drawn it for them, with just the right amount of creamy foam on the top and not a bit too much.

And so it was still many a 'Ho, Sally! 'Ere Sally! 'Ow long'll you be with that there beer!' or 'Say, Sally! A cut of your cheese and homebaked bread; and look sharp about it!' that resounded from end to end of the long, low-raftered coffee-room of *The Fisherman's Rest*, on this fine May day of the year of grace 1794.

Sally Waite, her muslin cap set at a becoming angle, her kerchief primly folded over her well-developed bosom, and her kirtle neatly raised above a pair of exceedingly shapely ankles, was in and out of the room, in and out of the kitchen, tripping it like a benevolent if somewhat substantial fairy, bandying chaff here, administering rebuke there, hot, panting and excited.

II

The while mine host, Master Jellyband, stood with stubby legs firmly planted upon his own hearth, wherein, despite the warmth of a glorious afternoon, a log fire blazed away merrily. He was giving forth his views upon the political situation of Europe generally with the self-satisfied assurance born of complete ignorance and true British insular prejudice.

Believe me, Mr Jellyband was in no two minds about 'them murderin' furriners over yonder' who had done away with their King and Queen and all their nobility and quality, and whom England had at last decided to lick into shape.

'And not a moment too soon, hark'ee, Mr 'Empseed,' he went on sententiously. 'And if I 'ad my way, we should 'ave punished 'em proper long before this – blown their bloomin' Paris into smithereens, and carried off the pore Queen afore those murderous villains 'ad 'er pretty 'ead off of 'er shoulders!'

Mr Hempseed, from his own privileged corner in the ingle-nook, was not altogether prepared to admit that.

'I am not for interfering with other folks' ways,' he said, raising his quaking treble so as to stem effectually the torrent of Master Jellyband's eloquence. 'As the Scriptures say—'

'Keep your dirty fingers from off my waist!' came in decisive tones from Mistress Sally Waite, whilst the shrill sound made by the violent contact of a feminine hand against a manly cheek froze the Scriptural quotation on Mr Hempseed's lips.

'Now then, now then, Sally!' Mr Jellyband thought fit to say in stern tones, not liking his customers to be thus summarily dealt with.

'Now then, father,' Sally retorted, with a toss of her brown curls, 'you just attend to your politics, and Mr 'Empseed to 'is Scriptures, and leave me to deal with them impudent jackanapes. You wait!' she added, turning once more with a parting shot directed against the discomfited offender. 'If my 'Arry catches you at them tricks, you'll see what you get – that's all!'

'Sally!' Mr Jellyband admonished, more sternly this time. 'You'll 'ave my lord Hastings 'ere before 'is dinner is ready.'

Which suggestion so overawed Mistress Sally that she promptly forgot the misdoings of the forward swain and failed to hear the sarcastic chuckle which greeted the mention of her husband's name. With an excited little cry, she ran quickly out of the room.

Mr Hempseed, loftily unaware of interruption, concluded his sententious remark:

'As the Scriptures say, Mr Jellyband: "'Ave no fellowship

with the unfruitful work of darkness." I don't 'old not with interfering. Remember what the Scriptures say: "'E that committeth sin is of the devil, and the devil sinneth from the beginning,"' he concluded with sublime irrelevance, sagely nodding his head.

But Mr Jellyband was not thus lightly to be confounded in his argument – no, not by any quotation, relevant or otherwise!

'All very fine, Mr 'Empseed,' he said, 'and good enough for them 'oo, like yourself, are willin' to side with them murderin' reprobates. . . .'

'Like myself, Mr Jellyband?' protested Mr Hempseed, with as much vigour as his shrill treble would allow. 'Nay, but I'm not for them children of darkness—'

'You may be or you may not,' Mr Jellyband went on, nothing daunted. 'There be many as are, and 'oo'd say "Let 'em murder," even now. But I say that them as 'oo talk that way are not true Englishmen; for 'tis we Englishmen 'oo can teach the furriner just what 'e may do and what 'e may not.'

For the nonce Mr Hempseed was silent. True, a Scriptural text did hover on his thin, quivering lips; but as no one paid any heed to him for the moment its appositeness will for ever remain doubtful. The honours of victory rested with Mr Jellyband. Such lofty patriotism, coupled with so much sound knowledge of political affairs, could not fail to leave its impress upon the more ignorant and the less fervent amongst the frequenters of *The Fisherman's Rest*.

Indeed, who was more qualified to pass an opinion on current events than the host of that much-frequented resort, seeing that the ladies and gentlemen of quality who came to England from over the water, so as to escape all them murtherin' reprobates in their own country, did most times halt at *The Fisherman's Rest* on their way to London or to

Bath? And though Mr Jellyband did not know a word of French – no furrin lingo for him, thank 'ee! – he nevertheless had mixed with all that nobility and gentry for over two years now, and had learned all that there was to know about the life over there, and about Mr Pitt's intentions to put a stop to all those abominations.

III

Even now, hardly had mine host's conversation with his favoured customers assumed a more domestic turn, than a loud clatter on the cobblestones outside, a jingle and a rattle, shouts, laughter and bustle, announced the arrival of guests who were privileged to make as much noise as they pleased.

Mr Jellyband ran to the door, shouted for Sally at the top of his voice, with a 'Here's my lord Hastings!' to add spur to Sally's hustle.

Three young gallants in travelling clothes, smart of appearance and debonair of mien, were ushering a party of strangers – three ladies and two men – into the hospitable porch of *The Fisherman's Rest*. The little party had walked across from the inner harbour, where the graceful masts of an elegant schooner lately arrived in port were seen gently swaying against the delicately coloured afternoon sky. Three or four sailors from the schooner were carrying luggage, which they deposited in the hall of the inn, then touched their forelocks in response to a pleasant smile and nod from the young lords.

'This way, my lord,' Master Jellyband reiterated with jovial obsequiousness. 'Everything is ready. This way! Hey, Sallee!'

he called again; and Sally, hot, excited, blushing, came tripping over from the kitchen, wiping her hot plump palms against her apron in anticipation of shaking hands with their lordships.

'Since Mr Waite isn't anywhere about,' my lord Hastings said gaily, as he put a bold arm round Mistress Sally's dainty waist, 'I'll e'en have a kiss, my pretty one.'

'And I, too, by gad, for old sake's sake!' Lord Tony asserted, and planked a hearty kiss on Mistress Sally's dimpled cheek.

'At your service, my lords, at your service!' Master Jellyband rejoined, laughing. Then added more soberly: 'Now then, Sally, show the ladies up into the blue room, the while their lordships 'ave a first shake down in the coffee-room. This way, gentlemen – your lordships – this way!'

The strangers in the meanwhile had stood by, wide-eyed and somewhat bewildered in face of this exuberant hilarity which was so unlike what they had pictured to themselves of dull, fog-ridden England – so unlike, too, the dreary morose-ness which of late had replaced the erstwhile lighthearted gaiety of their own countrymen. The porch and the narrow hall of *The Fisherman's Rest* appeared to them seething with vitality. Every one was talking, nobody seemed to listen; every one was merry, and every one knew everybody else and was pleased to meet them. Sonorous laughter echoed from end to end along the solid beams, black and shiny with age. It all seemed so homely, so happy. The deference paid to the young gallants and to them as strangers by the sailors and the innkeeper was so genuine and hearty, without the slightest sign of servility, that those five people who had left behind them so much class-hatred, enmity and cruelty in their own country, felt an unaccountable tightening of the heart, a few hot tears rise to their eyes, partly of joy, but partly too of regret.

IV

Lord Hastings, the youngest and merriest of the English party, guided the two Frenchmen toward the coffee-room, with many a jest in atrocious French and kindly words of encouragement, all intended to put the strangers at their ease.

Lord Anthony Dewhurst and Sir Andrew Ffoulkes lingered a moment longer in the hall, in order to speak with the sailors who had brought the luggage along.

'Do you know aught of Sir Percy?' Lord Tony asked.

'No, my lord,' the sailor gave answer; 'not since he went ashore early this morning. 'Er Ladyship was waitin' for 'im on the pier. Sir Percy just ran up the steps and then 'e shouted to us to get back quickly. "Tell their lordships," 'e says, "I'll meet them at *The Rest*." And then Sir Percy and 'er ladyship just walked off and we saw naun more of them.'

'That was many hours ago,' Sir Andrew Ffoulkes mused, with an inward smile. He too saw visions of meeting his pretty Suzanne very soon, and walking away with her into the land of dreams.

''Twas just six o'clock when Sir Percy 'ad the boat lowered,' the sailor rejoined. 'And we rowed quick back after we landed 'im. But the *Day-Dream*, she 'ad to wait for the tide. We wurr a long while gettin' into port.'

Sir Andrew nodded.

'You don't know,' he said, 'if the skipper had any further orders?'

'I don't know, sir,' the man replied. 'But we mun be in readiness always. No one knows when Sir Percy may wish to set sail again.'

The two young men said nothing more, and presently the sailors touched their forelocks and went away. Lord Tony and Sir Andrew exchanged knowing smiles. They could easily picture to themselves their beloved chief, indefatigable, like a boy let out from school, exhilarated by the deadly danger through which he had once more passed unscathed, clasping his adored wife in his arms and wandering off with her, heaven knew whither, living his life of joy and love and happiness during the brief hours which his own indomitable energy, his reckless courage, accorded to the sentimental side of his complex nature.

Far too impatient to wait until the tide allowed the *Day-Dream* to get into port, he had been rowed ashore in the early dawn, and his beautiful Marguerite – punctual to the assignation conveyed to her by one of those mysterious means of which Percy alone knew the secret – was there ready to receive him, to forget in the shelter of his arms the days of racking anxiety and of cruel terror for her beloved through which she had again and again been forced to pass.

Neither Lord Tony nor Sir Andrew Ffoulkes, the Scarlet Pimpernel's most faithful and devoted lieutenants, begrudged their chief these extra hours of bliss, the while they were left in charge of the party so lately rescued from horrible death. They knew that within a day or two – within a few hours, perhaps – Blakeney would tear himself away once more from the clinging embrace of his exquisite wife, from the comfort and luxury of an ideal home, from the adulation of friends, the pleasures of wealth and of fashion, in order mayhap to grovel in the squalor and filth of some outlandish corner of Paris, where he could be in touch with the innocents who suffered – the poor, the terror-stricken victims of the merciless revolution. Within a few hours, mayhap, he would be risking his life again every moment of the day, in order to save some poor hunted fellow-creature – man, woman or child – from death that threatened them at the hands of inhuman monsters who knew neither mercy nor compunction.

As for the nineteen members of the League, they took it in turns to follow their leader where danger was thickest. It was a privilege eagerly sought, deserved by all, and accorded to those who were most highly trusted. It was invariably followed by a period of rest in happy England, with wife, friends, joy and luxury. Sir Andrew Ffoulkes, Lord Anthony Dewhurst and my lord Hastings had been of the expedition which brought Mme de Serval with her three children and Bertrand Moncrif safely to England, after adventures more perilous, more reckless of danger, than most. Within a few hours they would be free to forget in the embrace of clinging arms every peril and every adventure save the eternal one of love, free to forswear everything outside that, save their veneration for their chief and their loyalty to his cause.

CHAPTER 14

The Castaway

I

An excellent dinner served by Mistress Sally and her attendant little wenches put everybody into rare good-humour. Madame de Serval even contrived to smile, her heart warmed by the genuine welcome, the rare gaiety that irradiated this fortunate corner of God's earth. Wars and rumours of war reached it only as an echo of great things that went on in the vast outside world; and though more than one of Dover's gallant sons had perished in one or the other of the Duke of York's unfortunate incursions into Holland, or in one of the numerous naval engagements off the Western shores of France, on the whole, the war, intermittent and desultory, had not yet cast its heavy gloom over the entire country.

Joséphine and Jacques de Serval, whose enthusiasm for martyrdom had received so severe a check in the course of the Fraternal Supper in the Rue St Honoré, had at first with the self-consciousness of youth adopted an attitude of obstinate and irreclaimable sorrow, until the antics of Master Harry Waite, pretty Sally's husband – jealous as a young turkey-cock of every gallant who dared to ogle his buxom wife – brought laughter to their lips. My lord Hastings' comical attempts at speaking French, the droll mistakes he made, easily did the rest; and soon their lively, high-pitched Latin voices mingled with unimpaired gaiety with the more mellow sound of Anglo-Saxon tongues.

Even Régine de Serval had smiled when my lord Hastings had asked her with grave solemnity whether Mme de Serval would wish 'le fou de descendre' – the lunatic to come downstairs – meaning all the while whether she wanted the fire in the big hearth to be let down, seeing that the atmosphere in the coffee-room was growing terribly hot.

The only one who seemed quite unable to shake off his moroseness was Bertrand Moncrif. He sat next to Régine, silent, somewhat sullen, a look that seemed almost one of dull resentment lingering in his eyes. From time to time, when he appeared peculiarly moody or when he refused to eat, her little hand would steal out under the table and press his with a gentle, motherly gesture.

II

It was when the merry meal was over and while Master Jellyband was going the round with a fine bottle of smuggled brandy, which the young gentlemen sipped with unmistakable relish, that a commotion arose outside the inn; whereupon Master Harry Waite ran out of the coffee-room in order to see what was amiss.

Nothing very much apparently. Waite came back after a moment or two and said that two sailors from the barque *Angela* were outside with a young French lad, who seemed more dead than alive, and whom it appears the barque had picked up just outside French waters, in an open boat, half perished with terror and inanition. As the lad spoke nothing but French, the sailors had brought him along to

The Fisherman's Rest, thinking that maybe some of the quality would care to interrogate him.

'Let the lad be taken into the parlour, Jellyband,' Sir Andrew commanded. 'You've got a fire there, haven't you?'

'Yes, yes, Sir Andrew! We always keep fires going here until past the 15th of May.'

'Well then, get him in there. Then give him some of your smuggled brandy first, you old dog! then some wine and food. After that we'll find out something more about him.'

He himself went along in order to see that his orders were carried out. Jellyband, as usual, had already deputed his daughter to do the necessary, and in the hall there was Mistress Sally, capable and compassionate, supporting, almost carrying, a youth who in truth appeared scarce able to stand.

She led him gently into the small private parlour, where a cheerful log-fire was blazing, sat him down in an arm-chair beside the hearth, after which Master Jellyband himself poured half a glass of brandy down the poor lad's throat. This revived him a little, and he looked about him with huge, scared eyes.

'Sainte Mère de Dieu!' he murmured feebly. 'Where am I?'

'Never mind about that now, my lad,' replied Sir Andrew, whose knowledge of French was of a distinctly higher order than that of his comrades. 'You are among friends. That is enough. Have something to eat and drink now. Later we'll talk.'

He was eyeing the boy keenly. Contact with suffering and misery over there in France, under the leadership of the most selfless, most understanding man of this or any time, had intensified his powers of perception. Even the first glance had revealed to him the fact that here was no ordinary waif. The lad spoke with a gentle, highly refined voice; his skin was delicate, and his face exquisitely beautiful; his hands, though covered with grime, and his feet, encased in huge, coarse boots, were small and daintily shaped, like those of a woman. Already Sir Andrew had made up his mind that if the oilskin cap which sat so extraordinarily tightly on the boy's head were to be removed, a wealth of long hair would certainly be revealed.

However, all these facts, which threw over the young stranger a further veil of mystery, could not in all humanity be investigated now. Sir Andrew Ffoulkes, with the consummate tact born of kindliness, left the lad alone as soon as he appeared able to sit up and eat, and himself rejoined his friends in the coffee-room.

CHAPTER 15

The Nest

I

No one, save a very few intimates, knew of the little nest wherein Sir Percy Blakeney and his lady hid their happiness on those occasions when the indefatigable Scarlet Pimpernel was only able to spend a few hours in England, and when a journey to their beautiful home in Richmond could not be thought of. The house – it was only a cottage, timbered and creeper-clad – lay about a mile and a half outside Dover, off the main road, perched up high on rising ground over a narrow lane. It had a small garden round it, which in May was ablaze with daffodils and bluebells, and in June with roses. Two faithful servants, a man and his wife, looked after the place, kept the nest cosy and warm whenever her ladyship wearied of fashion, or else, actually expecting Sir Percy, would come down from London for a day or two in order to dream of that elusive and transient happiness for which her soul hungered, even while her indomitable spirit accepted the inevitable.

A few days ago the weekly courier from France had brought her a line from Sir Percy, together with the promise that she should rest in his arms on the Ist of May. And Marguerite had come down to the creeper-covered cottage knowing that, despite obstacles which might prove insuperable to others, Percy would keep his word.

She had stolen out at dawn to wait for him on the pier; and sure enough, as soon as the May-day sun had dissipated the morning mist, her yearning eyes had spied the smart white gig which had put off from the *Day-Dream*, leaving the graceful ship to await the turn of the tide before putting into port.

Since then, every moment of the day had been one of rapture. The first sight of her husband in his huge caped coat, which seemed to add further inches to his great height, his call of triumph when he saw her, his arms outstretched, there, far away in the small boat, with a gesture of such infinite longing that for a second or two tears obscured Marguerite's vision. Then the drawing up of the boat against the landing-stage; Percy's spring ashore; his voice, his look; the strength of his arms; the ardour of his embrace. Rapture, in truth, to which the thought of its brief duration alone lent a touch of bitterness.

After that, breakfast in the low, raftered room – the hot, savoury milk, the home-baked bread, the home-churned butter. Then the long, delicious, intimate talk of love, and of yearnings, of duty and gallant deeds. Blakeney kept nothing secret from his wife; and what he did not tell her, that she easily guessed. But it was from the members of the League that she learned all there was to know of heroism and selflessness in the perilous adventures through which her husband passed with so lighthearted a gaiety.

'You should see me as an asthmatic reprobate, m'dear,' he would say, with his infectious laugh. 'And hear that cough! Lud love you, but I am mightily proud of that cough! Poor old Rateau does not do it better himself; and he is genuinely asthmatic.'

He gave her an example of his prowess; but she would not allow him to go on. The sound was too weird, and conjured up visions which today she would fain forget.

'Rateau was a real find,' he went on more seriously; 'because he is three parts an imbecile and as obedient as a dog. When some of those devils are on my track, lo! the real Rateau appears and yours truly vanishes where no one can find him!'

'Pray God,' she murmured involuntarily, 'they never may!'

'They won't, m'dear, they won't!' he asserted with light-hearted conviction. 'They have become so confused now between Rateau the coal-heaver, the mysterious Scarlet Pimpernel, and the problematic English milor, that all three of these personalities can appear before their eyes and they will let 'em all escape! I assure you that the con-fusion between the Scarlet Pimpernel who was in the ante-chamber of Mother Théot on that fateful afternoon, and again at the Fraternal Supper in the Rue Honoré, and the real Rateau who was at Mother Théot's while that same exciting supper party was going on, was so great that not one of those murdering reprobates could trust his own eyes and ears, and that we got away as easily as rabbits out of a torn net.'

Thus did he explain and laugh over the perilous adven-ture where he had faced a howling mob disguised as Rateau the coal-heaver, and with almost superhuman pluck and boldness had dragged Mme de Serval and her children into the derelict house which was one of the League's head-quarters. That is how he characterised the extraordinary feat of audacity when in order to give his gallant lieutenants time to smuggle the unfortunates out of the house through a back and secret way, he showed himself on the balcony above the multitude, and hurled dummy figures into the brazier below.

Then came the story of Bertrand Moncrif, snatched half-unconscious out of the apartment of fair Theresia Cabarrus, whilst Robespierre himself sat not half a dozen yards away, with only the thickness of a wall between him and his arch enemy.

'How the woman must hate you!' Marguerite murmured, with a slight shudder of acute anxiety which she did her best to conceal. 'There are things that a woman like the Cabarrus will never forgive. Whether she cares for Bertrand Moncrif or no, her vanity will suffer intensely, and she will never forgive you for taking him out of her clutches.'

He laughed.

'Lud, m'dear!' he said lightly. 'If we were to take heed of all the people who hate us we should spend our lives pondering rather than doing. And all I want to ponder over,' he added, whilst his glance of passionate earnestness seemed to envelop her like an exquisite warm mantle, 'is your beauty, your eyes, the scent of your hair, the delicious flavour of your kiss!'

II

It was some hours later on that same glorious day, when the shadows of ash and chestnut lay right across the lane and the arms of evening folded the cosy nest in their mysterious embrace, that Sir Percy and Marguerite sat in the deep window-embrasure of the tiny living-room.

It was one of those perfect spring evenings, rare enough in northern climes, without a breath of wind, when every sound carries clear and sharp through the stillness around.

The air was soft and slightly moist, with a tang in it of wakening life and of rising sap, and with the scent of wild narcissus and of wood violets rising like intoxicating incense to the nostrils. It was in truth one of those evenings when happiness itself seems rudely out of place, and nature – exquisite, but so cruelly transient in her loveliness – demands the tribute of gentle melancholy.

Then it was that suddenly a man's voice, hoarse but distinct, broke in upon the perfect peace around. What it said could not at first be gathered. It took some time ere Marguerite became sufficiently conscious of the disturbing noise to raise her head and listen. As for Sir Percy, he was wrapped in the contemplation of the woman he worshipped, and nothing short of an earthquake would have dragged him back to reality, had not Marguerite raised herself on her knees and quickly whispered:

'Listen!'

The man's voice had been answered by a woman's, raised as if in defiance that seemed both pitiful and futile.

'You cannot harm me now. I am in England!'

Marguerite leaned out of the window, tried to peer into the darkness which was fast gathering over the lane. The voices had come from there: first the man's, then the woman's, and now the man's again; both speaking in French, the woman obviously terrified and pleading, the man harsh and commanding. Now it was raised again, more incisive and distinct than before, and Marguerite had in truth some difficulty in repressing the cry that rose to her lips. She had recognised the man's voice.

'Chauvelin!' she murmured.

'Aye, in England, citoyenne!' that ominous voice went on dryly. 'But the arm of justice is long. And remember that you are not the first who has tried – unsuccessfully, let me tell you! – to evade punishment by flying to the enemies of

France. Wherever you may hide, I will know how to find you. Have I not found you here, now? – and you but a few hours in Dover!'

'But you cannot touch me!' the woman protested.

'Are you really simple enough, citoyenne,' he said, 'to be convinced of that?'

This sarcastic retort was followed by a moment or two of silence, then by a woman's cry; and in an instant Sir Percy was on his feet and out of the house. Marguerite followed him as far as the porch, whence the sloping ground, aided by flagged steps here and there, led down to the gate and thence on to the lane.

It was close beside the gate that a human-looking bundle lay huddled, when Sir Percy came upon the scene, even whilst, some fifty yards away at the sharp bend of the lane, a man could be seen walking rapidly away, his pace wellnigh at a run. Sir Percy's instinct was for giving chase, but the huddled-up figure put out a pair of arms and clung to him so desperately, with smothered cries of: 'For pity's sake, don't leave me!' that it would have been inhuman to go. And so he bent down, raised the human bundle from the ground, and carried it bodily up into the house.

Here he deposited his burden upon the window seat, where but a few moments ago he had been wrapped in the contemplation of Marguerite's eyelashes, and with his habitual quaint good-humour, said:

'I leave the rest to you, m'dear. My French is too atrocious for dealing with the case.'

Marguerite understood the hint. Sir Percy, whose command of French was nothing short of phenomenal, never used the language save when engaged in his perilous undertakings. His perfect knowledge of every idiom would have set any ill-intentioned eavesdropper thinking.

III

The human bundle looked very pathetic lying there upon the window seat, propped up with cushions. It appeared to be a youth, dressed in rough fisherman's clothes and with a cap that fitted tightly round the head; but with hands delicate as a woman's and a face of exquisite beauty.

Without another word, Marguerite quietly took hold of the cap and gently removed it. A wealth of blue-black hair fell like a cascade over the recumbent shoulders. 'I thought as much!' Sir Percy remarked quietly, even whilst the stranger, apparently terrified, jumped up and burst into tears, moaning piteously:

'Oh, mon Dieu! mon Dieu! Sainte Vierge, protégez-moi!'

There was nothing to do but to wait; and anon the first paroxysm of grief and terror passed. The stranger, with a wry little smile, took the handkerchief which Lady Blakeney was holding out to her and proceeded to dry her tears. Then she looked up at the kind Samaritans who had befriended her.

'I am an impostor, I know,' she said, with lips that quivered like those of a child in grief. 'But if you only knew . . . !'

She sat bolt upright now, squeezing and twirling the wet handkerchief between her fingers.

'Some kind English gentlemen were good to me, down in the town,' she went on more glibly. 'They gave me food and shelter, and I was left alone to rest. But I felt stifled in the narrow room. I could hear every one talking and laughing, and the evening air was so beautiful. So I ventured out. I only meant to breathe a little fresh air; but it was all so lovely, so peaceful . . . here in England . . . so different to . . .'

She shuddered a little and looked as if she was going to cry again. But Marguerite interposed gently:

'So you prolonged your walk, and found this lane?'

'Yes. I prolonged my walk,' the woman replied. 'I did not notice that the road had become lonely. Then suddenly I realised that I was being followed, and I ran. Mon Dieu, how I ran! Whither, I knew not! I just felt that something horrible was at my heels!'

Her eyes, dilated with terror, looked as black as sloes. They were fixed upon Marguerite, never once raised on Sir Percy, who, standing some way apart from the two women, was looking down on them, silent and apparently unmoved.

The stranger shuddered again; her face was almost grey in its expression of fear, and her lips seemed quite bloodless. Marguerite gave her trembling hands an encouraging pat.

'It was lucky,' she said gently, 'that you found your way here.'

'I had seen the light,' the woman continued more calmly. 'And I believe that at the back of my mind there was the instinct to run for shelter. Then suddenly my foot knocked against a stone, and I fell. I tried to raise myself quickly, but I had not the time, for the next moment I felt a hand on my shoulder, and a voice – oh, a voice I dread, citoyenne! – called to me by name.'

'The voice of citizen Chauvelin?' Marguerite asked simply.

The woman looked up quickly.

'You knew—?' she murmured.

'I knew his voice.'

'But you know him?' the other insisted.

'I know him – yes,' Marguerite replied. 'I am a compatriot of yours. Before I married, I was Marguerite St Just.'

'St Just?'

'We are cousins, my brother and I, of the young deputy, the friend of Robespierre.'

'God help you!' the woman murmured.

'He has done so already, by bringing us both to England. My brother is married, and I am Lady Blakeney now. You too will feel happy and safe now that you are here.'

'Happy?' the woman ejaculated, with a piteous sob. 'And safe? Mon Dieu, if only I could think it!'

'But what have you to fear? Chauvelin may have retained some semblance of power over in France. He has none over here.'

'He hates me!' the other murmured. 'Oh, how he hates me!'

'Why?'

The stranger made no immediate reply. Her eyes, dark as the night, glowing and searching, seemed to read the very soul behind Marguerite's serene brow. Then after awhile she went on, with seeming irrelevance:

'It all began so foolishly! . . . mon Dieu, how foolishly! And I really meant nothing treacherous to my own country – nothing unpatriotic, quoi?' She suddenly seized Marguerite's two hands and exclaimed with childlike enthusiasm: 'You have heard of the Scarlet Pimpernel, have you not?'

'Yes,' Marguerite replied. 'I have heard of him.'

'You know then that he is the finest, bravest, most wonderful man in all the world?'

'Yes, I know that,' Marguerite assented with a smile.

'Of course, in France they hate him. Naturally! He is the enemy of the republic, quoi? He is against all those massacres, the persecution of the innocent. He saves them and helps them when he can. So they hate him. Naturally.'

'Naturally!'

'But I have always admired him,' the woman continued, enthusiasm glowing in her dark eyes. 'Always; always! Ever since I heard what he had done, and how he saved the Comte de Tournai, and Juliette Marny, and Esther Vincent, and – and countless others. Oh, I knew about them all! For I knew Chauvelin well, and one or two of the men on the Committee of Public Safety quite intimately, and I used to worm out of them all the true facts about the Scarlet Pimpernel. Can you wonder that with my whole soul I admired him? I worshipped him! I could have laid down my life to help him! He has been the guiding star of my dreary life – my hero and my king!'

She paused, and those deep, dark eyes of hers were fixed straight out before her, as if in truth she beheld the hero of her dreams.

'So now,' the woman concluded, coming back to the painful realities of life with a shudder, which extinguished the light in her eyes and took all the glow out of her cheeks, 'so now you understand perhaps why Chauvelin hates me!'

'You must have been rather indiscreet,' Marguerite remarked with a smile.

'I was, I suppose. And Chauvelin is so vindictive. He hates the Scarlet Pimpernel. Out of a few words, foolishly spoken perhaps, he has made out a case against me. A friend gave me warning. My name was already in the hands of Foucquier-Tinville. You know what that means! Perquisition! Arrest! Judgment! Then the guillotine! Oh, mon Dieu! And I had done nothing! – nothing! I fled out of Paris. An influential friend just contrived to arrange this for me. A faithful servant accompanied me. We reached Boulogne. How, I know not! I was so weak, so ill, so wretched, I hardly lived. I just allowed François – that was my servant – to take me whithersoever he wished. But we had no passports, no papers – nothing! And Chauvelin was on our track. We had to hide – in barns . . . in pig-styes . . . anywhere! But we reached Boulogne at last . . . I had some money, fortunately. We bribed a fisherman to let us have his boat. Only a small

The Nest

boat – imagine! A rowing boat! And François and I alone in it! But it meant our lives if we didn't go; and perhaps it meant our lives if we went! A rowing boat on the great, big sea! . . . Fortunately the weather was fine, and François said that surely we would meet an English vessel which would pick us up. I was more dead than alive. And François lifted me into the boat. And I just remember seeing the coast of France receding, receding, receding – farther and farther from me. I was so tired. It is possible that I slept. Then suddenly something woke me. I had heard a cry. I knew I had heard a cry, and then a splash – an awful splash! I was wet through. One oar hung in the rowlock; the other had gone. And François was not there. I was all alone.'

She spoke in hard, jerky sentences, as if every word hurt her physically as she uttered it. For the most part she was looking down on her hands, that twitched convulsively and twisted the tiny wet handkerchief into a ball. But now and again she looked up, not at Marguerite always, rather at Sir Percy. Her glowing, tear-wet eyes fastened themselves on him from time to time with an appealing or a defiant gaze. He appeared silent and sympathetic, and his glance rested on her the whole while that she spoke, with an expression of detached if kindly interest, as if he did not quite understand everything that she said. Marguerite as usual was full of tenderness and compassion.

'How terribly you must have suffered!' she said gently. 'But what happened after that?'

'Oh, I don't know! I don't know!' the poor woman resumed. 'I was too numbed, too dazed with horror and fear, to suffer very much. I remember nothing after . . . after that awful cry . . . and the splash! I suppose my poor François fainted or fell asleep . . . and that he fell into the water. I never saw him again . . . and I remember nothing until – until I found myself on board a ship with a lot of rough sailors around me, who seemed very kind . . . They brought me ashore and took me to a nice warm place, where some English gentlemen took compassion on me. And . . . and . . . I have already told you the rest.'

She leaned back against the cushions of the seat as if exhausted with the prolonged effort. Her hands seemed quite cold now, almost blue, and Marguerite rose and closed the window behind her.

'How kind and thoughtful you are!' the stranger exclaimed, and after a moment added with a weary sigh, 'I must not trespass longer on your kindness. It is late now, and . . . I must go.'

She struggled to her feet, rose with obvious reluctance. 'The inn where I was,' she said, 'it is not far?'

'But you cannot go out alone,' Marguerite rejoined. 'You do not even know the way!'

'Ah, no! But perhaps your servant could accompany me . . . only as far as the town. . . . After that, I can ask the way . . . I should no longer be frightened.'

'You speak English then, Madame?'

'Oh, yes! My father was a diplomat. He was in England once for four years. I learned a little English. I have not forgotten it.'

'One of the servants shall certainly go with you. The inn you speak of must be *The Fisherman's Rest*, since you found English gentlemen there.'

'If Madame will allow me?' Sir Percy broke in, for the first time since the stranger had embarked upon her narrative.

The stranger looked up at him with a half-shy, half-eager smile.

'You, milor!' she exclaimed. 'Oh no! I would be ashamed—'

She paused, and her cheeks became crimson whilst she looked down in utter confusion on her extraordinary attire.

'I had forgotten,' she murmured tearfully. 'François made me put on these awful clothes when we left Paris.'

'Then I must lend you a cloak for tonight,' Marguerite interposed with a smile. 'But you need not mind your clothes, Madame. On this coast our people are used to seeing unfortunate fugitives landing in every sort of guise. Tomorrow we must find you something wherein to travel to London.'

'To London?' the stranger said with some eagerness. 'Yes! I would wish to go to London.'

'It will be quite easy. Mme de Serval, with her son and two daughters and another friend, is travelling by the coach tomorrow. You could join them, I am sure. Then you would not be alone. You have money, Madame?' Marguerite concluded, with practical solicitude.

'Oh yes!' the other replied. 'I have plenty for present needs . . . in a wallet . . . under my clothes. I was able to collect a little – and I have not lost it. I am not dependent,' she added, with a smile of gratitude. 'And as soon as I have found my husband—'

'Your husband?' Marguerite exclaimed.

'M. le Marquis de Fontenay,' the other answered simply. 'Perhaps you know him. You have seen him . . . in London? . . . Not?'

Marguerite shook her head.

'Not to my knowledge.'

'He left me – two years ago . . . cruelly . . . emigrated to England . . . and I was left all alone in the world . . . He saved his own life by running away from France; but I – I could not go just then . . . and so . . .'

She seemed on the verge of breaking down again, then recovered herself and continued more quietly:

'That was my idea, you see; to find my husband one day. I have never ceased to love him, though he was so cruel. And I think that . . . perhaps . . . he also has not quite forgotten me.'

'That were impossible,' Marguerite rejoined gently. 'But I have friends in London who are in touch with most of the emigrés here. We will see what can be done. It will not be difficult, methinks, to find M. de Fontenay.'

'You are an angel, milady!' the stranger exclaimed; and with a gesture that was perfect in its suggestion of gracious humility, she took Marguerite's hand and raised it to her lips. Then she once more mopped her eyes, picked up her cap and hastily hid the wealth of her hair beneath it. After which, she turned to Sir Percy.

'I am ready, milor,' she said. 'I have intruded far too long as it is upon your privacy. . . . But I am not brave enough to refuse your escort. Milady, forgive me! I will walk fast, very fast, so that milor will return to you very soon!'

She wrapped herself up in the cloak which, at Lady Blakeney's bidding, one of the servants had brought her, and a moment or two later the stranger and Sir Percy were out of the house, whilst Marguerite remained for awhile in the porch, listening to their retreating footsteps.

There was a frown of puzzlement between her brows, a look of troubled anxiety in her eyes. Somehow, the brief sojourn of that strange and beautiful woman in her house had filled her soul with a vague feeling of dread, which she tried vainly to combat. There was no real suspicion against the woman in her heart – how could there be? – but she – Marguerite – who as a rule was so compassionate, so understanding of those misfortunes, to alleviate which Sir Percy was devoting his entire life, felt cold and unresponsive in this case – most unaccountably so. Mme de Fontenay's story differed but little in all its grim detail of misery and humiliation from the thousand and one other similar tales which had been poured for the past three years into her sympathetic ear. She had always understood, had always been ready to comfort and to help. But this time she felt very much as if she had come across a sick or wounded reptile, something weak and dumb and helpless, and yet withal unworthy of compassion.

However, Marguerite Blakeney was surely not the woman to allow such fancies to dry the well of her pity. The gallant Scarlet Pimpernel was not wont to pause in his errands of mercy in order to reflect whether the objects of his selfless immolation were worthy of it or no. So Marguerite, with a determined little sigh, chided herself for her disloyalty and cowardice, and having dried her tears she went within.

CHAPTER 16

A Lover of Sport

I

For the first five minutes, Sir Percy Blakeney and Madame de
Fontenay walked side by side in silence. Then she spoke.

'You are silent, milor?' she queried, speaking in perfect
English.

'I was thinking,' he replied curtly.

'What?'

'That a remarkably fine actress is lost in the fashionable
Theresia Cabarrus.'

'Madame de Fontenay, I pray you, milor,' she retorted
drily.

'Theresia Cabarrus nevertheless. Madame Tallien probably tomorrow: for Madame divorced that weak-kneed
marquis as soon as the law "contre les emigrés" allowed
her to regain her freedom.'

'You seem very well informed, milor.'

'Almost as well as Madame herself,' he riposted with a
pleasant laugh.

'Then you do not believe my story?'

'Not one word of it!' he replied.

'Strange!' she mused. 'For every word of it is true.'

'Demmed strange!' he assented.

'Of course, I did not tell all,' she went on, with sudden

157

vehemence. 'I could not. My lady would not understand. She has become – what shall I say? – very English. Marguerite St Just understand . . . Lady Blakeney – no?'

'What would Lady Blakeney not understand?'

'Eh bien! About Bertrand Moncrif.'

'Ah?'

'You think I did harm to the boy . . . I know . . . you took him away from me . . . You! The Scarlet Pimpernel; . . . You see, I know! I know everything! Chauvelin told me. . . .'

'And guided you most dexterously to my door,' he concluded with a pleasant laugh. 'There to enact a delicious comedy of gruff-voiced bully and pathetic victim of a merciless persecution. It was all excellently done! Allow me to offer you my sincere congratulations!'

She said nothing for a moment or two, then queried abruptly:

'You think that I am here in order to spy upon you?'

'Oh!' he riposted lightly, 'how could I be so presumptuous as to suppose that the beautiful Cabarrus would bestow attention on so unworthy an object as I?'

' 'Tis you now, milor,' she rejoined drily, 'who choose to play a rôle. A truce on it, I pray you; and rather tell me what you mean to do.'

To this query he gave no reply, and his silence appeared to grate on Theresia's nerves, for she went on harshly:

'You will betray me to the police, of course. And as I am here without papers—'

'Oh!' he said, with his quiet little laugh, 'why should you think I would do anything so unchivalrous?'

'Unchivalrous?' she retorted with a pathetic sigh of weariness. 'I suppose, here in England, it would be called an act of patriotism or self-preservation . . . like fighting an enemy . . . or denouncing a spy—'

She paused for a moment or two, and as he once more

took refuge in silence, she resumed with sudden, moving passion:

'So it is to be a betrayal after all! The selling of an unfortunate woman to her bitterest enemy! Oh, what wrong have I ever done you, that you should persecute me thus?'

'Persecute you?' he exclaimed. 'Pardi, Madame; but this is a subtle joke which by your leave my dull wits are unable to fathom.'

'It is no joke, milor,' she rejoined earnestly. 'Will you let me explain? For indeed it seems to me that we are at cross purposes, you and I.'

She came to a halt, and he perforce had to do likewise. They had come almost to the end of the little lane; a few yards farther on it debouched on the main road. Theresia – divinely slender and divinely tall, graceful despite the rough masculine clothes which she wore – stood boldly in the full light; the tendrils of her jet black hair were gently stirred by an imperceptible breeze, her eyes dark and luminous, were fixed upwards at the man whom she had set out to subjugate.

'That boy,' she went on quite gently, 'Bertrand Moncrif, was just a young fool. But I liked him, and I could see the abyss to which his folly was tending. There was never anything but friendship between us; but I knew that sooner or later he would run his head into a noose, and then what good would his pasty-faced sweetheart have been to him? Whilst I – I had friends, influence – quoi? And I liked the boy; I was sorry for him. Then the catastrophe came ... the other night. There was what those ferocious beasts over in Paris were pleased to call a Fraternal Supper. Bertrand Moncrif was there. Like a young fool, he started to vilify Robespierre – Robespierre, who is the idol of France! There! – in the very midst of the crowd! They would have torn him limb from limb, it seems. I don't know just what happened, for I wasn't there; but he came to my apartment – at midnight – dishevelled – his clothes torn – more dead than alive. I gave him shelter; I tended him. Yes, I! – even whilst Robespierre and his friends were in my house, and risked my life every moment that Bertrand was under my roof! Chauvelin suspected something then. Oh, I knew it! Those awful, pale, deep-set eyes of his seemed to be searching my soul all the time! At which precise moment you came and took Bertrand away, I know not. But Chauvelin knew. He saw – he saw, I tell you! He had not been with us the whole time, but in and out of the apartment on some pretext or other. Then, after the others had left, he came back, accused me of having harboured not only Bertrand, but the Scarlet Pimpernel himself! – swore that I was in league with the English spies and had arranged with them to smuggle my lover out of my house. Then he went away. He did not threaten. You know him as well as I do. Threatening is not his way. But from his look I knew that I was doomed. Luckily I had François. We packed up my few belongings then and there. I left my woman Pepita in charge, and I fled. As for the rest, I swear to you that it all happened just as I told it to milady. You say you do not believe me. Very well! Will you then take me away from this sheltered land, which I have reached after terrible sufferings? Will you send me back to France, and drive me to the arms of a man who but waits to throw me into the tumbril with the next batch of victims for the guillotine? You have the power to do it, of course. You are in England; you are rich, influential, a power in your own country; whilst I am an alien, a political enemy, a refugee, penniless and friendless. You can do with me what you will, of course. But if you do *that*, milor, my blood will stain your hands for ever; and all the good you and your League have ever done in the cause of humanity will be wiped out by this execrable crime.'

She spoke very quietly and with soul-moving earnestness. But whatever his thoughts might be, when she paused, wearied and shaken with sobs which she vainly tried to suppress, he spoke to her quite gently.

'Believe me, dear lady,' he said, 'that I had no thought of wronging you when I owned to disbelieving your story. I have seen so many strange things in the course of my chequered career that, in verity, I ought to know by now how unbelievable truth often appears.'

'Had you known me better, milor—' she began.

'Ah, that is just it!' he rejoined quaintly. 'I did not know you, Madame. And now, meseems, that Fate has intervened, and that I shall never have the chance of knowing you.'

'How is that?' she asked.

But to this he gave no immediate answer, suggested irrelevantly:

'Shall we walk on? It is getting late.'

She gave a little cry, as if startled out of a dream, then started to walk by his side with her long, easy stride, so full of sinuous grace. Already they had passed the first group of town houses, and *The Running Footman*, which is the last inn outside the town. There was only the High Street now to follow and the Old Place to cross, and *The Fisherman's Rest* would be in sight.

'You have not answered my question, milor,' Theresia said presently.

'What question, Madame?' he asked.

'I asked you how Fate could intervene in the matter of our meeting again.'

'Oh!' he retorted simply. 'You are staying in England, you tell me.'

'If you will deign to grant me leave,' she said, with gentle submission.

'It is not in my power to grant or to refuse.'

'You will not betray me – to the police?'

'I have never betrayed a woman in my life.'

'Or to Lady Blakeney?'

As he made no answer, she began to plead with him.

'What could she gain – or you – by her knowing that I am that unfortunate, homeless waif, without kindred and without friends, Theresia Cabarrus – the beautiful Cabarrus! – once the fiancée of the great Tallien, now suspect of trafficking with her country's enemies in France ... and suspect of being a suborned spy in England! ... My God, where am I to go? What am I to do? Do not tell Lady Blakeney, milor! On my knees I entreat you, do not tell her! She will hate me – fear me – despise me! Oh, give me a chance to be happy! Give me – a chance – to be happy!'

Again she had paused and placed her hand on his arm. Once more she was looking up at him, her eyes glistening with tears, her full red lips quivering with emotion. And he returned her appealing, pathetic glance for a moment or two in silence; then suddenly, without any warning, he threw back his head and laughed.

'By Gad!' he exclaimed. 'But you are a clever woman!'

'Milor!' she protested, indignant.

'Nay: you need have no fear, fair one! I am a lover of sport. I'll not betray you.'

'I do not understand,' she murmured.

'Let us get back to *The Fisherman's Rest*,' he retorted with characteristic irrelevance. 'Shall we?'

'Milor,' she insisted, 'will you explain?'

'There is nothing to explain, dear lady. You have asked me – nay! challenged me – not to betray you to anyone, not even to Lady Blakeney. Very well! I accept your challenge. That is all.'

'You will not tell anyone – anyone, mind you! – that Mme de Fontenay and Theresia Cabarrus are one and the same?'

'You have my word for that.'

She drew a scarce perceptible sigh of relief.

'Very well then, milor,' she rejoined. 'Since I am allowed to go to London, we shall meet there, I hope.'

'Scarcely, dear lady,' he replied, 'since I go to France tomorrow.'

This time she gave a little gasp, quickly suppressed.

'You go to France tomorrow, milor?' she asked.

'As I had the honour to tell you, I go to France tomorrow, and leave you a free hand to come and go as you please.'

She chose not to notice the taunt; but suddenly, as if moved by an uncontrollable impulse, she said resolutely:

'If you go, I shall go too.'

'I am sure you will, dear lady,' he retorted with a smile. 'So there really is no reason why we should linger here. Our mutual friend M. Chauvelin must be impatient to hear the result of this interview.'

She gave a cry of horror and indignation.

'Oh! You – you still think *that* of *me*?'

He stood there, smiling, looking down on her with that half-amused, lazy glance of his. He did not actually say anything, but she felt that she had her answer. With a moan of pain, like a child who has been badly hurt, she turned abruptly, and burying her face in her hands, she sobbed as if her heart would break. Sir Percy waited quietly for a moment or two, until the first paroxysm of grief had quietened down, then he said gently:

'Madame, I entreat you to compose yourself and to dry your tears. If I have wronged you in my thoughts, I humbly crave your pardon. I pray you to understand that when a man holds human lives in his hands, when he is responsible for the life and safety of those who trust in him, he must be doubly cautious and in his turn trust no one. You have said yourself that now at last in this game of life and death, which

I and my friends have played so successfully these last three years, I hold the losing cards. Then must I watch every trick all the more closely, for a sound player can win through the mistakes of his opponent, even if he hold a losing hand.'

'You will never know, milor – never – how deeply you have wounded me,' she said through her tears. 'And I, who for months past – ever since I knew! – have dreamed of seeing the Scarlet Pimpernel one day! He was the hero of my dreams, the man who stood alone in the mass of self-seeking, vengeful, cowardly humanity as the personification of all that was fine and chivalrous. I longed to see him – just once – to hold his hand – to look into his eyes – and feel a better woman for the experience. Love? It was not love I felt, but hero-worship, pure as one's love for a starlit night or a spring morning, or a sunset over the hills. I dreamed of the Scarlet Pimpernel, milor; and because of my dreams, which were too vital for perfect discretion, I had to flee from home, suspected, vilified, already condemned. Chance brings me face to face with the hero of my dreams, and he looks on me as that vilest thing on earth: a spy! – a woman who would lie to a man first and send him afterwards to his death!'

They did not speak again with one another until they were under the porch of *The Fisherman's Rest*. Then Theresia stopped, and with a perfectly simple gesture she held out her hand to Sir Percy.

'We may never meet again on this earth, milor,' she said quietly. 'Indeed, I shall pray to le bon Dieu to keep me clear of your path.'

'I very much doubt, dear lady,' he said, 'that you will be in earnest when you utter that prayer!'

'You choose to suspect me, milor; and I'll no longer try to combat your mistrust. But to one more word you must listen: Remember the fable of the lion and the mouse. The invincible Scarlet Pimpernel might one day need the help of Theresia Cabarrus. I would wish you to believe that you can always count on it.'

She extended her hand to him, and he took it, the while his inveterately mocking glance challenged her earnest one. After a moment or two he stooped and kissed her finger-tips.

'Let me rather put it differently, dear lady,' he said. 'One day the exquisite Theresia Cabarrus – the Egeria of the Terrorists, the fiancée of the Great Tallien – might need the help of the League of the Scarlet Pimpernel.'

'I would sooner die than seek your help, milor.'

'Here in Dover, perhaps . . . but in France? . . . And you said you were going back to France, in spite of Chauvelin and his pale eyes, and his suspicions of you.'

'Since you think so ill of me,' she retorted, 'why should you offer me your help?'

'Because,' he replied lightly, 'with the exception of my friend Chauvelin, I have never had so amusing an enemy; and it would afford me intense satisfaction to render you a signal service.'

'You mean, that you would risk your life to save mine?'

'No. I should not risk my life, dear lady,' he said with his puzzling smile. 'But I should – God help me! – do my best, if the need arose, to save yours.'

After which, with another ceremonious bow, he took final leave of her, and she was left standing there, looking after his tall, retreating figure until the turn of the street hid him from view.

Who could have fathomed her thoughts and feelings at that moment? No one, in truth; not even herself. Theresia Cabarrus had met many men in her day, subjugated and fooled not a few. But she had never met anyone like this before. At one moment she had thought she had him: he appeared moved, serious, compassionate, gave her his word that he would not betray her; and in that word, her unerring instinct – the instinct of the adventuress, the woman who succeeds by her wits as well as by her charm – told her that she could trust. Did he fear her, or did he not? Did he suspect her? Theresia could not say.

But, he had defied and insulted her. The letter which he left for her after he had smuggled Bertrand Moncrif out of her apartment, rankled and stung her pride as nothing had ever done before. Therefore the man must be punished, and in a manner that would leave no doubt in his mind as to whence came the blow that struck him. But it was all going to be very much more difficult than the beautiful Theresia Cabarrus had allowed herself to believe.

CHAPTER 17

Reunion

I

It was a thoughtful Theresia who turned into the narrow hall of *The Fisherman's Rest* a few moments later. The inn, when she left it earlier in the evening, had still been all animation and bustle consequent on the arrival of their lordships with the party of ladies and gentlemen over from France, and the excitement of making all these grand folk comfortable for the night. Theresia Cabarrus, in her disguise as a young stowaway, had only aroused passing interest – refugees of every condition and degree were frequent enough in these parts – and when awhile ago she had slipped out in order to enact the elaborate rôle devised by her and Chauvelin, she had done so unperceived. Since then, no doubt there had been one or two cursory questions about the mysterious stowaway, who had been left to feed and rest in the tiny living-room; but equally no doubt, interest in him waned quickly when it was discovered that he had gone, without as much as thanking those who had befriended him.

The travellers from France had long since retired to their rooms, broken with fatigue after the many terrible experiences they had gone through. The young English gallants had gone, either to friends in the neighbourhood or – in the case of Sir Andrew Ffoulkes and Lord Anthony Dewhurst – ridden away in the early part of the evening, so as to reach Ashford mayhap or Maidstone before nightfall, and thus lessen the distance which still separated them from the loved ones at home.

A good deal of noise and laughter was still issuing from the coffee-room. Through the glass door Theresia could see the habitués of *The Fisherman's Rest* – yokels and fisherfolk – sitting over their ale, some of them playing cards or throwing dice. Mine host was there too, engaged as usual in animated discussion with some privileged guests who sat in the ingle-nook.

Theresia slipped noiselessly past the glass door. Straight in front of her a second passage ran at right angles; two or three steps led up to it. She tip-toed up these, and then looked about her, trying to reconstruct in her mind the disposition of the various rooms. On her left a glass partition divided the passage from the small parlour wherein she had found shelter on her arrival. On her right the passage obviously led to the kitchen, for much noise of crockery and shrill feminine voices and laughter came from there.

For a moment Theresia hesitated. Her original intention had been to find Mistress Waite and see if a bed for the night were still available; but a slight noise or movement issuing from the parlour caused her to turn. She peeped through the glass partition. The room was dimly lighted by a small oil-lamp which hung from the ceiling. A fire still smouldered in the hearth, and beside it, sitting on a low stool staring into the embers, his hands held between his knees, was Bertrand Moncrif.

Theresia Cabarrus had some difficulty in smothering the cry of surprise which had risen to her throat. Indeed, for the moment she thought that the dim light and her own imaginative fancy was playing her a fantastic trick. The next, she had opened the door quite noiselessly and slipped into the room. Bertrand had not moved. Apparently he had not heard; or if he had cursorily glanced up, he had disdained to notice the roughly clad fellow who was disturbing his solitude. Certain it is that he appeared absorbed in gloomy meditations; whilst Theresia, practical and deliberate, drew the curtains together that hung in front of the glass partition, and thus made sure that intruding eyes could not catch her unawares. Then she murmured softly:

'Bertrand!'

He woke as from a dream, looked up and saw her. He passed a shaking hand once or twice across his forehead, then suddenly realised that she was actually there, near him, in the flesh. A hoarse cry escaped him, and the next moment he was down on his knees at her feet, his arms around her, his face buried in the folds of her mantle.

Everything – anxiety, sorrow, even surprise – was forgotten in the joy of seeing her. He was crying like a child, and murmuring her name in the intervals of covering her knees, her hands, her feet in their rough boots with kisses. She stood there, quite still, looking down on him, yielding her hands to his caresses. Around her full red lips there was an indefinable smile; but the light in her eyes was certainly one of triumph.

After awhile he rose, and she allowed him to lead her to an arm-chair by the hearth. She sat down, and he knelt at her feet with one arm around her waist, and his head against her breast. He had never in his life been quite so exquisitely happy. This was not the imperious Theresia, impatient and disdainful, as she had been of late – cruel even sometimes, as on that last evening when he thought he would never see her again. It was the Theresia of the early days in Paris, when first she came back from Bordeaux, with a reputation for idealism as well as for beauty and wit, and with a gracious acceptance of his homage which had completely subjugated him.

She insisted on hearing every detail of his escape out of Paris and out of France, under the protection of the League of the Scarlet Pimpernel. In truth, he did not know who his rescuer was. He remembered but little of that awful night when, after the terrible doings at the Fraternal Supper, he had sought refuge in her apartment and then realised that, like a criminal and selfish fool, he was compromising her precious life by remaining under her roof.

He had resolved to go as soon as he was able to stand – resolved if need be to give himself up at the nearest Poste de Section, when in a semi-conscious state he became aware that someone was in the room with him. He had not the time or the power to rouse himself and to look about, when a cloth was thrown over his face and he felt himself lifted off the chair bodily and carried away by powerful arms, whither he knew not.

After that, a great deal had happened – it all seemed indeed like a dream. At one time he was with Régine de Serval in a coach; at others with her brother Jacques, in a hut at night, lying on straw, trying to get some sleep, and tortured with thoughts of Theresia and fear for her safety. There were halts and delays, and rushes through the night. He himself was quite dazed, felt like a puppet that was dragged hither and thither in complete unconsciousness. Régine was constantly with him. She did her best to comfort him, would try to wile away the weary hours in the coach or in various hiding-places by holding his hand and talking of the future – the happy future in England, when they would have a home of their own, secure from the terrors of the past two years, peaceful in complete oblivion of the cruel past. Happy and peaceful! My God! As if there could be any happiness or peace for him, away from the woman he worshipped!

Theresia listened to the tale, for the most part in silence. From time to time she would stroke his hair and forehead with her cool, gentle hand. She did ask one or two questions, but these chiefly on the subject of his rescuer: Had he seen him? Had he seen any of the English gentlemen who effected his escape?

Oh, yes; Bertrand saw a good deal of the three or four young gallants who accompanied him and the party all the way from Paris. He only saw the last of them here, in this inn, a few hours ago. One of them gave him some money to enable him to reach London in comfort. They were very kind, entirely unselfish. Mme de Serval, Régine, and the others were overwhelmed with gratitude, and oh, so happy! Joséphine and Jacques had forgotten all about their duty to their country in their joy at finding themselves united and safe in this new land.

But the Scarlet Pimpernel himself, Theresia insisted, trying to conceal her impatience under a veneer of tender solicitude – had Bertrand seen him?

'No!' Bertrand replied. 'I never once set eyes on him, though it was he undoubtedly who dragged me helpless out of your apartment. The others spoke of him – always as "the chief." They seem to reverence him. He must be fine and brave. Régine and her mother and the two young ones have learned to worship him. Small wonder! seeing what he did for them at that awful Fraternal Supper.'

'What did he do?' Theresia queried.

And the story had to be told by Bertrand, just as he had had it straight from Régine. The asthmatic coal-heaver – the quarrel – Robespierre's arrival on the scene – the shouts – the mob. The terror of that awful giant who had dragged them into the empty house, and there left them in the care of others scarce less brave than himself. Then the disguises – the wanderings through the streets – the deathly anxiety at the gates of the city – the final escape in a laundry cart. Miracles of self-abnegation! Wonders of ingenuity and of daring! What wonder that the name of the Scarlet Pimpernel was one to be revered!

'On my knees will I pay homage to him,' Bertrand concluded fervently; 'since he brought you to my arms!'

She had him by the shoulders, held him from her at arm's length, whilst she looked – inquiring, slightly mocking – into his eyes.

'Brought me to your arms, Bertrand?' she said slowly. 'What do you mean?'

'You are here, Theresia,' he riposted. 'Safe in England . . . through the agency of the Scarlet Pimpernel.'

'Aye!' she said drily; 'through his agency. But not as you imagine, Bertrand.'

'What do you mean?'

'The Scarlet Pimpernel, my friend, after he had dragged you away from the shelter which you had found under my roof, sent an anonymous denunciation of me to the nearest Poste de Section, as having harboured the traitor Moncrif and conspiring with him to assassinate Robespierre whilst the latter was in my apartment.'

'Impossible!' Bertrand exclaimed.

'The chief Commissary of the Section,' she went on glibly, earnestly – never taking her eyes off his, 'at risk of his life, gave me warning. Aided by him and a faithful servant, I contrived to escape – out of Paris first, then across country in the midst of unspeakable misery, and finally out of the country in an open boat, until I was picked up by a chance vessel and brought to this inn more dead than alive.'

She fell back against the cushion of the chair, her sinuous body shaken with sobs. Bertrand, speechless with horror, could but try and soothe his beloved as she had soothed him a while ago, when past terrors and past bitter experiences had unmanned him. After a while she became more calm, contrived to smile through her tears.

'You see, Bertrand, that your gallant Scarlet Pimpernel is as merciless in hate as he is selfless in love.'

'But why?' the young man ejaculated vehemently. 'Why?'

'Why he should hate me?' she rejoined with a pathetic little sigh and a shrug of the shoulders. '*Chien sabe*, my friend! Of course, he does not know that of late – ever since I have gained the regard of citizen Tallien – my life has been devoted to intervening on behalf of the innocent victims of our revolution. I suppose he takes me for the friend and companion of all those ruthless Terrorists whom he abhors. He has forgotten what I did in Bordeaux, and how I risked my life there, and did so daily in Paris for the sake of those whom he himself befriends. It may all be a question of misunderstanding,' she added, with gentle resignation, 'but 'tis one that wellnigh did cost me my life.'

Bertrand folded her in his arms, held her against him, as if to shield her with his body against every danger. It was his turn now to comfort and to console, and she rested her head against his shoulder – a perfect woman rather than an unapproachable divinity, giving him through her weakness more exquisite bliss than he had ever dreamed of before. The minutes sped on, winged with happiness, and time was forgotten in the infinity of joy.

II

Theresia was the first to rouse herself from this dream of happiness and oblivion. She glanced up at the clock. It was close upon ten. Confused, adorable, she jumped to her feet.

'You will ruin my reputation, Bertrand,' she said with a smile, 'thus early in a strange land!'

She would arrange with the landlord's daughter, she said, about a bed for herself, as she was very tired. What did he mean to do?

'Spend the night in this room,' he replied, 'if mine host will let me. I could have such happy dreams here! These four walls will reflect your exquisite image, and 'tis your dear face will smile down on me ere I close mine eyes in sleep.'

She had some difficulty in escaping from his clinging arms, and 'twas only the definite promise that she gave him to come back in a few minutes and let him know what she had arranged, that ultimately enabled him to let her go.

Bertrand drew a deep sigh, partly of happiness, partly of utter weariness. He was more tired than he knew. She had promised to come back and say good night . . . in a few minutes . . . But the minutes seemed leaden-footed now . . . and he was half-dead with fatigue.

CHAPTER 18

Night and Morning

I

Theresia waited for a moment or two at the turn of the passage, until her keen ear had told her that Bertrand was no longer on the watch and had closed the door behind him. Then she retraced her steps – on tiptoe, lest he should hear.

She found her way to the front door; it was still on the latch. She opened it and peered out into the night. The little porch was deserted, but out there on the quay a few passers-by still livened the evening with chatter or song. Theresia was on the point of stepping out of the porch, when a familiar voice hailed her softly by name:

'Citoyenne Cabarrus!'

A man, dressed in dark clothes, with high boots and sugar-loaf hat, came out from the dark angle behind the porch.

'Not here!' Theresia whispered eagerly. 'Out on the quay. Wait for me there, my little Chauvelin. I'll be with you anon. I have so much to tell you!'

Silently, he did as she desired. She waited for a moment in the porch, watching the meagre figure in the dark cloak making its way across to the quay, then walking rapidly in the direction of the Pent. The moon was dazzlingly brilliant. The harbour and the distant sea glistened like diamond-studded sheets of silver. From afar there came the sound of the castle clock striking ten. The groups of passers-by had dwindled down to an occasional amorous couple strolling homewards, whispering soft nothings and gazing enraptured at the moon; or half-a-dozen sailors lolling down the quays arm in arm, on their way back to their ship, obstructing the road, yelling and singing the refrain of the newest ribald song; or perhaps a belated pedlar, weary of an unprofitable beat, wending his way dejectedly home.

One of these poor wretches – a cripple with a wooden leg and bent nearly double with the heavy load on his back – paused for a moment beside the porch, held out a grimy hand to Theresia, with a pitiable cry.

'Of your charity, kind sir! Buy a little something from the pore ole man, to buy a bit of bread!'

He looked utterly woebegone, with lank grey hair blown about by the breeze and a colourless face covered with sweat, that shone like painted metal in the moonlight.

'Buy a little something, kind sir!' he went on, in a shrill, throaty voice. 'I've a sick wife at 'ome, and pore little gran'childer!'

Theresia – a little frightened, and not at all charitably inclined at this hour – turned hastily away and went back into the house, whither the cripple's vigorous curses followed her.

'May Satan and all his armies—'

She shut the door on him and hastened up the passage. That cadaverous old reprobate had caused her to shudder as with the presentiment of coming evil.

II

With infinite precaution, Theresia peeped into the room where she had left Bertrand. She saw him lying on the sofa, fast asleep.

On the table in the middle of the room there was an old ink-horn, a pen, and a few loose sheets of paper. Noiseless as a mouse, Theresia slipped into the room, sat at the table, and hurriedly wrote a few lines. Bertrand had not moved. Having written her missive, Theresia folded it carefully, and still on tiptoe, more stealthily even than before, she slipped the paper between the young man's loosely clasped fingers. Then, as soundlessly as she had come, she glided out of the room, ran down the passage, and was out in the porch once more, breathless but relieved.

Bertrand had not moved; and no one had seen her. Theresia only paused in the porch long enough to recover her breath, then, without hesitation and with rapid strides, she crossed over to the water's edge and walked along in the direction of the Pent.

Whereupon, the figure of the old cripple emerged from out the shadows. He gazed after the fast retreating figure of Theresia for a moment or two, then threw down his load, straightened out his back, and stretched out his arms from the shoulders with a sigh of content. After which amazing proceedings he gave a soft, inward chuckle, unstrapped his wooden leg, slung it with his discarded load across his broad shoulders, and turning his back upon harbour and sea, turned up the High Street and strode rapidly away.

III

When Bertrand Moncrif woke, the dawn was peeping in through the uncurtained window. He felt cold and stiff. It took him some time to realise where he was, to collect his scattered senses. He had been dreaming . . . here in this room . . . Theresia had been here . . . and she had laid her head against his breast and allowed him to soothe and comfort her. Then she said that she would come back . . . and he . . . like a fool . . . had fallen asleep.

He jumped up, fully awake now; and as he did so a folded scrap of paper fell out of his hand.

Controlling his apprehension, his nervousness, Bertrand at last contrived to unfold the mysterious epistle. He read the few lines that were traced with a delicate, feminine hand, and with a sigh of infinite longing and of ardent passion, he pressed the paper to his lips. Theresia had sent him a message. Finding him asleep, she had slipped it into his hand. The marvel was that he did not wake when she stooped over him, and perhaps even touched his forehead with her lips.

'A kind soul,' so the message ran, 'hath taken compassion on me. There was no room for me at the inn, and she has offered me a bed in her cottage, somewhere close by. I do not know where it is. I have arranged with the landlord that you shall be left undisturbed in the small room where we found one another, and where the four walls will whisper to you of me. Good night, my beloved! Tomorrow you will go to London with the de Servals. I will follow later. It is better so. In London you will find me at the house of Mme de Neufchateau, a friend of my father's who lives at No. 54 in Soho Square, and who offered me hospitality in the days when I thought I might visit London for pleasure. She will receive me now that I am poor and an exile. Come to me there. Until then my heart will feed on the memory of your kiss.'

The letter was signed 'Theresia.'

Bertrand pressed it time and again to his lips. Never in his wildest dreams had he hoped for this; never even in those early days of rapture had he tasted such perfect bliss.

With that letter in his possession, Bertrand felt that he could not remain indoors. He was pining for open spaces, the sea, the mountains, God's pure air – the air which she too was breathing even now. He snatched up his hat and made his way out of the little building. The kitchen wench paused in her scrubbing and looked up smiling as he ran past her, singing and shouting for joy. For Régine – the tender, loving heart that pined for him and for his love – he had not a thought. She was the past, the dull, drabby past wherein he had dwelt before he knew how glorious a thing life could be, how golden the future, how rosy that horizon far away.

By the time he reached the harbour, the sun had risen in all its glory. Way out against the translucent sky, the graceful silhouette of the schooner swayed gently in the morning breeze, her outspread sails gleaming like wings that are tinged with gold. Bertrand watched her for awhile. He thought of the mysterious Scarlet Pimpernel and the hideous vengeance which he had wrought against his beloved. And the rage which possessed his soul at the thought obscured for a moment the beauty of the morning and the glory of the sky. With a gesture characteristic of his blood and of his race, he raised his fist and shook it in the direction of the distant ship.

CHAPTER 19

A Rencontre

I

For Marguerite, that wonderful May-day, like so many others equally happy and equally wonderful, came to an end all too soon. To dwell on those winged hours were but to record sorrow, anxiety, a passionate resentment coupled with an equally passionate acceptance of the inevitable. Her intimate friends often marvelled how Marguerite Blakeney bore the strain of these constantly recurring farewells. Every time that in the early dawn she twined her loving arms round the neck of the man she worshipped, feeling that mayhap she was looking into those dear, lazy, laughing eyes for the last time on earth – every time, it seemed to her as if earth could not hold greater misery.

Then after that came that terrible half-hour, whilst she stood on the landing-stage – his kisses still hot upon her lips, her eyes, her throat – and watched and watched that tiny speck, the fast-sailing ship that bore him away on his errand of mercy and self-sacrifice, leaving her lonely and infinitely desolate. And then the days and hours, when he was away and it was her task to smile and laugh, to appear to know nothing of her husband save that he was a society butterfly, the pet of the salons, an exquisite, something of a fool, whose frequent absences were accounted for by deer-stalking in Scotland or fishing in the Tweed, or hunting in the shires – anything and everything that would throw dust in the eyes of the fashionable crowd of whom she and he formed an integral part.

People would talk and ask questions, throw out suggestions and innuendoes. Society a few months ago had been greatly agitated because the beautiful Lady Blakeney, the most fashionable woman about town, had taken a mad fancy for – you'll never believe it, my dear! – for her own husband. She had him by her side at routs and river-parties, in her opera-box and on the Mall. It was positively indecent! Sir Percy was the pet of Society, his sallies, his inane laugh, his lazy, delicious, impertinent ways and his exquisite clothes, made the success of every salon in which he chose to appear. His Royal Highness was never so good-tempered as when Sir Percy was by his side. Then, for his own wife to monopolise him was preposterous, abnormal, extravagant! Some people put it down to foreign eccentricity; others to Lady Blakeney's shrewdness in thus throwing dust in the eyes of her none-too-clever lord, in order to mask some intrigue or secret amour, of which Society had not as yet the key.

Fortunately for the feelings of the fashionable world, this phase of conjugal affection did not last long. It had been at its height last year, and had waned perceptibly since. Of late, so it was averred, Sir Percy was hardly ever at home, and his appearances at Blakeney Manor – his beautiful house at Richmond – were both infrequent and brief. He had evidently tired of playing second fiddle to his exquisite wife, or been irritated by her caustic wit, which she was wont to sharpen at his expense; and the ménage of these two leaders of fashion had, in the opinion of those in the know, once more resumed a more normal aspect.

When Lady Blakeney was in Richmond, London or Bath,

Sir Percy was shooting or fishing or yachting – which was just as it should be. And when he appeared in society, smiling, elegant, always an exquisite, Lady Blakeney would scarce notice him, save for making him a butt for her lively tongue.

II

What it cost Marguerite to keep up this rôle none but a very few ever knew. The identity of one of the greatest heroes of this or any time was known to his most bitter enemy – not to his friends. So Marguerite went on smiling, joking, flirting, while her heart ached and her brain was at times wellnigh numb with anxiety. His intimates rallied round her, of course: the splendid little band of heroes who formed the League of the Scarlet Pimpernel – Sir Andrew Ffoulkes and his pretty wife; Lord Anthony Dewhurst and his lady, whose great dark eyes still wore the impress of the tragedy which had darkened the first month of her happy wedded life. Then there was my Lord Hastings; and Sir Evan Cruche, the young Squire of Holt, and all the others.

As for the Prince of Wales, it is more than surmised by those competent to judge that His Royal Highness did indeed guess at the identity of the Scarlet Pimpernel, even if he had not actually been apprised of it. Certain it is that his tact and discretion did on more than one occasion save a situation which might have proved embarrassing for Marguerite.

In all these friends then – in their conversation, their happy laughter, their splendid pluck and equally splendid gaiety, the echo of the chief whom they adored – Marguerite found just the solace that she needed. With Lady Ffoulkes and Lady Anthony Dewhurst she had everything in common. With those members of the League who happened to be in England, she could talk over and in her mind trace the various stages of the perilous adventure on which her beloved and the others were even then engaged.

III

Of Madame de Fontenay – for as such Marguerite still knew her – she saw but little. Whether the beautiful Theresia had gone to London or no, whether she had succeeded in finding her truant husband, Marguerite did not know and cared less. The unaccountable antipathy which she had felt on that first night of her acquaintance with the lovely Spaniard still caused her to hold herself aloof. Sir Percy, true to his word, had not betrayed the actual identity of Theresia Cabarrus to his wife; but in his light, insouciant manner had dropped a word or two of warning, which had sharpened Marguerite's suspicions and strengthened her determination to avoid Mme de Fontenay as far as possible.

But one day, walking alone in Richmond Park, she came face to face with Theresia. It was a beautiful afternoon in July, the end of a day which had been a comparatively happy one for Marguerite – the day when a courier had come from France with news of Sir Percy; a letter from him, telling her that he was well and hinting at the possibility of another of those glorious days together at Dover.

With that message from her beloved just to hand, Marguerite had felt utterly unable to fulfil her social engagements in London. There was nothing of any importance that claimed her presence. His Royal Highness was at Brighton; the opera and the rout at Lady Portarles' could well get on without her. The evening promised to be more than ordinarily beautiful, with a radiant sunset and the soft, sweet-scented air of a midsummer's evening.

After dinner, Marguerite had felt tempted to stroll out alone. She threw a shawl over her head and stepped out on to the terrace. The vista of velvet lawns, of shady paths and rose borders in full bloom, stretched out into the dim distance before her; and beyond these, the boundary wall, ivy-clad, overhung with stately limes, and broken into by the finely wrought iron gates that gave straight into the Park.

IV

Marguerite strolled through the grounds with a light foot, and anon reached the monumental gates, through which the exquisite peace and leafy solitude of the Park seemed to beckon insistently to her. The gate was on the latch; she slipped through and struck down a woodland path bordered by tangled undergrowth and tall bracken, and thus reached the pond, when suddenly she perceived Mme de Fontenay.

Theresia was dressed in a clinging gown of diaphanous black silk, which gave value to the exquisite whiteness of her skin and to the vivid crimson of her lips. She wore a transparent shawl round her shoulders, which with the new-modish, high-waisted effect of her gown, suited her sinuous grace to perfection. But she wore no jewellery, no ornaments of any kind: only a magnificent red rose at her breast.

The sight of her at this place and at this hour was so unexpected that, to Marguerite's super-sensitive intuition, the appearance of this beautiful woman, strolling listless and alone beside the water's edge, seemed like a presage of evil. Her first instinct had been to run away before Mme de Fontenay was aware of her presence; but the next moment she chided herself for this childish cowardice, and stood her ground, waiting for the other woman to draw near.

A minute or two later, Theresia had looked up and in her turn had perceived Marguerite. She did not seem surprised, rather came forward with a glad little cry, and her two hands outstretched.

'Milady!' she exclaimed. 'Ah, I see you at last! I have oft wondered why we never met.'

Mme de Fontenay had not much to relate. She had found refuge in the French convent of the Assumption at Twickenham, where the Mother Superior had been an intimate friend of her mother's in the happy olden days. She went out very little, and never in society. But she was fond of strolling in this beautiful Park. The sisters had told her that Lady Blakeney's beautiful house was quite near. She would have liked to call – but never dared – hoping for a chance rencontre which hitherto had never come.

She asked kindly after milor, and seemed to have heard a rumour that he was at Brighton, in attendance on his royal friend. Of her husband, Mme de Fontenay had as yet found no trace. He must be living under an assumed name, she thought – no doubt in dire poverty – Theresia feared it, but did not know – would give worlds to find out.

Then she asked Lady Blakeney whether she knew aught of the de Servals.

'I was so interested in them,' she said, 'because I had heard something of them while I was in Paris, and seeing that we arrived in England the same day, though under such different circumstances. But we could not journey to London together, as you, milady, so kindly suggested, because I was very ill the next day ... Ah, can you wonder? ... A kind friend in Dover took care of me. But I remember their name, and have oft marvelled if we should ever meet.'

Yes; Marguerite did see the de Servals from time to time. They rented a small cottage not very far from here – just outside the town. One of the daughters, Régine, was employed all day at a fashionable dressmaker's in Richmond. The younger girl, Joséphine, was a pupil-teacher at a young ladies' finishing school, and the boy, Jacques, was doing work in a notary's office. It was all very dreary for them, but their courage was marvellous; and though the children did not earn much, it was sufficient for their wants.

Madame de Fontenay was vastly interested. She hoped that Régine's marriage with the man of her choice would bring a ray of real happiness into the household.

'I hope so too,' Lady Blakeney assented.

'Milady has seen the young man – Régine's fiancé?'

'Oh, yes! Once or twice. But he is engaged in business all day, it seems. He is inclined to be morbid and none too full of ardour. It is a pity; for Régine is a sweet girl and deserves happiness.'

Madame de Fontenay took her leave with a gracious inclination of the head and a cordial au revoir. Then she turned off into a small path under the trees, cut through the growing bracken; and Marguerite watched the graceful figure thoughtfully, until the leafy undergrowth hid her from view.

CHAPTER 20

Departure

I

The next morning's sun rose more radiant than before. Marguerite greeted it with a sigh that was entirely a happy one. Another round of the clock had brought her a little nearer to the time when she would see her beloved. The next courier might indeed bring a message naming the very day when she could rest once more in his arms for a few brief hours, which were so like the foretaste of heaven.

Soon after breakfast she ordered her coach, intending to go to London in order to visit Lady Ffoulkes and give Sir Andrew the message which was contained for him in Percy's last letter. Whilst waiting for the coach, she strolled out into the garden, which was gay with roses and blue larkspur, sweet william and heliotrope, alive with a deafening chorus of blackbirds and thrushes, the twittering of sparrows and the last call of the cuckoo.

Then suddenly she became aware of hurrying footsteps on the gravelled path close by. She turned, and saw a young man whom at first she did not recognise, running with breathless haste towards her. He was hatless, his linen crumpled, his coat-collar awry. At sight of her he gave a queer cry of excitement and relief.

'Lady Blakeney! Thank God! Thank God!'

Then she recognised him. It was Bertrand Moncrif.

He fell on his knees and seized her gown. He appeared entirely overwrought, unbalanced, and Marguerite tried in vain at first to get a coherent word out of him. All that he kept on repeating was:

'Will you help me? Will you help us all?'

'Indeed I will, if I can, M. Moncrif,' Marguerite said gently. 'Do try and compose yourself and tell me what is amiss.'

She persuaded him to rise, and presently to follow her to a garden seat, where she sat down. He remained standing in front of her. His eyes still looked wild and scared, and he passed a shaking hand once or twice through his unruly hair.

He paused a moment, then cried abruptly:

'Régine has gone!'

Marguerite frowned, puzzled, and murmured slowly, not understanding:

'Gone? Whither?'

'To Dover,' he replied, 'with Jacques.'

'Jacques?' she reiterated, still uncomprehending.

'Her brother,' he rejoined. 'You know the boy?' Marguerite nodded.

'Hot-headed, impulsive,' Moncrif went on, trying to speak calmly. 'He and the girl Joséphine always had it in their minds that they were destined to liberate France from her present state of anarchy and bloodshed.'

'Like you yourself, M. Moncrif!' Marguerite put in with a smile.

'Oh, I became sobered, reasonable, when I realised how futile it all was. We all owe our lives to that noble Scarlet Pimpernel. They were no longer ours to throw away. At least, that was my theory, and Régine's. I have been engaged in business; and she works hard. . . . Oh, but you know!' he exclaimed impulsively.

'Yes, I know all your circumstances.'

'Jacques of late has been very excited, feverish. We did not know what was amiss. Régine and I oft spoke of him. And Mme de Serval has been distraught with anxiety. She worships the boy. He is her only son. But Jacques would not say what was amiss. He spoke to no one. Went to his work every day as usual. Last night he did not come home. A message came for Mme de Serval to say that a friend in London had persuaded him to go to the play and spend the night with him. Mme de Serval thought nothing of that. She was pleased to think that Jacques had some amusement to distract him from his brooding thoughts. But Régine, it seems, was not satisfied. After her mother had gone to bed, she went into Jacques' room; found some papers, it seems . . . letters . . . I know not . . . proof in fact that the boy was even then on his way to Dover, having made arrangements to take ship for France.'

'Mon Dieu!' Marguerite exclaimed involuntarily. 'What senseless folly!'

'Ah! but that is not the worst.'

With the same febrile movements that characterised his whole attitude, he drew a stained and crumpled letter from his pocket.

'She sent me this, this morning,' he said. 'That is why I came to you.'

'You mean Régine?' Marguerite asked, and took the letter.

'Yes! She must have brought it round herself . . . to my lodgings . . . in the early dawn. I did not know what to do . . . whom to consult. . . . A blind instinct brought me here . . . I have no other friend . . .'

In the meanwhile Marguerite was deciphering the letter, turning a deaf ear to his ramblings.

'My Bertrand,' so the letter ran, 'Jacques is going to France.

Nothing will keep him back. He says it is his duty. I think that
he is mad, and I know that it will kill maman. So I go with
him. Perhaps at the last – at Dover – my tears and entreaties
might yet prevail. If not, and he puts this senseless project in
execution, I can watch over him there, and perhaps save him
from too glaring a folly. We go by the coach to Dover, which
starts in an hour's time. Farewell, my beloved, and forgive
me for causing you this anxiety; but, I feel that Jacques has
more need of me than you.'

Below the signature 'Régine de Serval' there were a few
more lines written as if with an afterthought:

'I have told maman that my employer is sending me
down into the country about some dresses for an important
customer, and that as Jacques can get a few days' leave from
his work, I am taking him with me, for I feel the country air
would do him good.

'Maman will be astonished and no doubt hurt that Jacques
did not send her a word of farewell, but is best that she
should not learn the truth too suddenly. If we do not return
from Dover within the week, you will have to break the
news as gently as you can.'

Whilst Marguerite read the letter, Bertrand had sunk upon
the seat and buried his head in his hands. He looked utterly
dejected and forlorn, and she felt a twinge of remorse at the
thought of how she had been wronging him all this while
by doubting his love for Régine. She placed a kindly hand
on the young man's shoulder.

'What was your idea,' she asked, 'in coming to me? What
can I do?'

'Give me advice, milady!' he implored. 'I am so helpless,
so friendless. When I had the letter, I could think of nothing
at first. You see, Régine and Jacques started early this
morning, by the coach from London, long before I had it. I
thought you could tell me what to do, how to overtake them.

Régine loves me – oh, she loves me! If I knelt at her feet I could bring her back. But they are marked people, those two. The moment they attempt to enter Paris, they will be recognised, arrested. Oh, my God! have mercy on us all!'

'You think you can persuade Régine, M. Moncrif?'

'I am sure,' he asserted firmly. 'And you, milady! Régine thinks the whole world of you!'

'But there is the boy – Jacques!'

'He is just a child – he acted on impulse – and I always had great authority over him. And you, milady! The whole family worship you! . . . They know what they owe to you. Jacques has not thought of his mother; but if he did—'

Marguerite rose without another word.

'Very well,' she said simply. 'We'll go together and see what we can do with those two obstinate young folk.'

Bertrand gave a gasp of surprise and of hope. His whole face lighted up and he gazed upon the beautiful woman before him as a worshipper would on his divinity.

'You, milady?' he murmured. 'You would . . . really . . . help me . . . like that?'

Marguerite smiled.

'I really would help you like that,' she said. 'My coach is ordered; we can start at once. We'll get relays at Maidstone and at Ashford, and easily reach Dover tonight, before the arrival of the public coach. In any case, I know every one of any importance in Dover. We could not fail to find the runaways.'

'But you are an angel, milady!' Bertrand contrived to stammer, although obviously he was overwhelmed with gratitude.

'You are ready to start?' Marguerite retorted, gently checking any further display of emotion.

He certainly was hatless, and his clothes were in an untidy condition; but such trifles mattered nothing at a moment like this. Marguerite's household, on the other hand, were accustomed to these sudden vagaries and departures of their mistress, either for Dover, Bath, or any known and unknown destination, often at a few minutes' notice.

In this case the coach was actually at the gates. The maids packed the necessary valise; her ladyship changed her smart gown for a dark travelling one, and less than half an hour after Bertrand Moncrif's first arrival at the Manor, he was seated beside Lady Blakeney in her coach. The coachman cracked his whip, the postilion swung himself into the saddle, and the servants stood at attention as the vehicle slowly swung out of the gates; and presently, the horses putting on the pace, disappeared along the road, followed by a cloud of dust.

II

Bertrand Moncrif, brooding, absorbed in thoughts, said little or nothing while the coach swung along at a very brisk pace. Marguerite, who always had plenty to think about, did not feel in the mood to try and make conversation. She was very sorry for the young man, who in very truth must have suffered also from remorse. His lack of ardour – obviously only an outward lack – toward his fiancée and the members of her family, must to a certain extent have helped to pre-cipitate the present catastrophe. Coolness and moroseness on his part gave rise to want of confidence on the other. Régine, heartsick at her lover's seeming indifference, was no doubt all the more ready to lavish love and self-sacrifice upon the young brother. Marguerite was sorry enough for the latter – a young fool, with the exalté Latin temperament, brimming over with desires for self-immolation as futile as they were senseless – but her generous heart went out to Régine de Serval, a girl who appeared predestined to sorrow and disappointments, endowed with an exceptionally warm nature and cursed with the inability to draw wholehearted affection to herself. She worshipped Bertrand Moncrif; she idolised her mother, her brother, her sister. But though they, one and all, relied on her, brought her the confidences of their troubles and their difficulties, it never occurred to any one of them to give up something – a distraction, a fancy, an ideal – for the sake of silent, thoughtful Régine.

Marguerite allowed her thoughts thus to dwell on these people, whom her husband's splendid sacrifice on their behalf had rendered dear. Indeed, she loved them like she loved so many others, because of the dangers which he had braved for their sakes. Their lives had become valuable because of his precious one, daily risked because of them. And at the back of her mind there was also the certainty that if these two young fools did put their mad project in execution and endeavoured to return to Paris, it would again be the gallant Scarlet Pimpernel who would jeopardise his life to save them from the consequences of their own folly.

III

Luncheon and a brief halt was taken at Farningham and Maidstone reached by three o'clock in the afternoon. Here Lady Blakeney's own servants took leave of her, and post-horses were engaged to take her ladyship on to Ashford. Two hours later, at Ashford, fresh relays were obtained.

The public coach at this hour was only some nine or ten miles ahead, it seems, and there was now every chance that Dover would be reached by nightfall and the young runaways met by their pursuers on arrival.

All was then for the best. Bertrand, after the coach had rattled out of Ashford, appeared to find comfort and courage. He began to talk, long and earnestly – of himself, his plans and projects, his love for Régine, to which he always found it so difficult to give expression; of Régine herself and the de Servals, mother, son and daughters. His voice was toneless and very even. The monotony of his diction acted after awhile as a soporofic on Marguerite's nerves. The rumble of the coach, the closeness of this long afternoon in July, the rocking of the springs, made her feel drowsy. After a while too, a curious scent pervaded the interior of the coach – a sweet, heady scent that appeared to weigh her eyelids down and gave her a feeling of delicious and lazy beatitude. Bertrand Moncrif droned on, and his voice came to her fast-fading senses as through a thick pulpy veil. She closed her eyes. That sweet, intoxicating scent came, more marked, more insistent, to her nostrils. She laid her head against the cushions, and still she heard the dreary monotone of Bertrand's voice, quite inarticulate now, like the hum of a swarm of bees. . . .

Then, all of a sudden she was fully conscious; only just in time to feel the weight of an iron hand against her mouth and to see Bertrand's face, ghastly of hue, eyes distorted more with fear than rage, quite close to her own. She had not the time to scream, and her limbs felt as heavy as lead, so that she could not struggle. The next moment a thick woollen scarf was wound quickly and tightly round her head, covering her mouth and eyes, only barely giving her room to breathe, and her hands and arms were tied together with cords.

This brutal assault had been so quick and sudden that at first it seemed to Marguerite like part of a hideous dream. She was not fully conscious, and was half suffocated by the thick folds of the scarf and that persistent odour, which by its sickening sweetness caused her wellnigh to swoon.

Through this semi-consciousness, however, she was constantly aware of her enemy, Bertrand Moncrif – the black-hearted traitor who had carried out this execrable outrage: why and for what purpose, Marguerite was too dazed to attempt to guess. He was there, that she knew. She was conscious of his hands making sure of the cords round her wrists, tightening the scarf around her mouth; then presently she felt him leaning across her body and throwing down the window, and she heard him shouting to the driver:

'Her ladyship has fainted. Drive as fast as ever you can till you come to that white house yonder on the right, the one with the green shutters and the tall yew at the gate!'

The driver's reply she could not hear, nor the crack of his whip. Certain it is that, though the coach had rattled on at a great pace before, the horses, as if in response to Bertrand's commands, now burned the ground under their hooves. A few minutes went by – an eternity. Then that terrible cloying perfume was again held close to her nostrils; an awful dizziness and nausea seized her; after which she remembered nothing more.

CHAPTER 21

Memories

I

When Marguerite Blakeney finally recovered consciousness, the sun was low down in the west. She was in a coach – not her own – which was being whisked along the road at terrific speed. She was alone, her mouth gagged, her wrists and her ankles tied with cords, so that she could neither speak nor move – a helpless log, being taken . . . whither? . . . and by whom?

Bertrand was not there. Through the front window of the coach she could perceive the vague outline of two men sitting on the driver's seat, whilst another was riding the off-leader. Four horses were harnessed to the light coach. It flew along in a south-easterly direction, the while the shades of evening were fast drawing in.

Lying pinioned and helpless as she was, Marguerite had but the one thought: in what way would those fiends who had her a prisoner use her as a leverage against the life and the honour of the Scarlet Pimpernel? They had held her once before – not so very long ago – in Boulogne, and he had emerged unscathed, victorious over them all.

Marguerite forced her thoughts to dwell on that time, when his enemies had filled to the brim the cup of humiliation and of dread which was destined to reach him through her hands, and his ingenuity and his daring dashed the cup to the ground ere it reached her lips. In truth, her plight then, at Boulogne, was in no way less terrible, less seemingly hopeless than now. She was a prisoner then, just as she was now; in the power of men whose whole life and entire range of thought had for the past two years been devoted to the undoing and annihilation of the Scarlet Pimpernel. And there was a certain grim satisfaction for the pinioned, helpless woman in recalling the many instances where the daring adventurer had so completely outwitted his enemies, as well as in the memory of those days at Boulogne when the life of countless innocents was to be the price of her own.

II

The embarkation took place somewhere on the coast around Birchington. When, at dead of night, the coach came to a halt, and the tang of sea air and salt spray reached Marguerite's burning cheeks and parched lips, she tried with all her might to guess at her exact position. But that was impossible.

She was lifted out of the coach, and at once a shawl was thrown over her face, so that she could not see. It was more instinct than anything else that guided her perceptions. Even in the coach she had been vaguely conscious of the direction in which she had been travelling. All that part of the country was entirely familiar to her. So often had she driven down with Sir Percy, either to Dover or more often to some lonely part of the coast, where he took ship for unknown destinations, that in her mind she could, even blinded with tears and half-conscious as she was, trace in her mind the various turnings and side-roads along which she was being borne at unabating speed.

Birchington – one of the favourite haunts of the smuggling fraternity, with its numberless caves and retreats dug by the sea in the chalk cliffs, as if for the express benefit of n'er-do-wells – seemed the natural objective of the miscreants who had her in their power. In fact, at one moment she was quite sure that the square tower of old Minster church flitted past her vision through the window of the coach, and that the horses immediately after that sprinted the hill between Minster and Acoll.

Be that as it may, there was no doubt that the coach came to a halt at a desolate spot. The day which had begun in radiance and sunshine, had turned to an evening of squall and drizzle. A thin rain soon wetted Marguerite's clothes and the shawl on her head through and through, greatly adding to her misery and discomfort. Though she saw nothing, she could trace every landmark of the calvary to the summit of which she was being borne like an insentient log.

For a while she lay at the bottom of a small boat, aching in body as well as in mind, her eyes closed, her limbs cramped by the cords which owing to the damp were cutting into her flesh, faint with cold and want of food, wet to the skin yet with eyes and head and hands burning hot, and her ears filled with the dreary, monotonous sound of the oars creaking in the rowlocks and the boom of the water against the sides of the boat.

She was lifted out of the boat and carried, as she judged, by two men up a companion ladder, then down some steps and finally deposited on some hard boards; after which the wet shawl was removed from her face. She was in the dark. Only a tiny streak of light found its way through a chink somewhere close to the floor. A smell of tar and of stale food gave her a wretched sense of nausea. But she had by now reached a stage of physical and mental prostration wherein even acute bodily suffering counts as nothing, and is endurable because it is no longer felt.

After a while the familiar motion, the well-known sound of a ship weighing anchor, gave another blow to her few lingering hopes. Every movement of the ship now bore her farther and farther from England and home, and rendered her position more utterly miserable and hopeless.

III

She was taken ashore in the early dawn, at a spot not very far from Boulogne. Precautions were no longer taken against her possible calls for help; even the cords had been removed from her wrists and ankles as soon as she was lowered into the boat that brought her to shore. Cramped and stiff though she was, she disdained the help of an arm which was held out to her to enable her to step out of the boat.

All the faces around her were unfamiliar. There were four or five men, surly and silent, who piloted her over the rocks and cliffs and then along the sands, to the little hamlet of Wimereux, which she knew well. The coast at this hour was still deserted; only at one time did the little party meet with a group of buxom young women, trudging along barefooted with their shrimping nets over their shoulders. They stared wide-eyed but otherwise indifferent, at the unfortunate woman in torn, damp clothes, and with golden hair all dishevelled, who was bravely striving not to fall whilst urged on by five rough fellows in ragged jerseys, tattered breeches, and bare-kneed.

Just for one moment – a mere flash – Marguerite at sight of

these girls had the wild notion to run to them, implore their assistance in the name of their sweethearts, their husbands, their sons; to throw herself at their feet and beg them to help her, seeing that they were women and could not be without heart or pity. But it was a mere flash, the wild vagary of an over-excited brain, the drifting straw that mocks the drowning man. The next moment the girls had gone by, laughing and chattering. One of them intoned the 'Ça ira!' and Marguerite, fortunately for her own dignity, was not seriously tempted to essay so futile, so senseless an appeal.

Later on, in a squalid little hovel on the outskirts of Wimereux, she was at last given some food which, though of the poorest and roughest description, was nevertheless welcome, for it revived her spirit and strengthened her courage, of which she had sore need.

The rest of the journey was uneventful. Within the first hour of making a fresh start, she had realised that she was being taken to Paris. A few words dropped casually by the men who had charge of her apprised her of that fact. Otherwise they were very reticent – not altogether rough or unkind.

The coach in which she travelled during this stage of the journey was roomy and not uncomfortable, although the cushions were ragged and the leatherwork mildewed. Above all, she had the supreme comfort of privacy. She was alone in the coach, alone during the halts at wayside hostelries when she was allowed food and rest, alone throughout those two interminable nights when, with brief intervals whilst relays of horses were put into the shafts or the men took it in turns to get food or drink in some house unseen in the darkness, she vainly tried to get a snatch or two of sleep and a few moments of forgetfulness; alone throughout that next long day, whilst frequent summer showers sent heavy raindrops beating against the windowpanes of the coach, and familiar landmarks on the way to Paris flitted like threatening ghouls past her aching eyes.

Paris was reached at dawn of the third day. Seventy-two hours had crept along leaden-footed, since the moment when she had stepped into her own coach outside her beautiful home in Richmond, surrounded by her own servants, and with that traitor Moncrif by her side. Since then, what a load of sorrow, of anxiety, of physical and mental suffering had she borne! And yet, even that sorrow, even those sufferings and that anxiety, seemed as nothing beside the heartrending thoughts of her beloved, as yet ignorant of her terrible fate and of the schemes which those fiends who had so shamefully trapped her were even now concocting for the realisation of their vengeance against him.

CHAPTER 22

Waiting

I

The house to which Marguerite was ultimately driven, and where she presently found herself ushered up the stairs into a small, well-furnished apartment, appeared to be situated somewhere in an outlying quarter of Paris.

The apartment consisted of three rooms – a bedroom, a sitting-room, and small cabinet de toilette – all plainly but nicely furnished. The bed looked clean and comfortable, there was a carpet on the floor, one or two pictures on the wall, an arm-chair or two, even a few books in an armoire. An old woman, dour of mien but otherwise willing and attentive, did all she could to minister to the poor wearied woman's wants. She brought up some warm milk and home-baked bread. Butter, she explained, was not obtainable these days, and the household had not seen sugar for weeks.

Marguerite, tired out and hungry, readily ate some breakfast; but what she longed for most and needed most was rest. So presently, at the gruff invitation of the old woman, she undressed and stretched her weary limbs between the sheets, with a sigh of content. Anxiety, for the moment, had to yield to the sense of well-being, and with the name of her beloved on her lips Marguerite went to sleep like a child.

When she woke, it was late afternoon. On a chair close by her bedside was some clean linen laid out, a change of stockings, clean shoes, and a gown – a perfect luxury, which made this silent and lonely house appear more like the enchanted abode of ogres or fairies than before. Marguerite rose and dressed. The linen was fine, obviously the property of a woman of refinement, whilst everything in the tiny dressing-room – a comb, hand-mirror, soap, and scented water – suggested that the delicate hand of a cultured woman had seen to their disposal. A while later, the dour attendant brought her some soup and a dish of cooked vegetables.

Every phase of the situation became more and more puzzling as time went on. Marguerite, with the sense of well-being further accentuated by the feel of warm, dry clothes and of wholesome food, had her mind free enough to think and to ponder. Where was she? Why was she being treated with a kindness and consideration altogether at variance with the tactics usually adopted by the enemies of the Scarlet Pimpernel? She was not in prison. She was not being starved, or threatened, or humiliated. The day wore on, and she was not confronted with one or other of those fiends who were so obviously using her as a decoy for her husband.

But though Marguerite Blakeney was not in prison, she was a prisoner. This she had ascertained five minutes after she was alone in the apartment. She could wander at will from room to room; but only in them, not out of them. The door of communication between the rooms was wide open; those that obviously gave on a landing outside were securely locked; and when a while ago the old woman had entered with the tray of food, Marguerite had caught sight of a group of men in the well-known tattered uniform of the National Guard, standing at attention in a wide, long antechamber.

Yes; she was a prisoner! She could open the windows of her apartment and inhale the soft moist air which came across the wide tract of barren land; but these windows were thirty feet above the ground.

Thus for twenty-four hours was she left to meditate, thrown upon her own resources, with no other company save that of her own thoughts, and they were anything but cheerful. The uncertainty of the situation soon began to prey upon her nerves. She had been calm in the morning; but as the day wore on the loneliness, the mystery, the silence, began to tell upon her courage. Soon she got to look upon the woman who waited on her as upon her jailer, and when she was alone she was for ever straining her ears to hear what the men who were guarding her door might be saying among themselves.

The next night she hardly slept.

II

Twenty-four hours later she had a visit from citizen Chauvelin. She had been expecting that visit all along, or else a message from him. When he came she had need of all her pluck and all her determination, not to let him see the emotion which his presence caused her. Dread! Loathing! These were her predominant sensations. But dread above all; because he looked perfectly urbane and self-possessed; because he was dressed with scrupulous care and affected the manners and graces of a society which had long since cast him out. It was not the rough, out-at-elbows Terrorist who stood before her, the revolutionary demagogue who hits out right and left against a caste that has always spurned him and held

itself aloof; it was the broken-down gentleman at war with
fortune, who strives by his wits to be revenged against the
buffetings of Fate and the arrogance which ostracised him
as soon as he was down.

He began by asking solicitously after her well-being;
hoped the journey had not over-fatigued her; humbly begged her pardon for the discomfort which a higher power
compelled him to put upon her.

'The point is,' said he suavely, 'that you should be
comfortable and have no cause to complain whilst you
are under this roof.'

'And how long am I to remain a prisoner under it?'
she asked.

'Until Sir Percy has in turn honoured this house with his
presence,' he replied.

To this she made no answer for a time, but sat quite still
looking at him, as if detached and indifferent. He waited for
her to speak, his pale eyes, slightly mocking, fixed upon
her. Then she said simply:

'I understand.'

'I was quite sure you would, dear lady,' he rejoined
blandly. 'You see, the phase of heroics is past. I will confess
to you that it proved of no avail when measured against the
lofty coolness of that peerless exquisite. So we over here
have shed our ardour like a mantle. We, too, now are quite
calm, quite unperturbed, quite content to wait. The beautiful
Lady Blakeney is a guest under this roof. Well, sooner or
later that most gallant of husbands will desire to approach
his lady. Sooner or later he will learn that she is no longer
in England. Then he will set his incomparable wits to work
to find out where she is. Again, I may say that sooner or
later, perhaps, even aided by us, he will know that she is
here. Then he will come. Am I not right?'

Of course he was right. Sooner or later Percy would learn

where she was; and then he would come. He would come to her, despite every trap set for his undoing, despite every net laid to catch him, despite danger of death that waited for him if he came.

Chauvelin said little more. In truth, the era of heroics was at an end.

CHAPTER 23

Mice and Men

I

It was on her return from England that Theresia Cabarrus took to consulting the old witch in the Rue de la Planchette, driven thereto by ambition, and also no doubt by remorse. There was nothing of the hardened criminal about the fair Spaniard; she was just a spoilt woman who had been mocked and thwarted, and desired to be revenged. The Scarlet Pimpernel had appeared before her as one utterly impervious to her charms, and, egged on by Chauvelin, who used her for his own ends, she entered into a callous conspiracy, the aim of which was the destruction of that gang of English spies who were the enemies of France, and the first stage of which was the heartless abduction of Lady Blakeney and her incarceration as a decoy for the ultimate capture of her own husband.

A cruel, abominable act! Theresia, who had plunged headlong into this shameful crime, would a few days later have given much to undo the harm she had wrought. But she had yet to learn that, once used as a tool by the Committee of Public Safety and by Chauvelin, its most unscrupulous agent, no man or woman could hope to become free again until the work demanded had been accomplished to the end. There was no freedom from that taskmaster save in death; and Theresia's fit of compunction did not carry her to the lengths of self-sacrifice. Marguerite Blakeney was her prisoner, the decoy which would bring the English milor inevitably to the spot where his wife was incarcerated; and Theresia, who had helped to bring this state of things about, did her best to smother remorse, and having done Chauvelin's dirty work for him she set to to see what personal advantage she could derive from it.

Firstly, the satisfaction of her petty revenge: the Scarlet Pimpernel caught in a trap, would surely regret his interference in Theresia's love affairs. Theresia cared less than nothing about Bertrand Moncrif, and would have been quite grateful to the English milor for having spirited that embarrassing lover of hers away but for a letter which had wounded the beautiful Spaniard's vanity to the quick, and still rankled sufficiently to ease her conscience on the score of her subsequent actions. That the letter was a bogus one, concocted and written by Chauvelin himself in order to spur her on to a mean revenge, Theresia did not know.

But far stronger than thoughts of revenge were Theresia's schemes for her own future. She had begun to dream of Robespierre's gratitude, of her triumph over all those who had striven for over two years to bring that gang of English spies to book. She saw her name writ largely on the roll of fame; she even saw in her mind, the tyrant himself as her willing slave . . . and something more than that.

For her tool Bertrand she had no further use. By way of a reward for the abominable abduction of Lady Blakeney, he had been allowed to follow the woman he worshipped like a lackey attached to her train. Dejected, already spurned, he returned to Paris with her, here to resume the life of humiliation and of despised ardour which had broken his spirit and warped his nature, before his gallant rescuer had snatched him out of the toils of the beautiful Spaniard.

Within an hour of setting his foot on French soil, Bertrand had realised that he had been nothing in Theresia's sight. He had realised that her ambition soared far above linking her fate to an obscure and penniless lover, when the coming man of the hour – citizen Tallien – was already at her feet.

II

Thus Theresia had attained one of her great desires: the Scarlet Pimpernel was as good as captured, and when he finally succumbed he could not fail to know whence came the blow that struck him.

With regard to her future, matters were more doubtful. She had not yet subjugated Robespierre sufficiently to cause him to give up his more humble love and to lay his power and popularity at her feet; whilst the man who had offered her his hand and name – citizen Tallien – was for ever putting a check upon her ambition and his own advancement by his pusillanimity and lack of enterprise.

Whilst she was aching to push him into decisive action, into seizing the supreme power before Robespierre and his friends had irrevocably established theirs, Tallien was for temporising, fearing that in trying to snatch a dictatorship he and his beloved with him would lose their heads.

'While Robespierre lives,' Theresia would argue passionately, 'no man's head is safe. Every rival, sooner or later, becomes a victim. St Just and Couthon aim at a dictatorship for him. Sooner or later they will succeed; then death to every man who has ever dared oppose them.'

'Therefore 'tis wiser not to oppose,' the prudent Tallien would retort. 'The time will come—'

'Never!' she riposted hotly. 'While you plot, and argue and ponder, Robespierre acts or signs your death-warrant.'

'Robespierre is the idol of the people; he sways the Convention with a word. His eloquence would drag an army of enemies to the guillotine.'

'Robespierre!' Theresia retorted with sublime contempt. 'Ah, when you have said that, you think you have said everything! France, humanity, the people, sovereign power! – all that, you assert, is embodied in that one man. But, my friend, listen to me!' she went on earnestly. 'Listen, when I assert that Robespierre is only a name, a fetish, a manikin set up on a pedestal! And the pedestal is composed of that elusive entity which you call the people and which will disintegrate from beneath his feet as soon as the people have realised that those feet are less than clay. One touch of a firm finger against that manikin, I tell you, and he will fall as dust before you; and you can rise upon that same elusive pedestal – popularity, to the heights which he hath so easily attained.'

But, though Tallien was at times carried away by her vehemence, he would always shake his head and counsel prudence, and assure her that the time was not yet. Theresia, impatient and dictatorial, had more than once hinted at rupture.

'I could not love a weakling,' she would aver; and at the back of her mind there would rise schemes, which aimed at transferring her favours to the other man, who she felt would be more worthy of her.

'Robespierre would not fail me, as this coward does!' she mused, even while Tallien, blind and obedient, was bidding her farewell at the very door of the charlatan to whom Theresia had turned in her ambition and her difficulties.

III

Something of the glamour which had originally surrounded Mother Théot's incantations had vanished since sixty-two of her devotees had been sent to the guillotine on a charge of conspiring for the overthrow of the Republic. Robespierre's enemies, too cowardly to attack him in the Convention or in the Clubs, had seized upon the mystery which hung over the séances in the Rue de la Planchette in order to undermine his popularity in the one and his power in the other.

Spies were introduced into the witch's lair. The names of its chief frequenters became known, and soon wholesale arrests were made, which were followed by the inevitable condemnations. Robespierre had not actually been named; but the identity of the sycophants who had proclaimed him the Messenger of the Most High, the Morning Star, or the Regenerator of Mankind, were hurled across from the tribune of the Convention, like poisoned arrows aimed at the tyrant himself.

But Robespierre had been too wary to allow himself to be dragged into the affair. He never raised his voice nor yet one finger to save them from death, and whilst he – the bloodthirsty autocrat – remained firmly installed upon his self-constituted throne, those who had acclaimed him as second only to God, perished upon the scaffold.

Mother Théot, for some inexplicable reason, escaped this wholesale slaughter; but her séances were henceforth shorn of their splendour. Robespierre no longer dared frequent them even in disguise. The house in the Rue de la Planchette became a marked one to the agents of the Committee of Public Safety, and the witch herself was reduced to innumerable shifts to eke out a precarious livelihood and to keep herself in the good graces of those agents, by rendering them various unavowable services.

To those, however, who chose to defy public opinion and to disregard the dangers which attended the frequentation of Mother Théot's sorceries, these latter had lost little or nothing of their pristine solemnity. There was the closely curtained room; the scented, heavy atmosphere; the chants, the coloured flames, the ghost-like neophytes. Draped in her grey veils, the old witch still wove her spells and called on the powers of light and of darkness to aid her in fore-telling the future. The neophytes chanted and twisted their bodies in quaint contortions; alone, the small blackamoor grinned at what experience had taught him was nothing but quackery and charlatanism.

Theresia, sitting on the dais, with the heady fumes of Oriental scents blurring her sight and the clearness of her intellect, was drinking in the honeyed words and flattering prophecies of the old witch.

'Thy name will be the greatest in the land! Before thee will bow the mightiest thrones! At thy word heads will fall and diadems will totter!' Mother Théot announced in sepulchral tones, whilst gazing into the crystal before her.

'As the wife of citizen Tallien?' Theresia queried in an awed whisper.

'That the spirits do not say,' the old witch replied. 'What is a name to them? I see a crown of glory, and thy head surrounded by a golden light; and at thy feet lies something which once was scarlet, and now is crimson and crushed.'

'What does it mean?' Theresia murmured.

'That is for thee to know,' the sybil replied sternly. 'Commune with the spirits; lose thyself in their embrace; learn from the great truths, and the future will be made clear to thee.'

With which cryptic utterance she gathered her veils

around her, and with weird murmurs of, 'Evohe! Evohe! Sammael! Zamiel! Evohe!' glided out of the room, mysterious and inscrutable, presumably in order to allow her bewildered client to meditate on the enigmatical prophecy in solitude.

But directly she had closed the door behind her, Mother Théot's manner underwent a change. She became just an ugly old woman, wrinkled and hook-nosed, dressed in shabby draperies that were grey with age and dirt, and with claw-like hands that looked like the talons of a bird of prey.

As she entered the room, a man who had been standing at the window opposite, staring out into the dismal street below, turned quickly to her.

'Art satisfied?' she asked at once.

'From what I could hear, yes!' he replied, 'though I could have wished thy pronouncements had been more clear.'

The hag shrugged her lean shoulders and nodded in the direction of her lair.

'O!' she said. 'The Spaniard understands well enough. She never consults me or invokes the spirits but they speak to her of that which is scarlet. She knows what it means. You need not fear, citizen Chauvelin, that in the pursuit of her vaulting ambition, she will forget that her primary duty is to you!'

'No,' Chauvelin asserted calmly, 'she'll not forget that. The Cabarrus is no fool. She knows well enough that when citizens of the State have been employed to work on its behalf, they are no longer free agents afterwards. The work must be carried through to the end.'

'You need not fear the Cabarrus, citizen,' the sybil rejoined drily. 'She'll not fail you. Her vanity is immense. She believes that the Englishman insulted her by writing that flippant letter, and she'll not leave him alone till she has had her revenge.'

'No!' Chauvelin assented. 'She'll not fail me. Nor thou either, citoyenne.'

'I!' she exclaimed, with a quiet laugh. 'Is that likely? You promised me ten thousand livres the day the Scarlet Pimpernel is captured!'

'And the guillotine,' Chauvelin broke in grimly, 'if thou shouldst allow the woman upstairs to escape.'

'I know that,' the old woman rejoined drily. 'If she escapes 'twill not be through my connivance.'

'In the service of the State,' Chauvelin riposted, 'even carelessness becomes a crime.'

Catherine Théot was silent for a moment or two, pressed her thin lips together; then rejoined quite quietly:

'She'll not escape. Have no fear, citizen Chauvelin.'

'That's brave! And now, tell me what has become of the coal-heaver Rateau?'

'Oh, he comes and goes. You told me to encourage him.'

'Yes.'

'So I give him potions for his cough. He has one foot in the grave.'

'Would he had both!' Chauvelin broke in savagely. 'That man is a perpetual menace to my plans. It would have been so much better if we could have sent him last April to the guillotine.'

'It was in your hands,' Mother Théot retorted. 'The Committee reported against him. His measure was full enough. Aiding that execrable Scarlet Pimpernel to escape . . . ! Name of a name! it should have been enough!'

'It was not proved that he did aid the English spies,' Chauvelin retorted moodily. 'And Foucquier-Tinville would not arraign him. He vowed it would anger the people –

the rabble – of which Rateau himself forms an integral part. We cannot afford to anger the rabble these days, it seems.'

'And so Rateau, the asthmatic coal-heaver, walked out of prison a free man, whilst my neophytes were dragged up to the guillotine, and I was left without means of earning an honest livelihood!' Mother Théot concluded with a doleful sigh.

'Honest?' Chauvelin exclaimed, with a sarcastic chuckle. Then, seeing that the old witch was ready to lose her temper, he quickly added: 'Tell me more about Rateau. Does he often come here?'

'Yes; very often. He must be in my anteroom now. He came directly he was let out of prison, and has haunted this place ever since. He thinks I can cure him of his asthma, and as he pays me well—'

'Pays you well?' Chauvelin broke in quickly. 'That starveling?'

'Rateau is no starveling,' the old woman asserted. 'Many an English gold piece hath he given me.'

'But not of late?'

'Not later than yesterday.'

'Then he is still in touch with that cursed Englishman!'

Mother Théot shrugged her shoulders.

'Does one ever know which is the Englishman and which the asthmatic Rateau?' she queried, with a dry laugh.

Whereupon a strange thing happened – so strange indeed that Chauvelin's next words turned to savage curses, and that Mother Théot, white to the lips, her knees shaking under her, tiny beads of perspiration rising beneath her scanty locks, had to hold on to the table to save herself from falling.

'Name of a name of a dog!' Chauvelin muttered hoarsely, whilst the old woman, shaken by that superstitious dread which she liked to arouse in her clients, could only stare at him and mutely shake her head.

And yet nothing very alarming had occurred. Only a man had laughed, light-heartedly and long; and the sound of that laughter had come from somewhere near – the next room probably, or the landing beyond Mother Théot's anteroom. It had come low and distinct, slightly muffled by the intervening wall. Nothing in truth to frighten the most nervous child!

Chauvelin, cursing himself now for his cowardice, passed a still shaking hand across his brow, and a wry smile distorted momentarily his thin, set lips.

'One of your clients is of good cheer,' he said with well-assumed indifference.

'There is no one in the anteroom at this hour,' the old hag murmured under her breath. 'Only Rateau . . . and he is too scant of breath to laugh . . . he . . .'

But Chauvelin no longer heard what she had to say. With an exclamation which no one who heard it could have defined, he turned on his heel and almost ran out of the room.

CHAPTER 24

By Order of the State

I

The antechamber, wide and long, ran the whole length of Mother Théot's apartment. Her witch's lair and the room where she had just had her interview with Chauvelin gave directly on it on the one side, and two other living rooms on the other. At one end of the antechamber there were two windows, usually kept closely shuttered; and at the other was the main entrance door, which led to landing and staircase.

The antechamber was empty. It appeared to mock Chauvelin's excitement, with its grey-washed walls streaked with grime, its worm-eaten benches and tarnished chandelier. Mother Théot, voluble and quaking with fear, was close at his heels. Curtly he ordered her to be gone; her mutterings irritated him, her obvious fear of something unknown grated unpleasantly on his nerves. He cursed himself for his cowardice, and cursed the one man who alone in this world had the power to unnerve him.

'I was dreaming, of course,' he muttered aloud to himself between his teeth. 'I have that arch-devil, his laugh, his voice, his affectations, on the brain!'

He was on the point of going to the main door, in order

to peer out on the landing or down the stairs, when he heard his name called immediately behind him. Theresia Cabarrus was standing under the lintel of the door which gave on the sybil's sanctum, her delicate hand holding back the portière.

'Citizen Chauvelin,' she said, 'I was waiting for you.'

'And I, citoyenne,' he retorted gruffly, 'had in truth forgotten you.'

'Mother Théot left me alone for a while, to commune with the spirits,' she explained.

'Ah!' he riposted, slightly sarcastic. 'With what result?'

'To help you further, citizen Chauvelin,' she replied; 'if you have need of me.'

'Ah!' he exclaimed with a savage curse. 'In truth, I have need of every willing hand that will raise itself against mine enemy. I have need of you, citizeness; of that old witch; of Rateau, the coal-heaver; of every patriot who will sit and watch this house, to which we have brought the one bait that will lure the goldfish to our net.'

'Have I not proved my willingness, citizen?' she retorted, with a smile. 'Think you 'tis pleasant to give up my life, my salon, my easy, contented existence, and become a mere drudge in your service?'

'A drudge,' he broke in with a chuckle, 'who will soon be greater than a Queen.'

'Ah, if I thought that! . . .' she exclaimed.

'I am as sure of it as that I am alive,' he replied firmly. 'You will never do anything with citizen Tallien, citoyenne. He is too mean, too cowardly. But bring the Scarlet Pimpernel to his knees at the chariot wheel of Robespierre, and even the crown of the Bourbons would be yours for the asking!'

'I know that, citizen,' she rejoined drily; 'else I were not here.'

'We hold all the winning cards,' he went on eagerly.

'Lady Blakeney is in our hands. So long as we hold her, we have the certainty that sooner or later the English spy will establish communication with her. Catherine Théot is a good jailer, and Captain Boyer upstairs has a number of men under his command – veritable sleuthhounds. But experience has taught me that that accursed Scarlet Pimpernel is never so dangerous as when we think we hold him. His extraordinary histrionic powers have been our undoing hitherto. No man's eyes are keen enough to pierce his disguises. That is why, citoyenne, I dragged you to England; that is why I placed you face to face with him, and said to you, "That is the man." Since then, with your help, we hold the decoy. Now you are my coadjutor and my help. In your eyes I place my trust; in your wits, your instinct. In whatever guise the Scarlet Pimpernel presents himself before you – and he *will* present himself before you, or he is no longer the impudent and reckless adventurer I know him to be! – I feel that you at least will recognise him.'

'Yes; I think I should recognise him,' she mused.

'Think you that I do not appreciate the sacrifice you make – the anxiety, the watchfulness to which you so nobly subject yourself? But 'tis you above all who are the lure which must inevitably attract the Scarlet Pimpernel into my hands.'

'Soon, I hope,' she sighed wearily.

'Soon,' he asserted firmly. 'I dare swear it! Until then, citizeness, in the name of your own future, and in the name of France, I adjure you to watch. Watch and listen! Oh, think of the stakes for which we are playing, you and I! Bring the Scarlet Pimpernel to his knees, citoyenne, and Robespierre will be as much your slave as he is now the prey to a strange dread of that one man. Robespierre fears the Scarlet Pimpernel. A superstitious conviction has seized hold of him that the English spy will bring about his downfall. We have all seen of late how aloof he holds himself. He no longer attends the Committees. He no longer goes to the Clubs; he shuns his friends; and his furtive glance is for ever trying to pierce some imaginary disguise, under which he alternately fears and hopes to discover his arch-enemy. He dreads assassination, anonymous attacks. In every obscure member of the Convention who walks up the steps of the tribune, he fears to find the Scarlet Pimpernel under a new, impenetrable mask. Ah, citoyenne! what influence you would have over him if through your agency all those fears could be drowned in the blood of that abominable Englishman!'

'Now, who would have thought that?' a mocking voice broke in suddenly, with a quiet chuckle. 'I vow, my dear M. Chambertin, you are waxing more eloquent than ever before!'

Like the laughter of a while ago, the voice seemed to come from nowhere. It was in the air, muffled by the clouds of Mother Théot's perfumes, or by the thickness of doors and tapestries. Weird, yet human.

'By Satan, this is intolerable!' Chauvelin exclaimed; and paying no heed to Theresia's faint cry of terror, he ran to the main door. It was on the latch. He tore it open and dashed out upon the landing.

II

From here a narrow stone staircase, dank and sombre, led downwards as well as upwards, in a spiral. The house had only the two stories, perched above some disused and dilapidated storage-rooms, to which a double outside door and wicket gave access from the street.

For an instant Chauvelin hesitated. Never a coward physically, he yet had no mind to precipitate himself down a dark staircase when mayhap his enemy was lying in wait for him down below.

Only for an instant however. The very next second had brought forth the positive reflection: 'Bah! Assassination, and in the dark, are not the Englishman's ways.'

Scarce a few yards from where he stood, the other side of the door, was the dry moat which ran round the Arsenal. From there, at a call from him, a dozen men and more would surge from the ground – sleuthhounds, as he had told Theresia a moment ago, who were there on the watch and whom he could trust to do his work swiftly and securely – if only he could reach the door and call for help. Elusive as that accursed Pimpernel was, successful chase might even now be given to him.

Chauvelin ran down half a dozen steps, peered down the shaft of the staircase, and spied a tiny light, which moved swiftly to and fro. Then presently, below the light a bit of tallow candle, then a grimy hand holding the candle, an arm, the top of a shaggy head crowned by a greasy red cap, a broad back under a tattered blue jersey. He heard the thump of heavy soles upon the stone flooring below, and a moment or two later the weird, sepulchral sound of a churchyard cough. Then the light disappeared. For a second or two the darkness appeared more impenetrably dense; then one or two narrow streaks of daylight showed the position of the outside door. Something prompted him to call:

'Is that you, citizen Rateau?'

It was foolish, of course. And the very next moment he had his answer. A voice – the mocking voice he knew so well – called up to him in reply:

'At your service, dear M. Chambertin! Can I do anything for you?'

Chauvelin swore, threw all prudence to the winds, and ran down the stairs as fast as his shaking knees would allow him. Some three steps from the bottom he paused for the space of a second, like one turned to stone by what he saw. Yet it was simple enough: just the same tiny light, the grimy hand holding the tallow candle, the shaggy head with the greasy cap. . . . The figure in the gloom looked preternaturally large, and the flickering light threw fantastic shadows on the face and neck of the colossus, distorting the nose to a grotesque length and the chin to weird proportions.

The next instant Chauvelin gave a cry like an enraged bull and hurled his meagre person upon the giant, who, shaken at the moment by a tearing fit of coughing, was taken unawares and fell backwards, overborne by the impact, dropping the light as he fell and still wheezing pitiably whilst trying to give vent to his feelings by vigorous curses.

Chauvelin, vaguely surprised at his own strength or the weakness of his opponent, pressed his knees against the latter's chest, gripped him by the throat, smothering his curses and wheezes, turning the funereal cough into agonised gasps.

'At my service, in truth, my gallant Pimpernel!' he murmured hoarsely, feeling his small reserve of strength oozing away by the strenuous effort. 'What you can do for me? Wait here, until I have you bound and gagged, safe against further mischief!'

His victim had in fact given a last convulsive gasp, lay now at full length upon the stone floor, with arms outstretched, motionless. Chauvelin relaxed his grip. His strength was spent, he was bathed in sweat, his body shook from head to foot. But he was triumphant! His mocking enemy, carried away by his own histrionics, had overtaxed his colossal strength. The carefully simulated fit of coughing had taken away his breath at the critical moment; the surprise attack had done the rest; and Chauvelin – meagre, feeble, usually the merest human insect beside the powerful Englishman – had conquered by sheer pluck and resource.

There lay the Scarlet Pimpernel, who had assumed the guise of asthmatic Rateau once too often, helpless and broken beneath the weight of the man whom he had hoodwinked and derided. And now at last all the intrigues, the humiliations, the schemes and the disappointments, were at an end. He – Chauvelin – free and honoured: Robespierre his grateful servant.

A wave of dizziness passed over his brain – the dizziness of coming glory. His senses reeled. When he staggered to his feet he could scarcely stand. Chauvelin lurched up to the door, fumbled for the latch of the wicket-gate, and finding it pulled the gate open and almost fell out into the open.

III

The Rue de la Planchette was as usual lonely and deserted. It was a second or two before Chauvelin spied a passer-by. That minute he spent in calling for help with all his might. The passer-by he quickly dispatched across to the Arsenal for assistance.

'In the name of the Republic!' he said solemnly.

But already his cries had attracted the attention of the sentries. Within two or three minutes, half a dozen men of the National Guard were speeding down the street. Soon they had reached the house, the door where Chauvelin, still breathless but with his habitual official manner that brooked of no argument, gave them hasty instructions.

'The man lying on the ground in there,' he commanded. 'Seize him and raise him. Then one of you find some cord and bind him securely.'

The men flung the double doors wide open. A flood of light illumined the store-room. There lay the huge figure on the floor, no longer motionless, but trying to scramble to his feet, once more torn by a fit of coughing. The men ran up to him; one of them laughed.

'Why, if it isn't old Rateau!'

They lifted him up by his arms. He was helpless as a child, and his face was of a dull purple colour.

'He will die!' another man said, with an indifferent shrug of the shoulders.

But, in a way, they were sorry for him. He was one of themselves. Nothing of the aristo about asthmatic old Rateau!

'Hast thou been playing again at being an English milor, poor old Rateau?' another man asked compassionately.

They had succeeded in propping him up and sitting him down upon a barrel. His fit of coughing was subsiding. He had breath enough now to swear. He raised his head and encountered the pale eyes of citizen Chauvelin fixed as if sightlessly upon him.

'Name of a dog!' he began; but got no farther. Giddiness seized him, for he was weak from coughing and from that strangling grip round his throat, after he had been attacked in the darkness and thrown violently to the ground.

The men around him recoiled at sight of citizen Chauvelin. His appearance was almost death-like. His cheeks and lips were livid; his hair dishevelled; his eyes of an unearthly paleness. One hand, clawlike and shaking, he held out before him, as if to ward off some horrible apparition.

This trance-like state made up of a ghastly fear and a sense of the most hideous, most unearthly impotence, lasted for several seconds. The men themselves were frightened. Unable to understand what had happened, they thought that citizen Chauvelin, whom they all knew by sight, had suddenly lost his reason or was possessed of a devil. For in truth there was nothing about poor old Rateau to frighten a child!

Fortunately the tension was over before real panic had seized on any of them. The next moment Chauvelin had pulled himself together with one of those mighty efforts of will of which strong natures are always capable. With an impatient gesture he passed his hand across his brow, then backwards and forwards in front of his face, as if to chase away the demon of terror that obsessed him. He gazed on Rateau for a moment or two, his eyes travelling over the uncouth, semi-conscious figure of the coal-heaver with a searching, undefinable glance. Then, as if suddenly struck with an idea, he spoke to the man nearest him:

'Sergeant Chazot? Is he at the Arsenal?'

'Yes, citizen,' the man replied.

'Run across quickly then,' Chauvelin continued; 'and bring him hither at once.'

Rateau, weary, cursing, not altogether in full possession of his faculties, sat huddled up on the barrel, his bleary eyes following every movement of citizen Chauvelin with an anxious, furtive gaze. The latter was pacing up and down the stone floor, like a caged, impatient animal. From time to time he paused, either to peer out into the open in the direction of the Arsenal, or to search the dark angles of the store-room, kicking the piles of rubbish about with his foot.

IV

Anon he uttered a sigh of satisfaction. The soldier had returned, was even now in the doorway with a comrade – a short, thick-set, powerful-looking fellow – beside him.

'Sergeant Chazot!' Chauvelin said abruptly.

'At your commands, citizen!' the sergeant replied, and at a sign from the other followed him to the most distant corner of the room.

'Bend your ear and listen,' Chauvelin murmured peremptorily. 'I don't want those fools to hear,' And, having assured himself that he and Chazot could speak without being overheard, he pointed to Rateau, then went on rapidly: 'You will take this lout over to the cavalry barracks. See the veterinary. Tell him—'

He paused, as if unable to proceed. His lips were trembling, his face, ashen-white, looked spectral in the gloom. Chazot, not understanding, waited patiently.

'That lout,' Chauvelin resumed more steadily after a while, 'is in collusion with a gang of dangerous English spies. One Englishman especially – tall, and a master of histrionics – uses this man as a kind of double. Perhaps you heard . . . ?'

Chazot nodded.

'I know, citizen,' he said sagely. 'The Fraternal Supper in the Rue St Honoré. Comrades have told me that no one could tell who was Rateau the coal-heaver and who the English milor.'

'Exactly!' Chauvelin rejoined drily, quite firmly now. 'Therefore, I want to make sure. The veterinary, you understand? He brands the horses for the cavalry. I want a brand on this lout's arm. Just a letter . . . a distinguishing mark . . .'

Chazot gave an involuntary gasp.

'But, citizen—!' he exclaimed.

'Eh? What?' the other retorted sharply. 'In the service of the Republic there is no "but", Sergeant Chazot.'

'I know that, citizen,' Chazot, abashed, murmured humbly. 'I only meant . . . it seems so strange. . . .'

'Stranger things than that occur every day in Paris, my friend,' Chauvelin said drily. 'We brand horses that are the property of the State; why not a man? Time may come,' he added with a vicious snarl, 'when the Republic may demand that every loyal citizen carry – indelibly branded in his flesh and by order of the State – the sign of his own allegiance.'

''Tis not for me to argue, citizen,' Chazot rejoined, with a careless shrug of the shoulders. 'If you tell me to take citizen Rateau over to the veterinary at the cavalry barracks and have him branded like cattle, why . . .'

'Not like cattle, citizen,' Chauvelin broke in blandly. 'You shall commence proceedings by administering to citizen Rateau a whole bottle of excellent eau de vie, at the Government's expense. Then, when he is thoroughly and irretrievably drunk, the veterinary will put the brand upon his left forearm . . . just one letter . . . Why, the drunken reprobate will never feel it!'

'As you command, citizen,' Chazot assented with perfect indifference. 'I am not responsible. I do as I'm told.'

'Like the fine soldier that you are, citizen Chazot!' Chauvelin concluded. 'And I know that I can trust to your discretion.'

'Oh, as to that—'

'It would not serve you to be otherwise; that's understood. So now, my friend, get you gone with the lout; and take these few words of instructions with you, for the citizen veterinary.'

He took tablet and point from his pocket and scribbled a few words; signed it 'Chauvelin' with that elegant flourish

which can be traced to this day on so many secret orders
that emanated from the Committee of Public Safety during
the two years of its existence.

Chazot took the written order and slipped it into his
pocket. Then he turned on his heel and briefly gave the
necessary orders to the men. Once more they hoisted the
helpless giant up on his feet. Rateau was willing enough
to go. He was willing to do anything so long as they took
him away from here, away from the presence of that small
devil with the haggard face and the pale, piercing eyes. He
allowed himself to be conducted out of the building without
a murmur.

Chauvelin watched the little party – the six men, the
asthmatic coal-heaver and lastly the sergeant – file out of
the place, then cross the Rue de la Planchette and take the
turning opposite, the one that led through the Porte and
the Rue St Antoine to the cavalry barracks in the Quartier
Bastille. After which, he carefully closed the double outside
doors and, guided by instinct since the place down here was
in darkness once more, he groped his way to the foot of the
stairs and slowly mounted to the floor above.

V

He reached the first-floor landing. The door which led into
Mother Théot's apartments was on the latch, and Chauvelin
had just stretched out his hand with a view to pushing
it open, when the door swung out on its hinges, as if
moved by an invisible hand, and a pleasant, mocking voice
immediately behind him said, with grave politeness:

'Allow me, my dear M. Chambertin!'

CHAPTER 25

Four Days

I

What occurred during the next few seconds Chauvelin himself would have been least able to say. Whether he stepped
of his own accord into the antechamber of Catherine Théot's
apartment, or whether an unseen hand pushed him in, he
could not have told you. Certain it is that, when he returned
to the full realisation of things, he was sitting on one of the
benches, his back against the wall, whilst immediately in
front of him, looking down on him through half-closed
lazy eyes, débonair, well groomed, unperturbed, stood his
arch-enemy, Sir Percy Blakeney.

Of Theresia Cabarrus there was not a sign. Chauvelin
looked about him, feeling like a goaded animal shut up in a
narrow space with its tormentor. He was making desperate
efforts to regain his composure, above all he made appeal to
that courage which was wont never to desert him. In truth,
Chauvelin had never been a physical coward, nor was he
afraid of death or outrage at the hands of the man whom he
had so deeply wronged, and whom he had pursued with
a veritable lust of hate. No! he did not fear death at the
hands of the Scarlet Pimpernel. What he feared was ridicule,
humiliation, those schemes – bold, adventurous, seemingly

impossible – which he knew were already seething behind the smooth, unruffled brow of his arch-enemy, behind those lazy, supercilious eyes, which had the power to irritate his nerves to the verge of dementia.

This impudent adventurer – no better than a spy, despite his aristocratic mien and air of lofty scorn – this meddlesome English brigand, was the one man in the world who had, when he measured his prowess against him, invariably brought him to ignominy and derision, made him a laughing-stock before those whom he had been wont to dominate.

He could not understand why Theresia Cabarrus had deserted him. Even a woman, if she happened to be a friend, would by her presence have afforded him moral support.

'You are looking for Mme de Fontenay, I believe, dear M. Chambertin,' Sir Percy said lightly, as if divining his thoughts. 'The ladies – ah, the ladies! They add charm, piquancy, eh? to the driest conversations. Alas!' he went on with mock affectation, 'that Mme de Fontenay should have fled at first sound of my voice! Now she hath sought refuge in the old witch's lair, there to consult the spirits as to how best she can get out again, seeing that the door is now locked . . . Demmed awkward, a locked door, when a pretty woman wants to be on the other side. What think you, M. Chambertin?'

'I only think, Sir Percy,' Chauvelin contrived to retort, calling all his wits and all his courage to aid him in his humiliating position, 'I only think of another pretty woman, who is in the room just above our heads, and who would also be mightily glad to find herself on the other side of a locked door.'

'Your thoughts,' Sir Percy retorted with a light laugh, 'are always so ingenuous, my dear M. Chambertin. Strangely

enough, mine just at this moment run on the possibility
– not a very unlikely one, you will admit – of shaking
the breath out of your ugly little body, as I would that
of a rat.'

'Shake, my dear Sir Percy, shake!' Chauvelin riposted with
well-simulated calm. 'I grant you that I am a puny rat and
you the most magnificent of lions; but even if I lie mangled
and breathless on this stone floor at your feet, Lady Blakeney
will still be a prisoner in our hands.'

'And you will still be wearing the worst-cut pair of
breeches it has ever been my bad fortune to behold,' Sir
Percy retorted, quite unruffled. 'Lud love you, man! Have
you guillotined all the good tailors in Paris?'

'You choose to be flippant, Sir Percy,' Chauvelin rejoined
drily. 'But, though you have chosen for the past few years
to play the rôle of a brainless nincompoop, I have cause to
know that behind your affectations there lurks an amount
of sound common sense.'

'Lud, how you flatter me, my dear sir!' quoth Sir Percy
airily. 'I vow you had not so high an opinion of me last time
I had the honour of conversing with you. It was at Nantes;
do you remember?'

'There, as elsewhere, you succeeded in circumventing
me, Sir Percy.'

'No, no!' he protested. 'Not in circumventing you. Only
in making you look a demmed fool!'

'Call it that, if you like, sir,' Chauvelin admitted, with an
indifferent shrug of the shoulders. 'Luck has favoured you
many a time. As I had the honour to tell you, you have had
the laugh of us in the past, and no doubt you are under the
impression that you will have it again this time.'

'I am such a believer in impressions, my dear sir. The
impression now that I have of your charming personality
is indelibly graven upon my memory.'

'Sir Percy Blakeney counts a good memory as one of his many accomplishments. Another is his adventurous spirit, and the gallantry which must inevitably bring him into the net which we have been at pains to spread for him. Lady Blakeney—'

'Name her not, man!' Sir Percy broke in with affected deliberation; 'or I verily believe that within sixty seconds you would be a dead man!'

'I am not worthy to speak her name, c'est entendu,' Chauvelin retorted with mock humility. 'Nevertheless, Sir Percy, it is around the person of that gracious lady that the Fates will spin their web during the next few days. You may kill me. Of course, I am at this moment entirely at your mercy. But before you embark on such a perilous undertaking, will you allow me to place the position a little more clearly before you?'

'Lud, man!' quoth Sir Percy with a quaint laugh. 'That's what I'm here for! Think you that I have sought your agreeable company for the mere pleasure of gazing at your amiable countenance?'

'I only desired to explain to you, Sir Percy, the dangers to which you expose Lady Blakeney, if you laid violent hands upon me. 'Tis you, remember, who sought this interview – not I.'

'You are right, my dear sir, always right; and I'll not interrupt again. I pray you to proceed.'

'Allow me then to make my point clear. There are at this moment a score of men of the National Guard in the room above your head. Every one of them goes to the guillotine if they allow their prisoner to escape; every one of them receives a reward of ten thousand livres the day they capture the Scarlet Pimpernel. A good spur for vigilance, what? But that is not all,' Chauvelin went on quite steadily, seeing that Sir Percy had apparently become thoughtful and absorbed.

'The men are under the command of Captain Boyer, and he understands that every day at a certain hour – seven in the evening, to be precise – I will be with him and interrogate him as to the welfare of the prisoner. If – mark me, Sir Percy! – if on any one day I do not appear before him at that hour, his orders are to shoot the prisoner on sight.'

The word was scarce out of his mouth; it broke in a hoarse spasm. Sir Percy had him by the throat, shook him indeed as he would a rat.

'You cur!' he said in an ominous whisper, his face quite close now to that of his enemy, his jaw set, his eyes no longer good-humoured and mildly scornful, but burning with the fire of a mighty, unbridled wrath. 'You damned – insolent – miserable cur! As there is a Heaven above us—'

Then suddenly his grip relaxed, the whole face changed as if an unseen hand had swept away the fierce lines of anger and of hate. The eyes softened beneath their heavy lids, the set lips broke into a mocking smile. He let go his hold of the Terrorist's throat; and the unfortunate man, panting and breathless, fell heavily against the wall. He tried to steady himself as best he could, but his knees were shaking, and faint and helpless, he finally collapsed upon the nearest bench, the while Sir Percy straightened out his tall figure, with unruffled composure rubbed his slender hands one against the other, as if to free them from dust, and said, with gentle, good-humoured sarcasm:

'Do put your cravat straight, man! You look a disgusting object!'

He dragged the corner of a bench forward, sat astride upon it, and waited with perfect sang-froid, spy-glass in hand, while Chauvelin mechanically readjusted the set of his clothes.

'That's better!' he said approvingly. 'Just the bow at the back of your neck . . . a little more to the right . . . now your cuffs. . . . Ah, you look quite tidy again! . . . a perfect picture, I vow, my dear M. Chambertin, of elegance and of a well-regulated mind!'

'Sir Percy—!' Chauvelin broke in with a vicious snarl.

'I entreat you to accept my apologies,' the other rejoined with utmost courtesy. 'I was on the verge of losing my temper, which we in England would call demmed bad form. I'll not transgress again. I pray you, proceed with what you were saying. So interesting – demmed interesting! You were talking about murdering a woman in cold blood, I think—'

'In hot blood, Sir Percy,' Chauvelin rejoined more firmly. 'Blood fired by thoughts of a just revenge.'

'Pardon! My mistake! As you were saying—'

''Tis you who attack us. You – the meddlesome Scarlet Pimpernel, with your accursed gang! . . . We defend ourselves as best we can, using what weapons lie closest to our hand—'

'Such as murder, outrage, abduction . . . and wearing breeches the cut of which would provoke a saint to indignation!'

'Murder, abduction, outrage, as you will, Sir Percy,' Chauvelin retorted, as cool now as his opponent. 'Had you ceased to interfere in the affairs of France when first you escaped punishment for your machinations, you would not now be in the sorry plight in which your own intrigues have at last landed you. Had you left us alone, we should by now have forgotten you.'

'Which would have been such a pity, my dear M. Chambertin,' Blakeney rejoined gravely. 'I should not like you to forget me. Believe me, I have enjoyed life so much these past two years, I would not give up these pleasures even for that of seeing you and your friends have a bath or wear tidy buckles on your shoes.'

'You will have cause to indulge in those pleasures within the next few days, Sir Percy,' Chauvelin rejoined drily.

'What?' Sir Percy exclaimed. 'The Committee of Public Safety going to have a bath? Or the Revolutionary Tribunal? Which?'

But Chauvelin was determined not to lose his temper again. Indeed, he abhorred this man so deeply that he felt no anger against him, no resentment; only a cold, calculating hate.

'The pleasure of pitting your wits against the inevitable,' he riposted drily.

'Ah?' quoth Sir Percy airily. 'The inevitable has always been such a good friend to me.'

'Not this time, I fear, Sir Percy.'

'Ah? You really mean this time to——?' and he made a significant gesture across his own neck.

'In as few days as possible.'

Whereupon Sir Percy rose, and said solemnly:

'You are right there, my friend, quite right. Delays are always dangerous. If you mean to have my head, why – have it quickly. As for me, delays always bore me to tears.'

He yawned and stretched his long limbs.

'I am getting so demmed fatigued,' he said. 'Do you not think this conversation has lasted quite long enough?'

'It was none of my seeking, Sir Percy.'

'Mine, I grant you; mine, absolutely! But, hang it, man! I had to tell you that your breeches were badly cut.'

'And I, that we are at your service, to end the business as soon as may be.'

'To——?' And once more Sir Percy passed his firm hand across his throat. Then he gave a shudder.

'B-r-r-r!' he exclaimed. 'I had no idea you were in such a demmed hurry.'

'We wait your pleasure, Sir Percy. Lady Blakeney must

not be kept in suspense too long. Shall we say that, in three days . . . ?'

'Make it four, my dear M. Chambertin, and I am eternally your debtor.'

'In four days then, Sir Percy,' Chauvelin rejoined with pronounced sarcasm. 'You see how ready I am to meet you in a spirit of conciliation! Four days, you say? Very well then; for four days more we keep our prisoner in those rooms upstairs . . . After that—'

He paused, awed mayhap, in spite of himself, by the diabolical thought which had suddenly come into his mind. He looked the Scarlet Pimpernel – his enemy – squarely in the face. Conscious of his power, he was no longer afraid.

For a while complete silence reigned in the bare, dank room – a silence broken only by the stertorous, rapid breathing of the one man who appeared moved. That man was not Sir Percy Blakeney. He indeed had remained quite still, spy-glass in hand, the good-humoured smile still dancing round his lips. Somewhere in the far distance a church clock struck the hour. Then only did Chauvelin put his full fiendish project into words.

'For four days,' he reiterated with slow deliberation, 'we keep our prisoner in the room upstairs. . . . after that, Captain Boyer has orders to shoot her.'

Just one second, whilst Chauvelin waited for his enemy's answer to this monstrous pronouncement, and the very walls of the drabby apartment appeared to listen, expectant. Overhead, could be dimly heard the measured tramp of heavy feet upon the uncarpeted floor. And suddenly through the bare apartment there rang the sound of a quaint, light-hearted laugh.

'You really are the worst-dressed man I have ever come across, my good M. Chambertin,' Sir Percy said with rare good-humour. 'You must allow me to give you the address of a good little tailor I came across in the Latin Quarter the other day. No decent man would be seen walking up the guillotine in such a waistcoat as you are wearing. As for your boots—' He yawned again. 'You really must excuse me! I came home late from the theatre last night, and have not had my usual hours of sleep. So, by your leave—'

'By all means, Sir Percy!' Chauvelin replied complacently. 'At this moment you are a free man, because I happen to be alone and unarmed, and because this house is solidly built and my voice would not carry to the floor above. Also because you are so nimble that no doubt you could give me the slip long before Captain Boyer and his men came to my rescue. Yes, Sir Percy; for the moment you are a free man! Free to walk out of this house unharmed. But even now, you are not as free as you would wish to be, eh? You are free to despise me, to overwhelm me with lofty scorn, to sharpen your wits at my expense; but you are not free to indulge your desire to squeeze the life out of me, to shake me as you would a rat. And shall I tell you why? Because you know now that if at a certain hour of the day I do not pay my daily visit to Captain Boyer upstairs, he will shoot his prisoner without the least compunction.'

Whereupon Blakeney threw up his head and laughed heartily.

'You are absolutely priceless, my dear M. Chambertin!' he said gaily. 'But you really must put your cravat straight. It has once again become disarranged . . . in the heat of your oratory, no doubt. . . . Allow me to offer you a pin.'

And with inimitable affectation, he took a pin out of his own cravat and presented it to Chauvelin, who, unable to control his wrath, jumped to his feet.

'Sir Percy—!' he snarled.

But Blakeney placed a gentle, firm hand upon his shoulder, forcing him to sit down again.

'Easy, easy, my friend,' he said. 'Do not, I pray you, lose that composure for which you are so justly famous. There! Allow me to arrange your cravat for you. A gentle tug here,' he added, suiting the action to the word, 'a delicate flick there, and you are the most perfectly cravatted man in France!'

'Your insults leave me unmoved, Sir Percy,' Chauvelin broke in savagely, and tried to free himself from the touch of those slender, strong hands that wandered so uncomfortably in the vicinity of his throat.

'No doubt,' Blakeney riposted lightly, 'that they are as futile as your threats. One does not insult a cur, any more than one threatens Sir Percy Blakeney – what?'

'You are right there, Sir Percy. The time for threats has gone by. And since you appear so vastly entertained—'

'I *am* vastly entertained, my dear M. Chambertin! How can I help it, when I see before me a miserable shred of humanity who does not even know how to keep his tie straight or his hair smooth, calmly – or almost calmly – talking of – Let me see, what were you talking of, my amiable friend?'

'Of the hostage, Sir Percy, which we hold until the happy day when the gallant Scarlet Pimpernel is a prisoner in our hands.'

''M, yes! He was that once before, was he not, my good sir? Then, too, you laid down mighty schemes for his capture.'

'And we succeeded.'

'By your usual amiable methods – lies, deceit, forgery. The latter has been useful to you this time too, eh?'

'What do you mean, Sir Percy?'

'You had need of the assistance of a fair lady for your schemes. She appeared disinclined to help you. So when her inconvenient lover, Bertrand Moncrif, was happily dragged away from her path, you forged a letter, which the lady rightly looked upon as an insult. Because of that letter, she nourished a comfortable amount of spite against me, and lent you her aid in the fiendish outrage for which you are about to receive punishment.'

He had raised his voice slightly while he spoke, and Chauvelin cast an apprehensive glance in the direction of the door behind which he guessed that Theresia Cabarrus must be straining her ears to listen.

'A pretty story, Sir Percy,' he said with affected coolness. 'And one that does infinite credit to your imagination. It is mere surmise on your part.'

'What, my friend? What is surmise? That you gave a letter to Madame de Fontenay which you had concocted, and which I had never written? Why, man,' he added with a laugh, 'I saw you do it!'

'You? Impossible!'

'More impossible things than that will happen within the next few days, my good sir. I was outside the window of Madame de Fontenay's apartment during the whole of your interview with her. And the shutters were not as closely fastened as you would have wished. But why argue about it, my dear M. Chambertin, when you know quite well that I have given you a perfectly accurate exposé of the means which you employed to make a pretty and spoilt woman help you in your nefarious work?'

'Why argue, indeed?' Chauvelin retorted drily. 'The past is past. I'll answer to my country, which you outrage by your machinations, for the methods which I employ to circumvent them. Your concern and mine, my gallant friend, is solely with the future – with the next four days, in fact . . . After which, either the Scarlet Pimpernel is in our hands, or Lady Blakeney will be put against the wall upstairs and summarily shot.'

Then only did something of his habitual lazy nonchalance go out of Blakeney's attitude. Just for the space of a few seconds he drew himself up to his full magnificent height, and from the summit of his splendid audacity and the consciousness of his own power, he looked down at the mean, cringing figure of the enemy who had hurled this threat of death against the woman he worshipped.

'And you really believe,' Sir Percy Blakeney said slowly and deliberately, 'that you have the power to carry through your infamous schemes? That I – yes, I! – would allow you to come within measurable distance of their execution? Bah! my dear friend. You have learned nothing by past experience – not even this: that when you dared to lay your filthy hands upon Lady Blakeney, you and the whole pack of assassins who have terrorised this beautiful country far too long, struck the knell of your ultimate doom. You have dared to measure your strength against mine by perpetrating an outrage so monstrous in my sight that, to punish you, I – even I! – will sweep you off the face of the earth and send you to join the pack of unclean ghouls who have aided you in your crimes. After which – thank the Lord! – the earth, being purged of your presence, will begin to smell sweetly again.'

Chauvelin made a vain effort to laugh, to shrug his shoulders, to put on those airs of insolence which came so naturally to his opponent. No doubt the strain of this long interview with his enemy had told upon his nerves. His limbs felt heavy as lead, an icy shudder was coursing down his spine. It seemed in truth as if some uncanny ghoul had entered the dreary, dank apartment and with gaunt, invisible hand was tolling a silent passing bell – the death knell of all his ambitions and of all his hopes. He closed his eyes, for he felt giddy and sick. When he opened his eyes again he was alone.

CHAPTER 26

A Dream

I

Chauvelin had not yet regained full possession of his faculties, when a few seconds later he saw Theresia Cabarrus glide swiftly across the antechamber. She appeared to him like a ghost – a pixie who had found her way through a keyhole. But she threw him a glance of contempt that was very human, very feminine indeed, and the next moment she was gone.

Outside on the landing she paused. Straining her ears, she caught the sound of a firm footfall slowly descending the stairs. She ran down a few steps, then called softly:

'Milor!'

The footsteps paused, and a pleasant voice gave quiet reply:

'At your service, fair lady!'

Theresia, shrewd as well as brave, continued to descend. She was not in the least afraid. Instinct had told her before now that no woman need ever have the slightest fear of that elegant milor with the quaint laugh and gently mocking mien, whom she had learned to know over in England.

Midway down the stairs she came face to face with him, and when she paused, panting, a little breathless with excitement, he said with perfect courtesy:

'You did me the honour to call me, Madame?'

'Yes, milor,' she replied, in a quick, eager whisper. 'I heard every word that passed between you and citizen Chauvelin.'

'Of course you did, dear lady,' he rejoined with a smile. 'If a woman once resisted the temptation of putting a shell-like ear to a keyhole, the world would lose many a cause for entertainment.'

'That insulting letter to me . . . when you took Moncrif away. . . . You never wrote it?'

'Did you really think that I did?' he retorted.

'No. I ought to have guessed . . . the moment that I saw you in England. . . .'

'And realised that I was not a cad – what?'

'Oh, milor!' she protested. 'But why – why did you not tell me before?'

'It had escaped my memory. And if I remember rightly, you spent most of the time when I had the honour of walking with you, in giving me elaborate and interesting accounts of your difficulties, and I, in listening to them.'

'Oh!' she exclaimed vehemently. 'I hate that man! I hate him!'

'In truth, he is not a lovable personality. But, by your leave, I presume that you did not desire to speak with me so that we might discuss our friend Chauvelin's amiable qualities.'

'No, no, milor!' she rejoined quickly. 'I called to you because—'

Then she paused for a moment or two, as if to collect her thoughts. Her eager eyes strove to pierce the gloom that enveloped the figure of the bold adventurer. She could only see the dim outline of his powerful figure, the light from above striking on his smooth hair, the elegantly tied bow at the nape of his neck, the exquisite filmy lace at his throat and wrists.

'Milor,' she said abruptly, 'you told me once – you remember? – that you were what you English call a sportsman. Is that so?'

'I hope always to remain that, dear lady,' he replied with a smile.

'Does that mean,' she queried, with a pretty air of deference and hesitation, 'does that mean a man who would under no circumstances harm a woman?'

'I think so.'

'Not even if she – if she has sinned – transgressed against him?'

'I don't quite understand, Madame,' he rejoined simply. 'And, time being short— Are you perchance speaking of yourself?'

'Yes. I have done you an injury, milor.'

'A very great one indeed,' he assented gravely.

'Could you,' she pleaded, raising earnest, tear-filled eyes to his, 'could you bring yourself to believe that I have been nothing but a miserable, innocent tool?'

'So was the lady upstairs innocent, Madame,' he broke in quietly.

'I know,' she retorted with a sigh. 'I know. I would never dare to plead, as you must hate me so.'

'Oh!' he said. 'Does a man ever hate a pretty woman?'

'He forgives her, milor,' she entreated, 'if he is a true sportsman.'

'Indeed? You astonish me, dear lady. But in verity you all in this unhappy country are full of surprises for a plain, blunt-headed Britisher. Now what, I wonder,' he added, with a light, good-humoured laugh, 'would my forgiveness be worth to you?'

'Everything!' she replied earnestly. 'I was deceived by that abominable liar, who knew how to play upon a woman's pique. I am ashamed, wretched. . . . Oh, cannot you believe me? And I would give worlds to atone!'

He laughed in his quiet, gently ironical way.

'You do not happen to possess worlds, dear lady. All that you have is youth and beauty and ambition, and life. You would forfeit all those treasures if you really tried to atone.'

'But—'

'Lady Blakeney is a prisoner. . . . You are her jailer. . . . Her precious life is the hostage for yours.'

'Milor—' she murmured.

'From my heart, I wish you well, fair one,' he broke in lightly. 'Believe me, the pagan gods that fashioned you did not design you for tragedy . . . and if you ran counter to your friend Chauvelin's desires, I fear me that that pretty neck of yours would suffer. A thing to be avoided at all costs! And now,' he added, 'have I your permission to go? My position here is somewhat precarious, and for the next four days I cannot afford the luxury of entertaining so fair a lady, by running my head into a noose.'

'Milor!' she pleaded.

'At your service, dear lady!'

'Is there naught I can do for you?'

He looked at her for a moment or two, and even through the gloom she caught his quizzical look and the mocking lines around his firm lips.

'You can ask Lady Blakeney to forgive you,' he said, with a thought more seriousness than was habitual to him. 'She is an angel; she might do it.'

'And if she does?'

'She will know what to do, to convey her thoughts to me.'

'Nay! but I'll do more than that, milor,' Theresia continued excitedly. 'I will tell her that I shall pray night and day for your deliverance and hers. I will tell her that I have seen you, and that you are well.'

'Ah, if you did that—!' he exclaimed, almost involuntarily.

'You would forgive me, too?' she pleaded.

'I would do more than that, fair one. I would make you Queen of France, in all but name.'

'What do you mean?' she murmured.

'That I would then redeem the promise which I made to you that evening, in the lane – outside Dover. Do you remember?'

She made no reply, closed her eyes; and her vivid fancy, rendered doubly keen by the mystery which seemed to encompass him as with a supernal mantle, conjured up the vision of that unforgettable evening: the moonlight, the scent of the hawthorn, the call of the thrush. She saw him stooping before her, and kissing her finger-tips, even whilst her ears recalled every word he had spoken and every inflexion of his mocking voice:

'Let me rather put it differently, dear lady,' he had said then. 'One day the exquisite Theresia Cabarrus, the Egeria of the Terrorists, the fiancée of the great Tallien, might need the help of the Scarlet Pimpernel.'

And she, angered, piqued by his coolness, thirsting for revenge for the insult which she believed he had put upon her, had then protested earnestly:

'I would sooner die,' she had boldly asserted, 'than seek your help, milor!'

And now, at this hour, here in this house where Death lurked in every corner, she could still hear his retort:

'Here in Dover, perhaps. . . . But in France?'

How right he had been! . . . How right! She – who had

thought herself so strong, so powerful – what was she indeed but a miserable tool in the hands of men who would break her without scruple if she ran counter to their will? Remorse was not for her – atonement too great a luxury for a tool of Chauvelin to indulge in. The black, hideous taint, the sin of having dragged this splendid man and that innocent woman to their death, must rest upon her soul for ever. Even now she was jeopardising his life, every moment that she kept him talking in this house. And yet the impulse to speak with him, to hear him say a word of forgiveness, had been unconquerable. One moment she longed for him to go; the next she would have sacrificed much to keep him by her side.

He seemed to divine her thoughts, remained quite still while she stood there with eyes closed, in one brief second reviewing the past. All! All! It all came back to her: her challenge to him, his laughing retort.

'You mean,' she had said at parting, 'that you would risk your life to save mine?'

'I should not risk my life, dear lady,' he had said, with his puzzling smile. 'But I should – God help me! – do my best, if the need arose, to save yours.'

Then he had gone, and she had stood under the porch of the quaint old English inn and watched his splendid figure as it disappeared down the street. Ah! if it had been her good fortune to have come across such a man, to have aroused in him that admiration for herself which she so scorned in others, how different, how very different would life have been! And she fell to envying the poor prisoner upstairs, who owned the most precious treasure life can offer to any woman: the love of a fine man. Two hot tears came slowly through her closed eyes, coursing down her cheeks.

'Why so sad, dear lady?' he asked gently.

She could not speak for the moment, only murmured vaguely:

'Four days—'

'Four days,' he retorted gaily, 'as you say! In four days, either I or a pack of assassins will be dead.'

'Oh, what will become of me?' she sighed.

'Whatever you choose.'

'You are bold, milor,' she rejoined more calmly. 'And you are brave. Alas! what can you do, when the most powerful hands in France are against you?'

'Smite them, dear lady,' he replied airily. 'Smite them! Then turn my back upon this fair land. It will no longer have need of me.' Then he made her a courteous bow. 'May I have the honour of escorting you upstairs? Your friend M. Chauvelin will be awaiting you.'

The name of her taskmaster brought Theresia back to the realities of life. Gone was the dream of a while ago, when subconsciously her mind had dwelt upon a sweet might-have-been. The man was nothing to her – less than nothing; a common spy, so her friends averred. Even if he had not presumed to write her an insulting letter, he was still the enemy – the foe whose hand was raised against her own country and against those with whose fortunes she had thrown in her lot. Even now, she ought to be calling loudly for help, rouse the house with her cries, so that this spy, this enemy, might be brought down before her eyes. Instead of which, she felt her heart beating with apprehension lest his quiet, even voice be heard on the floor above, and he be caught in the snare which those who feared and hated him had laid for him.

Indeed, she appeared far more conscious of danger than he was; and while she chided herself for her folly in having called to him, he was standing before her as if he were in a drawing-room, holding out his arm to escort her in to dinner. His foot was on the step, ready to ascend, even whilst Theresia's straining ears caught the sound of other footsteps up above: footsteps of men – real men, those! – who were set up there to watch for the coming of the Scarlet Pimpernel, and whose vigilance had been spurred by promise of reward and by threat of death. She pushed his arm aside almost roughly.

'You are mad, milor!' she said, in a choked murmur. 'Such foolhardiness, when your life is in deadly jeopardy, becomes criminal folly—'

'The best of life,' he said airily, 'is folly. I would not miss this moment for a kingdom!'

She felt like a creature under a spell. He took her hand and drew it through his arm. She went up the steps beside him.

Every moment she thought that one or more of the soldiers would be coming down, or that Chauvelin, impatient at her absence, might step out upon the landing. The dank, murky air seemed alive with ominous whisperings, of stealthy treads upon the stone. Theresia dared not look behind her, fearful lest the grim presence of Death itself be suddenly made manifest before her.

On the landing he took leave of her, stooped and kissed her hand.

'Why, how cold it is!' he remarked with a smile.

His was perfectly steady and warm. The very feel of it seemed to give her strength. She raised her eyes to his.

'Milor,' she entreated, 'on my knees I beg of you not to toy with your life any longer.'

'Toy with my life?' he retorted gaily. 'Nothing is further from my thoughts.'

'You must know that every second which you spend in this house is fraught with the greatest possible danger.'

'Danger? Ne'er a bit, dear lady! I am no longer in danger, now that you are my friend.'

The next moment he was gone. For awhile, Theresia's straining ears still caught the sound of his firm footfall upon the stone steps. Then all was still; and she was left wondering if, in very truth, the last few minutes on the dark stairs had not all been part of a dream.

CHAPTER 27

Terror or Ambition

I

Chauvelin had sufficiently recovered from the emotions of the past half-hour to speak coolly and naturally to Theresia. He made no reference to his interview with the Scarlet Pimpernel, nor did he question her directly as to whether she had overheard what passed between them. Certainly his attitude was a more dictatorial one than it had been before. Some of his first words to her contained a veiled menace.

'Vigilance!' he said to Theresia, after a curt greeting. 'Incessant vigilance, night and day, is what your country demands of you now, citizeness! All our lives now depend upon our vigilance.'

'Yours perhaps, citizen,' she rejoined coolly. 'You seem to forget that I am not bound—'

'You? Not bound?' he broke in roughly, and with a strident laugh. 'Not bound to aid in bringing the most bitter enemy of your country to his knees? Not bound, now that success is in sight?'

'You only obtained my help by a subterfuge,' she retorted, 'by a forged letter and a villainous lie—'

'Bah! Are you going to tell me, citizeness, that all means are not justifiable when dealing with those whose hands are raised against France? Forgery?' he went on, with passionate earnestness. 'Why not? Outrage? Murder? I would commit every crime in order to serve the country which I love, and hound her enemies to death. The only crime that is unjustifiable, citoyenne, is indifference. You? Not bound? Wait! Wait, I say! And if by your indifference or your apathy we fail once more to bring that elusive enemy to book, wait then until you stand at the bar of the people's tribunal, and in the face of France, who called to you for help, of France, who, beset by a hundred foes, stretched appealing arms to you, her daughter, you turned a deaf ear to her entreaties, and, shrugging your fair shoulders, calmly pleaded, "Bah! I was not bound!"'

He paused, carried away by his own enthusiasm, feeling perhaps that he had gone too far, or else had said enough to enforce the obedience which he exacted. After awhile, since Theresia remained silent too, he added more quietly:

'If we capture the Scarlet Pimpernel this time, citizeness, Robespierre shall know from my lips that it is to you and to you alone that he owes this triumph over the enemy whom he fears above all. Without you, I could not have set the trap out of which he cannot now escape.'

'He can escape! He can!' she retorted defiantly. 'The Scarlet Pimpernel is too clever, too astute, too audacious, to fall into your trap.'

'Take care, citoyenne, take care! Your admiration for that elusive hero carries you beyond the bounds of prudence.'

'Bah! If he escapes, 'tis you who will be blamed—'

'And 'tis you who will suffer, citoyenne,' he riposted blandly. With which parting shaft he left her certain that she would ponder over his threats as well as over his bold promise of a rich reward.

Terror and ambition! Death, or the gratitude of Robespierre! How well did Chauvelin gauge the indecision, the shallowness of a fickle woman's heart. Theresia, left to herself, had only those two alternatives over which to ponder. Robespierre's gratitude, which meant that the admiration which already he felt for her would turn to stronger passion. He was still heart-whole, that she knew. The regard which he was supposed to feel for the humble cabinet-maker's daughter could only be a passing fancy. The dictator of France must choose a mate worthy of his power and of his ambition; his friends would see to that. Robespierre's gratitude! What a vista of triumphs and of glory did that eventuality open up before her, what dizzy heights of satisfied ambition! And what a contrast if Chauvelin's scheme failed in the end!

'Wait,' he had cried, 'until you stand at the bar of the people's tribunal and plead indifference!'

Theresia shuddered. Her loneliness, her isolation, here in this house, where an appalling and grim tragedy was even now in preparation, filled her with sickening dread. Overhead she could hear the soldiers moving about, and in one of the rooms close by her sensitive ear caught the sound of Mother Théot's shuffling tread.

But the sound that was most insistent, that hammered away at her heart until she could have screamed with the pain, was the echo of a lazy, somewhat inane laugh and of a gently mocking voice that said lightly:

'The best of life is folly, dear lady. I would not miss this moment for a kingdom.'

Impatient to get away from this atmosphere of tragedy and of mysticism which was preying on her nerves, Theresia called peremptorily to Mother Théot, and when the old woman came shuffling out of her room, demanded her cloak and hood.

'Have you seen aught of citizen Moncrif?' she asked, just before going away.

'I caught sight of him over the way,' Catherine Théot

replied, 'watching this house, as he always does when you, citoyenne, are in it.'

'Ah!' the imperious beauty retorted, with a thought of spite in her mellow voice. 'Would you could give him a potion, Mother, to cure him of his infatuation for me!'

'Despise no man's love, citoyenne,' the witch retorted sententiously. 'Even that poor vagabond's blind passion may yet prove thy salvation.'

A moment or two later Theresia was once more on the dark stairs where she had dreamed of the handsome milor. She still felt his presence through the gloom; and in the ghostly light that feebly illumined the corner whereon he had stood, she still vaguely saw in spirit his tall straight figure, stooping whilst he kissed her hand. At one moment she was quite sure that she heard his voice and the echo of his pleasant laugh.

Down below, Bertrand Moncrif was waiting for her, silent, humble, with the look of a faithful watch-dog upon his pale, wan face.

'You make yourself ill, my poor Bertrand,' Theresia said, not unkindly, seeing that he stood aside to let her pass, fearful of a rebuff if he dared speak to her. 'I am in no danger, I assure you; and this constant dogging of my footsteps can do no good to you or to me.'

'But it can do no harm,' he pleaded earnestly. 'Something tells me, Theresia, that danger does threaten you, unbeknown to you, from a quarter least expected.'

'Bah!' she retorted lightly. 'And if it did, you could not avert it.'

He made a desperate effort to check the words of passionate protestations which rose to his lips. But obviously he dared not say what lay nearest to his heart. All he could do now was to walk silently by her side as far as her lodgings in the Rue Villedot, grateful for this small privilege, uncomplaining and almost happy because she tolerated his presence, and because while she walked the ends of her long scarf stirred by the breeze would now and again flutter against his cheek.

Miserable Bertrand! He had laden his soul with an abominable crime for this woman's sake; and he had not even the satisfaction of feeling that she gave him an infinitesimal measure of gratitude.

CHAPTER 28

In the Meanwhile

I

Chauvelin, who, despite his many failures, was still one of the most conspicuous – since he was one of the most unscrupulous – members of the Committee of Public Safety, had not attended its sittings for some days. He had been too deeply absorbed in his own schemes to trouble about those of his colleagues. In truth, the coup which he was preparing was so stupendous, and if it succeeded his triumph would be so magnificent, that he could well afford to hold himself aloof. Those who were still inclined to scorn and to scoff at him today would be his most cringing sycophants on the morrow.

Robespierre, the tyrant, the autocrat whose mere word swayed the multitude, remained silent and impenetrable, absent from every gathering. He only made brief appearances at the Convention, and there sat moody and self-absorbed. Every one knew that this man, dictator in all but name, was meditating a Titanic attack upon his enemies. His veiled threats, uttered during his rare appearances at the speaker's tribune, embraced even the most popular, the most prominent, amongst the representatives of the people. Every one, in fact, who was likely to stand in his way when he was ready to snatch the supreme power. His intimates – Couthon, St Just, and the others – openly accused of planning a dictatorship for their chief, hardly took the trouble to deny the impeachment, even whilst Tallien and his friends, feeling that the tyrant had already decreed their doom, went about like ghostly shadows, not daring to raise their voice in the Convention lest the first word they uttered brought down the sword of his lustful wrath upon their heads.

The Committee of Public Safety – now re-named the Revolutionary Committee – strove on the other hand by a recrudescence of cruelty to ingratiate itself with the potential dictator and to pose before the people as alone pure and incorruptible, blind in justice, inexorable where the safety of the Republic was concerned. Thus an abominable emulation of vengeance and of persecution went on between the Committee and Robespierre's party, wherein neither side could afford to give in, for fear of being accused of apathy and of moderation.

Chauvelin, for the most part, had kept out of the turmoil. He felt that in his hands lay the destiny of either party. His one thought was of the Scarlet Pimpernel and of his imminent capture, knowing that, with the most inveterate opponent of revolutionary excesses in his hands, he would within an hour be in a position to link his triumph with one or the other of the parties – either with Robespierre and his herd of butchers, or with Tallien and the Moderates.

He was the mysterious and invisible deus ex machina, who anon, when it suited his purpose, would reveal himself in his full glory as the man who had tracked down and brought to the guillotine the most dangerous enemy of the revolutionary government. And, so easily is a multitude swayed, that that one fact would bring him popularity transcending that of every other man in France. He,

Chauvelin, the despised, the derided, whose name had become synonymous with Failure, would then with a word sweep those aside who had mocked him, hurl his enemies from their pedestals, and name at will the rulers of France. All within four days!

And of these, two had gone by.

II

For Marguerite Blakeney these days had gone by like a nightmare. Cut off from all knowledge of the outside world, without news from her husband for the past forty-eight hours, she was enduring mental agony such as would have broken a weaker or less trusting spirit.

Two days ago she had received a message, a few lines hastily scribbled by an unknown hand, and brought to her by the old woman who waited upon her.

'I have seen him,' the message said. 'He is well and full of hope. I pray God for your deliverance and his, but help can only come by a miracle.'

The message was written in a feminine hand, with no clue as to the writer.

Marguerite had not seen Chauvelin again, for which indeed she thanked Heaven on her knees. But every day at a given hour she was conscious of his presence outside her door. She heard his voice in the vestibule: there would be a word or two of command, the grounding of arms, then some whispered talking; and presently Chauvelin's stealthy footstep would slink up to her door. And Marguerite would remain still as a mouse that scents the presence of a cat, holding her breath, life almost at a standstill in this agony of expectation.

The remainder of the day time hung with a leaden weight on her hands. She was given no books to read, not a needle wherewith to busy herself. She had no one to speak to save old Mother Théot, who waited on her and brought her her meals, nearly always in silence, and with a dour mien which checked any attempt at conversation.

For company, the unfortunate woman had nothing but her own thoughts, her fears which grew in intensity, and her hopes which were rapidly dwindling, as hour followed hour and day succeeded day in dreary monotony. No sound around her save the incessant tramp, tramp of sentries at her door, and every two hours the changing of the guard in the vestibule outside; then the whispered colloquies, the soldiers playing at cards or throwing dice, the bibulous songs, the ribald laughter, the obscene words flung aloud like bits of filthy rag; the life, in fact, that revolved around her jailers and seemed at a standstill within her prison walls.

In the late afternoons the air would become insufferably hot, and Marguerite would throw open the window and sit beside it, her gaze fixed upon the horizon far away, her hands lying limp and moist upon her lap.

Then she would fall to dreaming. Her thoughts, swifter than a flight of swallows, would cross the sea and go roaming across country to her stately home in Richmond, where at this hour the moist, cool air was fragrant with the scent of late roses and of lime blossom, and the murmur of the river lapping the mossy bank whispered of love and of peace.

She would dream . . . only to wake up the next moment to hear the church clock of St Antoine striking seven, and a minute or two later that ominous shuffling footstep outside her door, those whisperings, the grounding of arms, a burst of cruel laughter, which brought her from the dizzy heights of illusive happiness back to the hideous reality of her own horrible position, and of the deadly danger which lay in wait for her beloved.

CHAPTER 29

The Close of the Second Day

I

Soon after seven o'clock that evening the storm which had threatened all day burst in its full fury. A raging gale tore at the dilapidated roofs of this squalid corner of the great city, and lashed the mud of the streets into miniature cascades.

Chauvelin, who had paid his daily visit to the Captain in charge of the prisoner in the Rue de la Planchette, was unable to proceed homewards. For the moment the street appeared impassable. Wrapped in his cloak, he decided to wait in the disused storage-room below until it became possible for an unfortunate pedestrian to sally forth into the open.

There seems no doubt that at this time the man's very soul was on the rack.

He trusted no one – not Mother Théot, not the men upstairs, not Theresia: least of all Theresia. And his tortured brain invented and elaborated schemes whereby he set one set of spies to watch another, one set of sleuthhounds to run after another, in a kind of vicious and demoniac circle of mistrust and denunciation. Nor did he trust himself any longer: neither his instinct nor his eyes, nor his ears.

It was impossible to keep the outer doors open, because

the rain beat in wildly on that side, and the place would have been in utter darkness but for an old grimy lanthorn which some prudent hand had set up on a barrel in the centre of the vast space, and which shed a feeble circle of light around. The latch of the wicket appeared to be broken, for the small door, driven by the wind, flapped backwards and forwards with irritating ceaselessness. At one time Chauvelin tried to improvise some means of fastening it, for the noise helped to exacerbate his nerves and, leaning out into the street in order to seize hold of the door, he saw the figure of a man, bent nearly double in the teeth of the gale, shuffling across the street from the direction of the Porte St Antoine.

It was then nearly eight o'clock, and the light treacherous, but despite the veil of torrential rain which intervened between him and that shuffling figure, something in the gait, the stature, the stoop of the wide, bony shoulders, appeared unpleasantly familiar. The man's head and shoulders were wrapped in a tattered piece of sacking, which he held close to his chest. His arms were bare, as were his shins, and on his feet he had a pair of sabots stuffed with straw.

Midway across the street he paused, and a tearing fit of coughing seemed to render him momentarily helpless. Chauvelin's first instinct prompted him to run to the stairs and to call for assistance from Captain Boyer. Indeed, he was half-way up to the first floor when, looking down, he saw that the man had entered the place through the wicket-door. Still coughing and spluttering, he had divested himself of his piece of sacking and was crouching down against the barrel in the centre of the room and trying to warm his hands by holding them against the glass sides of the old lanthorn.

From where he stood, Chauvelin could see the dim outline of the man's profile, the chin ornamented with a three-days' growth of beard, the lank hair plastered above the pallid forehead, the huge bones, coated with grime, that protruded through the rags that did duty for a shirt. The sleeves of this tattered garment hung away from the arm, displaying a fiery, inflamed weal, shaped like the letter 'M,' that had recently been burned into the flesh with a branding iron.

The sight of that mark upon the vagabond's arm caused Chauvelin to pause a moment, then to come down the stairs again.

'Citizen Rateau!' he called.

The man jumped as if he had been struck by a whip, tried to struggle to his feet, but collapsed on the floor, while a terrible fit of coughing took his breath away. Chauvelin, standing beside the barrel, looked down with a grim smile on this miserable wreckage of humanity whom he had so judiciously put out of the way of further mischief. The dim flicker of the lanthorn illumined the gaunt, bony arm, so that the charred flesh stood out like a crimson fiery string against a coating of grime.

Rateau appeared terrified, scared by the sudden appar-ition of the man who had inflicted the shameful punishment upon him. Chauvelin's face, lighted from below by the lanthorn, did indeed appear grim and forbidding. Some few seconds elapsed before the coal-heaver had recovered sufficiently to stand on his feet.

'I seem to have scared you, my friend,' Chauvelin remarked drily.

'I – I did not know,' Rateau stammered with a painful wheeze, 'that anyone was here . . . I came for shelter. . . .'

'I am here for shelter, too,' Chauvelin rejoined, 'and did not see you enter.'

'Mother Théot allows me to sleep here,' Rateau went on mildly. 'I have had no work for two days . . . not since . . .' And he looked down ruefully upon his arm. 'People think I am an escaped felon,' he explained with snivelling timidity. 'And as I have always lived just from hand to mouth . . .'

He paused, and cast an obsequious glance on the Terrorist, who retorted drily:

'Better men than you, my friend, live from hand to mouth these days. Poverty,' he continued with grim sarcasm, 'exalts a man in this glorious revolution of ours. 'Tis riches that shame him.'

Rateau's branded arm went up to his lanky hair, and he scratched his head dubiously.

'Aye,' he nodded, obviously uncomprehending; 'perhaps! But I'd like to taste some of that shame!'

Chauvelin shrugged his shoulders and turned on his heel. The thunder sounded a little more distant and the rain less violent for the moment, and he strode toward the door.

'The children run after me now,' Rateau continued dolefully. 'In my *quartier*, the concierge turned me out of my lodging. They keep asking me what I have done to be branded like a convict.'

'Tell them you've been punished for serving the English spy,' Chauvelin said.

'The Englishman paid me well, and I am very poor,' Rateau retorted meekly. 'I could serve the State now . . . if it would pay me well.'

'Indeed? How?'

'By telling you something, citizen, which you would like to know.'

'What is it?'

At once the instinct of the informer, of the sleuthhound, was on the *qui vive*. The coal-heaver's words, the expression of cunning on his ugly face, the cringing obsequiousness of his attitude, all suggested the spirit of intrigue, of underhand dealing, of lies and denunciations, which were as the breath of life to this master-spy. He retraced his steps, came and sat upon a pile of rubbish beside the barrel, and when Rateau, terrified apparently at what he had said, made a motion as if to slink away, Chauvelin called him back peremptorily.

'What is it, citizen Rateau,' he said curtly, 'that you could tell me, and that I would like to know?'

Rateau was cowering in the darkness, trying to efface his huge bulk and to smother his rasping cough.

'You have said too much already,' Chauvelin went on harshly, 'to hold your tongue. And you have nothing to fear . . . everything to gain. What is it?'

'Am I to be paid this time?' Rateau asked.

'If you speak the truth – yes.'

'How much?'

'That depends on what you tell me. And now, if you hold your tongue, I shall call to the citizen Captain upstairs and send you to jail.'

The coal-heaver appeared to crouch yet further into himself. He looked like a huge, shapeless mass in the gloom. His huge yellow teeth could be heard chattering.

'Citizen Tallien will send me to the guillotine,' he murmured.

'What has citizen Tallien to do with it?'

'He pays great attention to the citoyenne Cabarrus.'

'And it is about her?'

'She is playing you false, citizen,' Rateau murmured in a hoarse breath, and crawled like a long, bulky worm a little closer to the Terrorist.

'How?'

'She is in league with the Englishman.'

'How do you know?'

'I saw her here . . . two days ago . . . you remember, citizen . . . after you . . .'

'Yes, yes!' Chauvelin cried impatiently.

'Sergeant Chazot took me to the cavalry barracks. . . .

271

They gave me a drink ... and I don't remember much what happened. But when I was myself again, I know that my arm was very sore, and when I looked down I saw this awful mark on it ... I was just outside the Arsenal then. ... How I got there I don't know ... I suppose Sergeant Chazot brought me back. ... He says I was howling for Mother Théot. ... She has marvellous salves, you know, citizen.'

'Yes, yes!'

'I came in here. ... My head still felt very strange ... and my arm felt like living fire. Then I heard voices ... they came from the stairs ... I looked about me, and saw them standing there. ...'

Rateau, leaning upon one arm, stretched out the other and pointed to the stairs. Chauvelin, with a violent gesture, seized him by the wrist.

'Who?' he queried harshly. 'Who was standing there?'

His glance followed the direction in which the coal-heaver was pointing, then instinctively wandered back and fastened on that fiery letter 'M' which had been seared into the vagabond's flesh.

'The Englishman and citoyenne Cabarrus,' Rateau replied feebly, for he had winced with pain under the excited grip of the Terrorist.

'You are certain?'

'I heard them talking—'

'What did they say?'

'I do not know. ... But I saw the Englishman kiss the citoyenne's hand before they parted.'

'And what happened after that?'

'The citoyenne went to Mother Théot's apartment and the Englishman came down the stairs. I had just time to hide behind that pile of rubbish. He did not see me.'

Chauvelin uttered a savage curse of disappointment.

'Is that all?' he exclaimed.

'The State will pay me?' Rateau murmured vaguely.

'Not a sou!' Chauvelin retorted roughly. 'And if citizen Tallien hears this pretty tale . . .'

'I can swear to it!'

'Bah! Citoyenne Cabarrus will swear that you lied. 'Twill be her word against that of a mudlark!'

'Nay!' Rateau retorted. ''Twill be more that that.'

'What then?'

'Will you swear to protect me, citizen, if citizen Tallien—'

'Yes, yes! I'll protect you. . . . And the guillotine has no time to trouble about such muck-worms as you!'

'Well, then, citizen,' Rateau went on in a hoarse murmur, 'if you will go to the citoyenne's lodgings in the Rue Villedot, I can show you where the Englishman hides the clothes wherewith he disguises himself . . . and the letters which he writes to the citoyenne when . . .'

He paused, obviously terrified at the awesome expression of the other man's face. Chauvelin had allowed the coal-heaver's wrist to drop out of his grasp. He was sitting quite still, silent and grim, his thin, claw-like hands closely clasped together and held between his knees. The flickering light of the lanthorn distorted his narrow face, lengthened the shadows beneath the nose and chin, threw a high-light just below the brows, so that the pale eyes appeared to gleam with an unnatural flame. Rateau hardly dared to move. He lay like a huge bundle of rags in the inky blackness beyond the circle of light projected by the lanthorn; his breath came and went with a dragging, hissing sound, now and then broken by a painful cough.

For a moment or two there was silence in the great disused storeroom – a silence broken only by the thunder, dull and distant now, and the ceaseless, monotonous patter of the rain. Then Chauvelin murmured between his teeth:

'If I thought that she . . .' But he did not complete the

sentence, jumped to his feet and approached the big mass of rags and humanity that cowered in the gloom. 'Get up, citizen Rateau!' he commanded.

The asthmatic giant struggled to his knees. His wooden shoes had slipped off his feet. He groped for them, and with trembling hands contrived to put them on again.

'Get up!' Chauvelin reiterated, with a snarl like an angry tiger.

He took a small tablet and a leaden point from his pocket, and stooping toward the light he scribbled a few words, and then handed the tablet to Rateau.

'Take this over to the Commissary of the Section in the Place du Carrousel. Half a dozen men and a captain will be detailed to go with you to the lodgings of the citoyenne Cabarrus in the Rue Villedot. You will find me there. Go!'

Rateau's hand trembled visibly as he took the tablet. He was obviously terrified of what he had done. But Chauvelin paid no further heed to him. He had given him his orders, knowing well that they would be obeyed. The man had gone too far to draw back. It never entered Chauvelin's head that the coal-heaver might have lied. He had no cause for spite against the citoyenne Cabarrus, and the fair Spaniard stood on too high a pinnacle of influence for false denunciations to touch her. The Terrorist waited until Rateau had quietly slunk out by the wicket door; then he turned on his heel and quickly went up the stairs.

II

In the vestibule on the top floor he called to Captain Boyer.

'Citizen Captain,' he said at the top of his voice, 'you remember that tomorrow eve is the end of the third day?'

'Pardi!' the Captain retorted gruffly. 'Is anything changed?'

'No.'

'Then, unless by the eve of the fourth day that cursed Englishman is not in our hands, my orders are the same.'

'Your orders are,' Chauvelin rejoined loudly, and pointed with grim intention at the door behind which he felt Marguerite Blakeney to be listening for every sound, 'unless the English spy is in our hands on the evening of the fourth day, to shoot your prisoner.'

'It shall be done, citizen!' Captain Boyer gave reply.

Then he grinned maliciously, because from behind the closed door there had come a sound like a quickly smothered cry.

After which, Chauvelin nodded to the Captain and once more descended the stairs. A few seconds later he went out of the house into the stormy night.

CHAPTER 30

When the Storm Burst

I

Fortunately the storm only broke after the bulk of the audience was inside the theatre. The performance was timed to commence at seven, and a quarter of an hour before that time the citizens of Paris who had come to applaud citoyenne Vestris, citoyen Talma, and their colleagues, in Chénier's tragedy, *Henri VIII*, were in their seats.

The theatre in the Rue de Richelieu was crowded. Talma and Vestris had always been great favourites with the public and more so perhaps since their secession from the old and reactionary Comédie Française. Citizen Chénier's tragedy was in truth of a very poor order; but the audience was not disposed to be critical, and there was quite an excited hush in the house when citoyenne Vestris, in the part of 'Anne de Boulen,' rolled off the meretricious verses:

'Trop longtemps j'ai gardé le silence;
Le poids qui m'accablait tombe avec violence.'

It was a brilliant evening, not only because citoyenne Vestris was in magnificent form, but also because of the number of well-known people who sat in the various boxes and in the parterre and who thronged the foyer during the entr'actes.

It seemed as if the members of the Convention and those who sat upon the Revolutionary Committees, as well as the more prominent speakers in the various Clubs, had made a point of showing themselves to the public, gay, unconcerned, interested in the stage and in the audience, at this moment when every man's head was insecure upon his shoulders and no man knew whether on reaching home he would not find a posse of the National Guard waiting to convey him to the nearest prison.

Death indeed lurked everywhere.

The evening before, at a supper party given in the house of deputy Barrère, a paper was said to have dropped out of Robespierre's coat pocket, and been found by one of the guests. The paper contained nothing but just forty names. What those names were the general public did not know, nor for what purpose the dictator carried the list about in his pocket: but during the representation of *Henri VIII*, the more obscure citizens of Paris – happy in their own insignificance – noted that in the foyer during the entr'actes, citizen Tallien and his friends appeared obsequious, whilst those who fawned upon Robespierre were more than usually arrogant.

II

In one of the proscenium boxes, citizeness Cabarrus attracted a great deal of attention. Indeed, her beauty tonight was in the opinion of most men positively dazzling. Dressed with almost ostentatious simplicity, she drew all eyes upon her by her merry, ringing laughter, the ripple of conversation which flowed almost incessantly from her lips, and the graceful, provocative gestures of her bare hands and arms as she toyed with a miniature fan.

Indeed, Theresia Cabarrus was unusually light-hearted tonight. Sitting during the first two acts of the tragedy in her box, in the company of citizen Tallien, she became the cynosure of all eyes, proud and happy when, during the third interval, she received the visit of Robespierre.

He only stayed with her a few moments, and kept himself concealed for the most part at the back of the box; but he had been seen to enter, and Theresia's exclamation, 'Ah, citizen Robespierre! What a pleasant surprise! 'Tis not often you grace the theatre with your presence!' had been heard all over the house.

Indeed, with the exception of Eleonore Duplay, whose passionate admiration he rather accepted than reciprocated, the incorruptible and feline tyrant had never been known to pay attention to any woman. Great therefore was Theresia's triumph. Visions of that grandeur which she had always coveted and to which she had always felt herself predestined, danced before her eyes; and remembering Chauvelin's prophecies and Mother Théot's incantations, she allowed the dream-picture of the magnificent English milor to fade slowly from her ken, bidding it a reluctant adieu.

Though in her heart she still prayed for his deliverance – and did it with a passionate earnestness – some impish demon would hover at her elbow and repeat in her unwilling ear Chauvelin's inspired words: 'Bring the Scarlet Pimpernel to his knees at the chariot-wheel of Robespierre, and the crown of the Bourbons will be yours for the asking.' And if, when she thought of that splendid head falling under the guillotine, a pang of remorse and regret shot through her heart, she turned with a seductive smile to the only man who could place that crown at her feet. His popularity was still at its zenith. Tonight, whenever the audience caught sight of him in the Cabarrus' box, a wild cheer rang out from gallery to pit of the house. Then Theresia would lean over to him and whisper insinuatingly:

'You can do anything with that crowd, citizen! You hold the people by the magnetism of your presence and of your voice. There is no height to which you cannot aspire.'

'The greater the height,' he murmured moodily, 'the dizzier the fall. . . .'

''Tis on the summit you should gaze,' she retorted, 'not on the abyss below.'

'I prefer to gaze into the loveliest eyes in Paris,' he replied with a clumsy attempt at gallantry; 'and remain blind to the summits as well as to the depths.'

She tapped her daintily shod foot against the ground and gave an impatient little sigh. It seemed as if at every turn of fortune she was confronted with pusillanimity and indecision. Tallien fawning on Robespierre; Robespierre afraid of Tallien; Chauvelin a prey to nerves. How different to them all was that cool, self-possessed Englishman with the easy good-humour and splendid self-assurance!

'I would make you Queen of France in all but name!' He said this as easily, as unconcernedly as if he were promising an invitation to a rout.

When, a moment or two later, Robespierre took leave of her and she was left for a while alone with her thoughts, Theresia no longer tried to brush away from her mental vision the picture on which her mind loved to dwell. The tall, magnificent figure; the lazy, laughing eyes; the slender hand that looked so firm and strong amidst the billows of exquisite lace.

Ah, well! The dream was over!

Fate, in the guise of the one man she could have loved, was throwing Theresia into the arms of Robespierre.

III

The next moment she was rudely awakened from her dreams. The door of her box was torn open by a violent hand, and turning, she saw Bertrand Moncrif, hatless, with hair dishevelled, clothes dripping and mudstained, and linen soaked through. She was only just in time to arrest with a peremptory gesture the cry which was obviously hovering on his lips.

'Hush – sh – sh!' came at once from every portion of the audience, angered by this disturbing noise.

Tallien jumped to his feet.

'What is it?' he demanded in a quick whisper.

'A perquisition,' Moncrif replied hurriedly, 'in the house of the citoyenne!'

'Impossible!' she broke in harshly.

'Hush! . . . Silence!' the audience muttered audibly.

'I have come from there,' Moncrif murmured. 'I have seen . . . heard . . .'

'Come outside,' Theresia interjected. 'We cannot talk here.'

She led the way out, and Tallien and Moncrif followed.

The corridor fortunately was deserted. Only a couple of ouvreuses stood gossiping in a corner. Theresia, white to the lips – but more from anger than fear – dragged Moncrif with her to the foyer. Here there was no one.

'Now, tell me!' she commanded.

Bertrand passed his trembling hand through his soaking hair. His clothes were wet through. He was shaking from head to foot and appeared to have run till now he could scarcely stand.

'Tell me!' Theresia reiterated impatiently.

Tallien stood by, half paralysed with terror. He did not

question the younger man, but gazed on him with compelling, horror-filled eyes as if he would wrench the words out of him before they reached his throat.

'I was in the Rue Villedot,' Moncrif stammered breathlessly at last, 'when the storm broke. I sought shelter under the portico of a house opposite the citoyenne's lodgings. . . . I was there a long time. Then the storm subsided. . . . Men in uniform came along. . . . They were soldiers of the National Guard . . . I could see that, though the street was pitch dark . . . they passed quite close to me. . . . They were talking of the citoyenne. . . . Then they crossed over to her lodgings . . . I saw them enter the house . . . I saw citizen Chauvelin in the doorway . . . he chided them for being late. . . . There was a captain, and there were six soldiers, and that asthmatic coal-heaver was with them.'

'What!' Theresia exclaimed. 'Rateau?'

'What in Satan's name does it all mean?' Tallien exclaimed with a savage curse.

'They went into the house,' Moncrif went on, his voice rasping through his parched throat. 'I followed at a little distance, to make quite sure before I came to warn you. Fortunately I knew where you were . . . fortunately I always know. . . .'

'You are sure they went up to my rooms?' Theresia broke in quickly.

'Yes. Two minutes later I saw a light in your apartment.'

She turned abruptly to Tallien.

'My cloak!' she commanded. 'I left it in the box.'

He tried to protest.

'I am going,' she rejoined firmly. 'This is some ghastly mistake, for which that fiend Chauvelin shall answer with his life. My cloak!'

It was Bertrand who went back for the cloak and wrapped her in it. He knew – none better – that if his divinity desired to go, no power on earth would keep her back. She did not appear in the least afraid, but her wrath was terrible to see, and boded ill to those who had dared provoke it. Indeed, Theresia, flushed with her recent triumph and with Robespierre's rare if clumsy gallantries still ringing in her ear, felt ready to dare anything, to brave anyone – even Chauvelin and his threats. She even succeeded in reassuring Tallien, ordered him to remain in the theatre, and to show himself to the public as utterly unconcerned.

'In case a rumour of this outrage penetrates to the audience,' she said, 'you must appear to make light of it . . . Nay! you must at once threaten reprisals against its perpetrators.'

Then she wrapped her cloak about her and, taking Bertrand's arm, she hurried out of the theatre.

CHAPTER 31

Our Lady of Pity

I

It was like an outraged divinity in the face of sacrilege that Theresia Cabarrus appeared in the antechamber of her apartment, ten minutes later.

Her rooms were full of men; sentries were at the door; the furniture was overturned, the upholstery ripped up, cupboard doors swung open; even her bed and bedding lay in a tangled heap upon the floor. The lights in the rooms were dim, one single lamp shedding its feeble rays from the antechamber into the living-room, whilst another flickered on a wall-bracket in the passage. In the bedroom the maid Pepita, guarded by a soldier, was loudly lamenting and cursing in voluble Spanish.

Citizen Chauvelin was standing in the centre of the living-room, intent on examining some papers. In a corner of the antechamber cowered the ungainly figure of Rateau the coal-heaver.

Theresia took in the whole tragic picture at a glance; then with a proud, defiant toss of the head she swept past the soldiers in the antechamber and confronted Chauvelin, before he had time to notice her approach.

'Something has turned your brain, citizen Chauvelin,' she said coolly. 'What is it?'

'How wise was our young friend there to tell you of our visit, citoyenne!' he said suavely. And he looked with mild approval in the direction where Bertrand Moncrif stood between two soldiers, who had quickly barred his progress and were holding him tightly by the wrists.

'I came,' Theresia retorted harshly, 'as the forerunner of those who will know how to punish this outrage, citizen Chauvelin.'

'I shall be as ready to receive them,' he said quietly, 'as I am gratified to see the citoyenne Cabarrus. When they come, shall I direct them to call and see their beautiful Egeria at the Conciergerie, whither we shall have the honour to convey her immediately?'

Theresia threw back her head and laughed; but her voice sounded hard and forced.

'At the Conciergerie?' she exclaimed. 'I?'

'Even you, citoyenne,' Chauvelin replied.

'On what charge, I pray you?' she demanded, with biting sarcasm.

'Of trafficking with the enemies of the Republic.'

'You are mad, citizen Chauvelin!' she riposted with perfect sang-froid. 'I pray you, order your men to re-establish order in my apartment; and remember that I will hold you responsible for any damage that has been done.'

'Shall I also,' Chauvelin rejoined with equally perfect equanimity, 'replace these letters and other interesting objects, there where we found them?'

'Letters?' she retorted, frowning. 'What letters?'

'These, citoyenne,' he replied, and held up to her gaze the papers which he had in his hand.

'What are they? I have never seen them before.'

'Nevertheless, we found them in that bureau.' And Chauvelin pointed to a small piece of furniture which stood against the wall, and the drawers of which had obviously been forcibly torn open. Then as Theresia remained silent, apparently not understanding, he went on suavely: 'They are letters written at different times to Mme de Fontenay, née Cabarrus – *Our Lady of Pity*, as she was called by grateful Bordeaux.'

'By whom?' she asked.

'By the interesting hero of romance who is known to the world as the Scarlet Pimpernel.'

'It is false!' she retorted firmly. 'I have never received a letter from him in my life!'

'His handwriting is all too familiar to me, citoyenne; and the letters are addressed to you.'

'It is false!' she reiterated with unabated firmness. 'This is some devilish trick you have devised in order to ruin me. But take care, citizen Chauvelin, take care! If this is a trial of strength 'twixt you and me, the next few hours will show who will gain the day.'

'If it were a trial of strength 'twixt you and me, citoyenne,' he rejoined blandly, 'I would already be a vanquished man. But it is France this time who has challenged a traitor. That traitor is Theresia Fontenay, née Cabarrus. The trial of strength is between her and France.'

'You are mad, citizen Chauvelin! If there were letters writ by the Scarlet Pimpernel found in my rooms, 'tis you who put them there!'

'That statement you will be at liberty to substantiate tomorrow, citoyenne,' he retorted coldly, 'at the bar of the revolutionary tribunal. There, no doubt, you can explain away how citizen Rateau knew of the existence of those letters and led me straight to their discovery. I have an officer of the National Guard, the commissary of the section, and half a dozen men, to prove the truth of what I say, and to add that in a wall-cupboard in your antechamber we also found this interesting collection, the use of which you, citoyenne, will no doubt be able to explain.'

He stepped aside and pointed to a curious heap which littered the floor – rags for the most part: a tattered shirt, frayed breeches, a grimy cap, a wig made up of lank, colourless hair, the counterpart of that which adorned the head of the coal-heaver Rateau.

Theresia looked on those rags for a moment in a kind of horrified puzzlement. Her cheeks and lips became the colour of ashes. She put her hand up to her forehead, as if to chase a hideous, ghoulish vision away, and smothered a cry of horror. Puzzlement had given place to a kind of superstitious dread. The room, the rags, the faces of the soldiers began to whirl around her – impish shapes to dance a wild saraband before her eyes. And in the midst of this witch's cauldron the figure of Chauvelin, like a weird hobgoblin, was executing elf-like contortions and brandishing a packet of letters writ upon scarlet paper.

She tried to laugh, to speak defiant words; but her throat felt as if it were held in a vice, and losing momentary consciousness she tottered, and only saved herself from measuring her length upon the floor by clinging with both hands to a table immediately behind her.

As to what happened after that, she only had a blurred impression. Chauvelin gave a curt word of command, and a couple of soldiers came and stood to right and left of her. Then a piercing cry rang through the narrow rooms, and she saw Bertrand Moncrif for one moment between herself and the soldiers, fighting desperately, shielding her with his body, tearing and raging like a wild animal defending its young. The whole room appeared full of a deafening noise: cries and more cries – words of command – calls of rage and entreaty. Then suddenly the word 'Fire!' and the detonation of a pistol at close range, and the body of Bertrand Moncrif sliding down limp and impotent to the floor.

After that, everything became dark around her. Theresia

felt as if she were looking down an immeasurable abyss of inky blackness, and that she was falling, falling. . . .

A thin, dry laugh brought her back to her senses, her pride to the fore, her vanity up in arms. She drew her statuesque figure up to its full height and once more confronted Chauvelin like an august and outraged divinity.

'And at whose word,' she demanded, 'is this monstrous charge to be brought against me?'

'At the word of a free citizen of the State,' Chauvelin replied coldly.

'Bring him before me.'

Chauvelin shrugged his shoulders and smiled indulgently, like one who is ready to humour a wayward child.

'Citizen Rateau!' he called.

From the anteroom there came the sound of much shuffling, spluttering, and wheezing; then the dull clatter of wooden shoes upon the carpeted floor; and presently the ungainly, grime-covered figure of the coal-heaver appeared in the doorway.

Theresia looked on him for a few seconds in silence, then she gave a ringing laugh, and with exquisite bare arm outstretched she pointed to the scrubby apparition.

'That man's word against mine!' she called, with well-assumed mockery. 'Rateau the caitiff against Theresia Cabarrus, the intimate friend of citizen Robespierre! What a subject for a lampoon!'

Then her laughter broke. She turned once more on Chauvelin like an angry goddess.

'That vermin!' she exclaimed, her voice hoarse with indignation. 'That sorry knave with a felon's brand! In truth, citizen Chauvelin, your spite must be hard put to it to bring up such a witness against me!'

Then suddenly her glance fell upon the lifeless body of Bertrand Moncrif, and on the horrible crimson stain which discoloured his coat. She gave a shudder of horror, and for a moment her eyes closed and her head fell back, as if she were about to swoon. But she quickly recovered herself. Her will-power at this moment was unconquerable. She looked with unutterable contempt on Chauvelin; then she raised her cloak, which had slipped down from her shoulders, and wrapped it with a queenlike gesture around her, and without another word led the way out of the apartment.

Chauvelin remained standing in the middle of the room, his face quite expressionless, his clawlike hands still fingering the fateful letters. Two soldiers remained with him beside the body of Bertrand Moncrif. The maid Pepita, still shrieking and gesticulating violently, had to be dragged away in the wake of her mistress.

In the doorway between the living-room and the ante-chamber, Rateau, humble, snivelling, more than a little frightened, stood aside in order to allow the guard and their imperious prisoner to pass. Theresia did not condescend to look at him again; and he, shuffling and stumbling in his clumsy wooden shoes, followed the soldiers down the stairs.

II

It was still raining hard. The captain who was in charge of Theresia told her that he had a chaise ready for her. It was waiting out in the street. Theresia ordered him to send for it; she would not, she said, offer herself as a spectacle to the riff-raff who happened to be passing by. The captain had probably received orders to humour the prisoner as far as was compatible with safety. Certain it is that he sent one of his men to fetch the coach and to order the concierge to throw open the porte-cochère.

Theresia remained standing in the narrow vestibule at the foot of the stairs. Two soldiers stood on guard over the maid, whilst another stood beside Theresia. The captain, muttering with impatience, paced up and down the stone-paved floor. Rateau had paused on the stairs, a step or two just above where Theresia was standing. On the wall opposite, supported by an iron bracket, a smoky oil-lamp shed a feeble, yellowish flicker around.

A few minutes went by; then a loud clatter woke the echoes of the dreary old house, and a coach drawn by two ancient, half-starved nags lumbered into the courtyard and came to a halt in front of the open doorway. The captain gave a sigh of relief, and called out: 'Now then, citoyenne!' whilst the soldier who had gone to fetch the coach jumped down from the box-seat and, with his comrades, stood at attention. The maid was summarily bundled into the coach, and Theresia was ready to follow.

Just then the draught through the open door blew her velvet cloak against the filthy rags of the miserable ruffian behind her. An unexplainable impulse caused her to look up, and she encountered his eyes fixed upon her. A dull cry rose to her throat, and instinctively she put up her hand to her mouth, striving to smother the sound. Horror dilated her eyes, and through her lips one word escaped like a hoarse murmur:

'You!'

He put a grimy finger to his lips. But already she had recovered herself. Here then was the explanation of the mystery which surrounded this monstrous denunciation. The English milor had planned it as a revenge for the injury done to his wife.

'Captain!' she cried out shrilly. 'Beware! The English spy is at your heels!'

But apparently the captain's complaisance did not go to the length of listening to the ravings of his fair prisoner. He was impatient to get this unpleasant business over.

'Now then, citoyenne!' was his gruff retort. 'En voiture!'

'You fool!' she cried, bracing herself against the grip of the soldiers who were on the point of seizing her. ''Tis the Scarlet Pimpernel! If you let him escape—'

'The Scarlet Pimpernel?' the captain retorted with a laugh. 'Where?'

'The coal-heaver! Rateau! 'Tis he, I tell you!' And Theresia's cries became more frantic as she felt herself unceremoniously lifted off the ground. 'You fool! You fool! You are letting him escape!'

'Rateau, the coal-heaver?' the captain exclaimed. 'We have heard that pretty story before. Here, citizen Rateau!' he went on, and shouted at the top of his voice. 'Go and report yourself to citizen Chauvelin. Tell him you are the Scarlet Pimpernel! As for you, citoyenne, enough of this shouting – what? My orders are to take you to the Conciergerie, and not to run after spies – English, German, or Dutch. Now then, citizen soldiers! . . .'

Theresia, throwing her dignity to the winds, did indeed raise a shout that brought the other lodgers of the house to their door. But her screams had become inarticulate, as the soldiers, in obedience to the captain's impatient orders, had wrapped her cloak about her head. Thus the inhabitants of the dreary old house in the Rue Villedot could only ascertain that the citoyenne Cabarrus who lodged on the third floor had been taken to prison, screaming and fighting, in a manner that no self-respecting aristo had ever done.

Theresia Cabarrus was ignominiously lifted into the coach and deposited by the side of equally noisy Pepita. Through the folds of the cloak her reiterated cry could still faintly be heard:

'You fool! You traitor! You cursed, miserable fool!'

One of the lodgers on the second floor – a young woman who was on good terms with every male creature that wore uniform – leaned over the balustrade of the balcony and shouted gaily down:

'Hey, citizen captain! Why is the aristo screaming so?'

One of the soldiers looked up, and shouted back:

'She has hold of the story that citizen Rateau is an English milor in disguise, and she wants to run after him!'

Loud laughter greeted this tale, and a lusty cheer was set up as the coach swung clumsily out of the courtyard.

A moment or two later, Chauvelin, followed by the two soldiers, came quickly down the stairs. The noise from below had at last reached his ears. At first he too thought that it was only the proud Spaniard who was throwing her dignity to the winds. Then a word or two sounded clearly above the din:

'The Scarlet Pimpernel! The English spy!'

The words acted like a sorcerer's charm – a call from the vasty deep. In an instant the rest of the world ceased to have any importance in his sight. One thing and one alone mattered; his enemy.

Calling to the soldiers to follow him, he was out of the apartment and down in the vestibule below in a trice. The coach at that moment was turning out of the porte-cochère. The courtyard, wrapped in gloom, was alive with chattering and laughter which proceeded from the windows and balconies around. It was raining fast, and from the balconies the water was pouring down in torrents.

Chauvelin stood in the doorway and sent one of the soldiers to ascertain what the disturbance had all been about. The man returned with an account of how the aristo had screamed and raved like a mad-woman, and tried to escape by sending the citizen captain on a fool's errand, vowing that poor old Rateau was an English spy in disguise.

Chauvelin gave a sigh of relief. He certainly need not rack his nerves or break his head over that! He had good cause to know that Rateau, with the branded arm, could not possibly be the Scarlet Pimpernel!

CHAPTER 32

Grey Dawn

I

Ten minutes later the courtyard and approach of the old house in the Rue Villedot were once more wrapped in silence and in darkness. Chauvelin had with his own hands affixed the official seals on the doors which led to the apartments of citoyenne Cabarrus. In the living room, the body of the unfortunate Moncrif still lay uncovered and unwatched, awaiting what hasty burial the commissary of the section would be pleased to order for it. Chauvelin dismissed the soldiers at the door, and himself went his way.

Tallien hurried along on foot to the Rue Villedot. The last hour had been positive torture for him. Although his reason told him that no man would be fool enough to trump up an accusation against Theresia Cabarrus, who was the friend, the Egeria of every influential man in the Convention or the Clubs, and that she herself had always been far too prudent to allow herself to be compromised in any way – although he knew all that, his overwrought fancy conjured up visions which made him sick with dread. His Theresia in the hands of rough soldiery – dragged to prison – he himself unable to ascertain what had become of her – until he saw her at the bar of that awful tribunal, from which there was no issue save the guillotine!

And with this dread came unendurable, gnawing remorse. He himself was one of the men who had helped to set up the machinery of wild accusations, monstrous tribunals and wholesale condemnations which had been set in motion now by an unknown hand against the woman he loved. He – Tallien – the ardent lover, the future husband of Theresia, had aided in the constitution of that abominable Revolutionary Committee, which could strike at the innocent as readily and as ruthlessly as at the guilty.

Indeed at this hour, this man, who long since had forgotten how to pray, when he heard the tower-clock of a neighbouring church striking the hour, turned his eyes that were blurred with tears toward the sacred edifice which he had helped to desecrate, and found in his heart a half-remembered prayer which he murmured to the Fount of all Mercy and of Pardon.

II

Citizen Tallien turned into the Rue Villedot, the street where lodged his beloved. A minute or so later, he was making his way up the back staircase of the dingy house where his divinity had dwelt until now. On the second-floor landing two women stood gossiping. One of them recognised the influential Representative.

'It is citizen Tallien,' she said.

And the other woman at once volunteered the information:

'They have arrested the citoyenne Cabarrus,' she said; 'and the soldiers did not know whither they were taking her.'

Tallien did not want to listen further. He stumbled up the stairs to the third floor, to the door which he knew so well. His trembling fingers wandered over the painted panels. They encountered the official seals, which told their own mute tale.

The whole thing, then, was not a dream. Those assassins had taken his Theresia and dragged her to prison, would drag her on the morrow to an outrageous mockery of a tribunal first, and then to death! Who shall say what wild thoughts of retrospection and of remorse coursed through the brain of this man – himself one of the makers of a bloody revolution?

For hours citizen Tallien sat in the dark, on the staircase outside Theresia's door, his head buried in his hands. The grey dawn, livid and chill, which came peeping in through the skylight overhead, found him still sitting there, stiff and numb with cold.

Whether what happened after that was part of a dream, he never knew. Certain it is that presently something extraneous appeared to rouse him. He sat up and listened, leaned his back against the wall, for he was very tired. Then he heard – or thought he heard – firm, swift steps on the stairs, and soon after saw the figures of two men coming up the stairs. Both the men were very tall, one of them unusually so, and the ghostly light of dawn made him appear unreal and mysterious. He was dressed with marvellous elegance; his smooth, fair hair was tied at the nape of the neck with a satin bow; soft, billowy lace gleamed at his wrists and throat, and his hands were exquisitely white and slender. Both the men wore huge coats of fine cloth, adorned with many capes, and boots of fine leather, perfectly cut.

They paused on the vestibule outside the door of Theresia's apartment, and appeared to be studying the official seals affixed upon the door. Then one of them – the taller of the two – took a knife out of his pocket and cut through the tapes which held the seals together. Then together they stepped coolly into the apartment.

Tallien had watched them, dazed and fascinated. He was so numb and weary that his tongue – just like it does in dreams – refused him service when he tried to call. But now he struggled to his feet and followed in the wake of the two mysterious strangers. With him, the instinct of the official, the respect due to regulations and laws framed by his colleagues and himself, had been too strong to allow him to tamper with the seals, and there was something mysterious and awesome about that tall figure of a man, dressed with supreme elegance, whose slender, firm hands had so unconcernedly committed this flagrant breach of the law. It did not occur to Tallien to call for help. Somehow, the whole incident – the two men – were so ghostlike, that he felt that at a word they would vanish into thin air.

He stepped cautiously into the familiar little antechamber. The strangers had gone through to the living-room. One of them was kneeling on the floor. Tallien, who knew nothing of the tragedy which had been enacted inside the apartment of his beloved, marvelled what the men were doing. He crept stealthily forward and craned his neck to see. The window at the end of the room had been left unfastened. A weird grey streak of light came peeping in and illumined the awesome scene: the overturned furniture, the torn hangings; and on the ground, the body of a man, with the stranger kneeling beside it.

Tallien, weary and dazed, always of a delicate constitution, felt nigh to swooning. His knees were shaking, a cold dread of the supernatural held his heart with an icy grip and caused his hair to tingle at the roots. His tongue felt huge and as if paralysed, his teeth were chattering together. It was as much as he could do not to measure his length on the ground; and the vague desire to remain unobserved kept him crouching in the gloom.

He could just see the tall stranger pass his hands over the body on the floor, and could hear the other ask him a question in English.

A few moments went by. The strangers conversed in a low tone of voice. From one or two words which came clearly to his ear, Tallien gathered that they spoke in English – a language with which he himself was familiar. The taller man of the two appeared to be giving his friend some orders, which the latter promised to obey. Then, with utmost precaution, he took the body in his arms and lifted it from the floor.

'Let me help you, Blakeney,' the other said in a whisper.

'No, no!' the mysterious stranger replied quickly. 'The poor worm is as light as a feather! 'Tis better he died as he did. His unfortunate infatuation was killing him.'

'Poor little Régine!' the younger man sighed.

'It is better so,' his friend rejoined. 'We'll be able to tell her that he died nobly, and that we've given him Christian burial.'

No wonder that Tallien thought that he was dreaming! These English were a strange folk indeed! Heaven alone knew what they risked by coming here, at this hour, and into this house, in order to fetch away the body of their friend. They certainly were wholly unconscious of danger.

Tallien held his breath. He saw the splendid figure of the mysterious adventurer step across the threshold, bearing the lifeless body in his arms with as much ease as if he were carrying a child. The pale grey light of morning was behind him, and his fine head with its smooth fair hair was silhouetted against the neutral-tinted background. His friend came immediately behind him.

In the dark antechamber he paused, and called abruptly:

'Citizen Tallien!'

A cry rose to Tallien's throat. He had thought himself entirely unobserved, and the stranger a mere vision which he was watching in a dream. Now he felt that compelling eyes were gazing straight at him, piercing the darkness for a clearer sight of his face.

But the spell was still on him, and he only moved in order to straighten himself out and to force his trembling knees to be still.

'They have taken the citoyenne Cabarrus to the Conciergerie,' the stranger went on simply. 'Tomorrow she will be charged before the Revolutionary Tribunal. . . . You know what is the inevitable end—'

It seemed as if some subtle magic was in the man's voice, in his very presence, in the glance wherewith he challenged that of the unfortunate Tallien. The latter felt a wave of shame sweep over him. There was something so splendid in these two men – exquisitely dressed, and perfectly deliberate and cool in all their movements – who were braving and daring death in order to give Christian burial to their friend; whilst he, in face of the outrage put upon his beloved, had only sat on her desecrated doorstep like a dumb animal pining for its master. He felt a hot flush rush to his cheeks. With quick, nervy movements he readjusted the set of his coat, passed his thin hands over his rumpled hair; whilst the stranger reiterated with solemn significance:

'You know what is the inevitable end. . . . The citoyenne Cabarrus will be condemned. . . .'

Tallien this time met the stranger's eyes fearlessly. It was the magic of strength and of courage that flowed into him from them.

'Not while I live!' he said firmly.

'Theresia Cabarrus will be condemned tomorrow,' the

stranger went on calmly. 'Then the next day, the guillotine—'

'Never!'

'Inevitably! . . . Unless—'

'Unless what?' Tallien queried, and hung breathless on the man's lips as he would on those of an oracle.

'Theresia Cabarrus, or Robespierre and his herd of assassins. Which shall it be, citizen Tallien?'

'By heaven!—' Tallien exclaimed forcefully.

But he got no further. The stranger, bearing his burden, had already gone out of the room, closely followed by his friend.

Tallien was alone in the deserted apartment, where every broken piece of furniture, every torn curtain, cried out for vengeance in the name of his beloved. He said nothing. He neither protested nor swore. But he tiptoed into the apartment and knelt down upon the floor close beside the small sofa on which she was wont to sit. Here he remained quite still for a minute or two, his eyes closed, his hands tightly clasped together. Then he stooped very low and pressed his lips against the spot where her pretty, sandalled foot was wont to rest.

After that he rose, strode with a firm step out of the apartment, carefully closing the doors behind him.

The strangers had vanished into the night; and citizen Tallien went quietly back to his own lodgings.

CHAPTER 33

The Cataclysm

I

Forty names! Found on a list in the pocket of Robespierre's coat!

Forty names! And every one of these that of a known opponent of Robespierre's schemes of dictatorship: Tallien, Barrère, Vadier, Cambon, and the rest. Men powerful today, prominent Members of the Convention, leaders of the people, too – but opponents!

The inference was obvious, the panic general. That night – it was the 8th Thermidor, July the 26th of the old calendar – men talked of flight, of abject surrender, of appeal – save the mark! – to friendship, camaraderie, humanity! Friendship, camaraderie, humanity? An appeal to a heart of stone! They talked of everything, in fact, save of defying the tyrant; for such talk would have been folly.

Defying the tyrant? Ye gods! When with a word he could sway the Convention, the Committees, the multitude, bend them to his will, bring them to heel like any tamer of beasts when he cracks his whip?

So men talked and trembled. All night they talked and trembled; for they did not sleep, those forty whose names were on Robespierre's list. But Tallien, their chief, was nowhere to be found. 'Twas known that his fiancée, the beautiful Theresia Cabarrus, had been summarily arrested. Since then he had disappeared; and they – the others – were leaderless. But, even so, he was no loss. Tallien was ever pusillanimous, a temporiser – what?

And now the hour for temporising is past. Robespierre then is to be dictator of France. He *will* be dictator of France, in spite of any opposition led by those forty whose names are on his list! He *will* be dictator of France! He has not said it; but his friends have shouted it from the house-tops, and have murmured under their breath that those who oppose Robespierre's dictatorship are traitors to the land. Death then must be their fate.

What then, ye gods? What then?

II

And so the day broke – smiling, mark you! It was a beautiful warm July morning. It broke on what is perhaps the most stupendous cataclysm – save one – the world has ever known.

Behold the picture! A medley. A confusion. A whirl of everything that is passionate and cruel, defiant and desperate. Heavens, how desperate! Men who have thrown lives away as if lives were in truth grains of sand; men who have juggled with death, dealt it and tossed it about like cards upon a gaming table. They are desperate now, because their own lives are at stake; and they find now that life can be very dear.

So, having greeted their leader, the forty draw together,

watching the moment when humility will be most opportune.

Robespierre mounts the tribune. The hour has struck. His speech is one long, impassioned, involved tirade, full at first of vague accusations against the enemies of the Republic and the people, and is full of protestations of his own patriotism and selflessness. Then he warms to his own oratory; his words are prophetic of death, his voice becomes harsh – like a screech owl's, so we're told. His accusations are no longer vague. He begins to strike.

Corruption! Backsliding! Treachery! Moderatism! – oh, moderatism above all! Moderatism is treachery to the glorious revolution. Every victim spared from the guillotine is a traitor let loose against the people! A traitor, he who robs the guillotine of her prey! Robespierre stands alone incorruptible, true, faithful unto death!

And for all that treachery, what remedy is there? Why, death of course! Death! The guillotine! New power to the sovereign guillotine! Death to all the traitors!

And seven hundred faces become paler still with dread, and the sweat of terror rises on seven hundred brows. There were only forty names on that list . . . but there might be others somewhere else!

And still the voice of Robespierre thunders on. His words fall on seven hundred pairs of ears like on a sounding-board; his friends, his sycophants, echo them; they applaud, rise in wild enthusiasm. 'Tis the applause that is thundering now!

One of the tyrant's most abject slaves has put forward the motion that the great speech just delivered shall forthwith be printed, and distributed to every township, every village, throughout France, as a monument to the lofty patriotism of her greatest citizen.

The motion at one moment looks as if it would be carried with acclamations; after which, Robespierre's triumph would have risen to the height of deification. Then suddenly the note of dissension; the hush; the silence. The great Assembly is like a sounding-board that has ceased to respond. Something has turned the acclamations to mutterings, and then to silence. The sounding-board has given forth a dissonance. Citizen Tallien has demanded 'delay in printing that speech,' and asked pertinently:

'What has become of the Liberty of Opinion in this Convention?'

His face is the colour of ashes, and his eyes, ringed with purple, gleam with an unnatural fire. The coward has become bold; the sheep has donned the lion's skin.

There is a flutter in the Convention, a moment's hesitation. But the question *is* put to the vote, and the speech is *not* to be printed. A small matter, in truth – printing or not printing. . . . Does the Destiny of France hang on so small a peg?

It is a small matter; and yet how full of portent! Like the breath of mutiny blowing across a ship. But nothing more occurs just then. Robespierre, lofty in his scorn, puts the notes of his speech into his pocket. He does not condescend to argue. He, the master of France, will not deign to bandy words with his slaves. And he stalks out of the Hall surrounded by his friends.

There *has* been a breath of mutiny; but his is still the iron heel, powerful enough to crush a raging revolt. His withdrawal – proud, silent, menacing – is in keeping with his character and with the pose which he has assumed of late. But he is still the Chosen of the People; and the multitude is there, thronging the streets of Paris – there, to avenge the insult put upon their idol by a pack of slinking wolves.

III

And now the picture becomes still more poignant. It is painted in colours more vivid, more glowing than before. The morning breaks on the 9th Thermidor, and again the Hall of the Convention is crowded to the roof, with Tallien and his friends, in a close phalanx, early at their post!

Tallien is there, pale, resolute, the fire of his hatred kept up by anxiety for his beloved. The night before, at the corner of a dark street, a surreptitious hand slipped a scrap of paper into the pocket of his coat. It was a message written by Theresia in prison, and written with her own blood. How it ever came into his pocket Tallien never knew; but the few impassioned, agonised words seared his very soul and whipped up his courage:

'The Commissary of Police has just left me,' Theresia wrote. 'He came to tell me that tomorrow I must appear before the tribunal. This means the guillotine. And I, who thought that you were a *man* . . . !'

Not only is his own head in peril, not only that of his friends; but the life of the woman whom he worships hangs now upon the thread of his own audacity and of his courage.

St Just on this occasion is the first to mount the tribune; and Robespierre, the very incarnation of lustful and deadly Vengeance, stands silently by. He has spent the afternoon and evening with his friends at the Jacobins' Club, where deafening applause greeted his every word, and wild fury raged against his enemies.

To the guillotine all those who have dared to say one word against the Chosen of the People! St Just shall thunder Vengeance from the tribune at the Convention, whilst Henriot, the drunken and dissolute Commandant of the

Municipal Guard, shall, by the might of sword and fire, proclaim the sovereignty of Robespierre through the streets of Paris. That is the picture as it has been painted in the minds of the tyrant and of his sycophants: a picture of death paramount, and of Robespierre rising like a new Phoenix from out the fire of calumny and revolt, greater, more unassailable than before.

And lo! One sweep of the brush, and the picture is changed.

Ten minutes . . . less . . . and the whole course of the world's history is altered. No sooner has St Just mounted the tribune than Tallien jumps to his feet. His voice, usually meek and cultured, rises in a harsh crescendo, until it drowns that of the younger orator.

'Citizens,' he exclaims, 'I ask for truth! Let us tear aside the curtain behind which lurk concealed the real conspirators and the traitors!'

'Yes, yes! Truth! Let us have the truth!' One hundred voices – not forty – have raised the echo.

The mutiny is on the verge of becoming open revolt, is that already, perhaps. It is like a spark fallen – who knows where? – into a powder magazine. Robespierre feels it, sees the spark. He knows one movement, one word, one plunge into that magazine, foredoomed though it be to destruction, one stamp with a sure foot, may yet quench the spark, may yet smother the mutiny. He rushes to the tribune, tries to mount. But Tallien has forestalled him, elbows him out of the way, and turns to the seven hundred with a cry that rings far beyond the Hall, out into the streets.

'Citizens!' he thunders in his turn. 'I begged of you just now to tear aside the curtains behind which lurk the traitors. Well, the curtain is already rent. And if you dare not strike at the tyrant now, then 'tis I who will dare!' And from beneath his coat he draws a dagger and raises it above his head. 'And

I will plunge this into his heart!' he cries, 'if you have not the courage to smite!'

His words, that gleaming bit of steel, fan the spark into a flame. Within a few seconds, seven hundred voices are shouting, 'Down with the tyrant!' Arms are waving, hands gesticulate wildly, excitedly. Only a very few shout: 'Behold the dagger of Brutus!' All the others retort with 'Tyranny!' and 'Conspiracy!' and with cries of 'Vive la Liberté!'

At this hour all is confusion and deafening uproar. In vain Robespierre tries to speak. He demands to speak. He hurls insults, anathema, upon the President, who relentlessly refuses him speech and jingles his bell against him.

'President of Assassins,' the falling tyrant cries, 'I demand speech of thee!'

But the bell goes jingling on, and Robespierre, choked with rage and terror, 'turns blue' we are told, and his hand goes up to his throat.

'The blood of Danton chokes thee!' cries one man. And these words seem like the last blow dealt to the fallen foe. The next moment the voice of an obscure Deputy is raised, in order to speak the words that have been hovering on every lip:

'I demand a decree of accusation against Robespierre!'

'Accusation!' comes from seven hundred throats. 'The decree of accusation!'

The President jingles his bell, puts the question, and the motion is passed unanimously.

Maximilien Robespierre – erstwhile master of France – is decreed *accused*.

CHAPTER 34

The Whirlwind

I

It was then noon. Five minutes later, the Chosen of the People, the fallen idol, is hustled out of the Hall into one of the Committee rooms close by, and with his friends – St Just, Couthon, Lebas, his brother Augustin, and the others – all decreed accused and the order of arrest launched against them. As for the rest, 'tis the work of the Public Prosecutor – and of the guillotine.

At five o'clock the Convention adjourns. The deputies have earned food and rest. They rush to their homes, there to relate what has happened; Tallien to the Conciergerie, to get a sight of Theresia. This is denied him. He is not dictator yet; and Robespierre, though apparently vanquished, still dominates – and lives.

But from every church steeple the tocsin bursts; and a prolonged roll of drums ushers in the momentous evening.

In the city all is hopeless confusion. Men are running in every direction, shouting, brandishing pistols and swords. Henriot, Commandant of the Municipal Guard, rides through the streets at the head of his gendarmes like one possessed, bent on delivering Robespierre. Women and children fly screaming in every direction; the churches, so long deserted, are packed with people who, terror-stricken, are trying to remember long-forgotten prayers.

Proclamations are read at street corners; there are rumours of a general massacre of all the prisoners. At one moment – the usual hour – the familiar tumbril with its load of victims for the guillotine rattles along the cobblestones of the Rue St Antoine. The populace, vaguely conscious of something stupendous in the air – even though the decree of accusation against Robespierre has not yet transpired – loudly demand the release of the victims. They surround the tumbrils, crying, 'Let them be free!'

But Henriot at the head of his gendarmes comes riding down the street, and while the populace shouts, 'It shall not be! Let them be free!' he threatens with pistols and sabre, and retorts, bellowing: 'It shall be! To the guillotine!' And the tumbrils, which for a moment had halted, lumber on, on their way.

II

Up in the attic of the lonely house in the Rue de la Planchette, Marguerite Blakeney heard but a mere faint echo of the confusion and of the uproar.

During the previous long, sultry afternoon, it had seemed to her as if her jailers had been unwontedly agitated. There was much more moving to and fro on the landing outside her door than there had been in the last three days. Men talked, mostly in whispers; but at times a word, a phrase here and there, a voice raised above the others, reached her straining ears.

But it was all very vague, for her nerves by this time were on the rack. She had lost count of time, of place; she knew nothing. She was unable even to think. All her instincts were merged in the dread of that silent evening hour, when Chauvelin's furtive footsteps would once more resound upon the stone floor outside her door, when she would hear the quick word of command that heralded his approach, the grounding of arms, the sharp query and quick answer, and when she would feel again the presence of the relentless enemy who lay in wait to trap her beloved.

At one moment that evening he had raised his voice, obviously so that she might hear.

'Tomorrow is the fourth day, citizen Captain,' she had heard him say. 'I may not be able to come.'

'Then,' the voice of the Captain had said in reply, 'if the Englishman is not here by seven o'clock—'

Chauvelin had given a harsh, dry laugh, and retorted:

'Your orders are as they were, citizen. But I think that the Englishman will come.'

What it all meant Marguerite could not fail to conjecture. It meant death to her or to her husband – or both, in fact. And all today she had sat by the open window, her hands clasped in silent, constant prayer, her eyes fixed upon the horizon far away, longing with all her might for one last sight of her beloved, fighting against despair, striving for trust in him and for hope.

III

At this hour, the centre of interest is the Place de l'Hôtel de Ville, where Robespierre and his friends sit entrenched and – for the moment – safe. The prisons have refused one by one to close their gates upon the Chosen of the People; governors and jailers alike have quaked in the face of so monstrous a sacrilege. And the same gendarmes who have been told off to escort the fallen tyrant to his penultimate resting-place, have had a touch of the same kind of scruple – or dread – and at his command have conveyed him to the Hôtel de Ville.

In vain does the Convention hastily re-assemble. In vain – apparently – does Tallien demand that the traitor Robespierre and his friends be put outside the pale of the law. They are for the moment safe, redacting proclamations, sending out messengers in every direction; whilst Henriot and his gendarmes, having struck terror in the hearts of all peaceable citizens, hold the place outside the Town Hall and proclaim Robespierre dictator of France.

The sun sinks towards the west behind a veil of mist. Ferment and confusion are at their height. All around the city there is an invisible barrier that seems to confine agitation within its walls. Outside this barrier, no one knows what is happening. The guard at the several gates appear slack and undisciplined. Sentries are accosted by passers-by, eager for news. And, from time to time, from every direction, troops of the Municipal gendarmes ride furiously by, with shouts of 'Robespierre! Robespierre! Death to the traitors! Long live Robespierre!'

They raise a cloud of dust around them, trample unheedingly over every obstacle, human or otherwise, that happens to be in their way. They threaten peaceable citizens with their pistols and strike at women and children with the flat of their sabres.

As soon as they have gone by, excited groups close up in their wake.

'Name of a name, what is happening?' every one queries in affright.

And gossip, conjectures, rumours, hold undisputed sway.

'Robespierre is dictator of France!'

'He has ordered the arrest of all the Members of the Convention.'

'And the massacre of all the prisoners.'

'Pardi, a wise decree! As for me, I am sick of the eternal tumbrils and the guillotine!'

'Better finish with the lot, say I!'

'Robespierre! Robespierre!' comes as a far-off echo, to the accompaniment of thundering hoofs upon the cobblestones.

And so, from mouth to mouth! The meek and the peace-loving magnify these rumours into approaching cataclysm; the opportunists hold their tongue, ready to fall in with this party or that; the cowards lie in hiding and shout 'Robespierre!' with Henriot's horde or 'Tallien!' in the neighbourhood of the Tuileries.

Here the Convention has reassembled and here they are threatened presently by Henriot and his artillery. The members of the great Assembly remain at their post. The President has harangued them.

'Citizen deputies!' he calls aloud. 'The moment has come to die at our posts!'

Tallien, moved by a spirit of lofty courage, goes, followed by a few intimates, to meet Henriot's gunners boldly face to face.

'Citizen soldiers!' he calls aloud, and his voice has the resonance of undaunted courage. 'After covering yourselves with glory on the fields of honour, are you going to disgrace your country?' He points a scornful finger at Henriot who, bloated, purple in the face, grunting and spluttering like an old seal, is reeling in his saddle. 'Look at him, citizen soldiers!' Tallien commands. 'He is drunk and besotted! What man is there who, being sober, would dare to order fire against the representatives of the people?'

The gunners are moved, frightened too by the decree which has placed them 'outside the pale of the law.' Henriot, fearing mutiny if he persisted in the monstrous order to fire, withdraws his troops back to the Hôtel de Ville.

Some follow him; some do not. And Tallien goes back to the Hall of the Convention covered with glory.

Citizen Barras is promoted Commandant of the National Guard and of all forces at the disposal of the Convention, and ordered to recruit loyal troops that will stand up to the traitor Henriot and his ruffianly gendarmes. The latter are in open revolt against the Government; but, name of a name! Citizen Barras, with a few hundred patriots, will soon put reason – and a few charges of gunpowder – into them!

IV

So, at five o'clock in the afternoon, whilst Henriot had once more collected his gendarmes and the remnants of his artillery outside the Hôtel de Ville, citizen Barras, accompanied by two aides-de-camp, goes forth on his recruiting mission. He makes the round of the city gates, wishing to find out what loyal soldiers amongst the National Guard the Convention can rely upon.

Chauvelin, on his way to the Rue de Planchette, meets Barras at the Porte St Antoine; and Barras is full of the news.

'Why were you not at your place at the Assembly, citizen Chauvelin?' he asks of his colleague. 'It was the grandest moment I have ever witnessed! Tallien was superb, and Robespierre ignoble! And if we succeed in crushing that bloodthirsty monster once and for all, it will be a new era of civilisation and liberty!'

He halts, and continues with a fretful sigh:

'But we want soldiers – loyal soldiers! All the troops that we can get! Henriot has the whole of the Municipal Gendarmerie at his command, with muskets and guns; and Robespierre can always sway that rabble with a word. We want men! . . . Men! . . .'

But Chauvelin is in no mood to listen. Robespierre's fall or his triumph, what are they to him at this hour, when the curtain is about to fall on the final act of his own stupendous drama of revenge? Whatever happens, whoever remains in power, vengeance is his! The English spy in any event is sure of the guillotine. He is not the enemy of a party, but of the people of France. And the sovereignty of the people is not in question yet. Then, what matters if the wild beasts in the Convention are at one another's throat?

So Chauvelin listens unmoved to Barras' passionate tirades, and when the latter, puzzled at his colleague's indifference, reiterates frowning:

'I must have all the troops I can get. You have some capable soldiers at your command always, citizen Chauvelin. Where are they now?'

Chauvelin retorts drily:

'At work. On business at least as important as taking sides in a quarrel between Robespierre and Tallien.'

'Pardi! . . .' Barras protests hotly.

But Chauvelin pays no further attention to him. A neighbouring church clock has just struck six. Within the hour his arch-enemy will be in his hands! Never for a moment does he doubt that the bold adventurer will come to the lonely house in the Rue de la Planchette. Even hating the

Englishman as he does, he knows that the latter would not endanger his wife's safety by securing his own.

So Chauvelin turns on his heel, leaving Barras to fume and to threaten. At the angle of the Porte St Antoine, he stumbles against and nearly knocks over a man who sits on the ground, with his back to the wall, munching a straw, his knees drawn up to his nose, a crimson cap pulled over his eyes, and his two long arms encircling his shins.

Chauvelin swore impatiently. His nerves were on the rack, and he was in no pleasant mood. The man, taken unawares, had uttered an oath, which died away in a racking fit of coughing. Chauvelin looked down, and saw the one long arm branded with the letter 'M,' the flesh still swollen and purple with the fire of the searing iron.

'Rateau!' he ejaculated roughly. 'What are you doing here?'

'I have finished my work at Mother Théot's, citizen,' he said humbly. 'I was resting.'

Chauvelin kicked at him with the toe of his boot.

'Then go and rest elsewhere,' he muttered. 'The gates of the city are not refuges for vagabonds.'

After which act of unnecessary brutality, his temper momentarily soothed, he turned on his heel and walked rapidly through the gate.

Barras had stood by during this brief interlude, vaguely interested in the little scene. But now, when the coal-heaver lurched past him, one of his aide-de-camp remarked audibly:

'An unpleasant customer, citizen Chauvelin! Eh, friend?'

'I believe you!' Rateau replied readily enough. Then, with the mulish persistence of a gaby who is smarting under a wrong, he thrust out his branded arm, right under citizen Barras' nose. 'See what he has done to me!'

'A convict, what? Then, how is it you are at large?'

'I am not a convict,' Rateau protested with sullen emphasis. 'I am an innocent man, and a free citizen of the Republic. But I got in citizen Chauvelin's way, what? He is always full of schemes—'

'You are right there!' Barras retorted grimly. But the subject was not sufficiently interesting to engross his attention further. He had so many and such momentous things to do. Already he had nodded to his men and turned his back on the grimy coal-heaver, who, shaken by a fit of coughing, unable to speak for the moment, had put out his grimy hand and gripped the deputy firmly by the sleeve.

'What is it now?' Barras ejaculated roughly.

'If you will but listen, citizen,' Rateau wheezed painfully, 'I can tell you—'

'What?'

'You were asking citizen Chauvelin where you could find some soldiers of the Republic to do you service.'

'Yes; I did.'

'Well,' Rateau rejoined, and an expression of malicious cunning distorted his ugly face. 'I can tell you.'

'What do you mean?'

'I lodge in an empty warehouse over yonder,' Rateau went on eagerly, and pointed in the direction where Chauvelin's spare figure had disappeared a while ago. 'The floor above is inhabited by Mother Théot, the witch. You know her, citizen?'

'Yes, yes! I thought she had been sent to the guillotine along with—'

'She was let out of prison, and has been doing some of citizen Chauvelin's spying for him.'

Barras frowned. This was none of his business, and the dirty coal-heaver inspired him with an unpleasant sense of loathing.

'To the point, citizen!' he said curtly.

319

'Citizen Chauvelin has a dozen or more soldiers under his command, in that house,' Rateau went on with a leer. 'They are trained troops of the National Guard—'

'How do you know?' Barras broke in harshly.

'Pardi!' was the coal-heaver's dry reply. 'I clean their boots for them.'

'Where is the house?'

'In the Rue de la Planchette. But there is an entrance into the warehouse at the back of it.'

'Allons!' was Barras' curt word of command, to the two men who accompanied him.

He strode up the street toward the gate, not caring whether Rateau came along or no. But the coal-heaver followed in the wake of the three men. He had buried his grimy fists once more in the pockets of his tattered breeches; but not before he had shaken them, each in turn, in the direction of the Rue de la Planchette.

V

Chauvelin in the meanwhile had turned into Mother Théot's house, and without speaking to the old charlatan, who was watching for him in the vestibule, he mounted to the top floor. Here he called peremptorily to Captain Boyer.

'There is half an hour yet,' the latter muttered gruffly; 'and I am sick of all this waiting! Let me finish with this cursed aristo in there. My comrades and I want to see what is going on in the city, and join in the fun, if there is any.'

'Half an hour, citizen,' Chauvelin rejoined drily. 'You'll

lose little of the fun, and you'll certainly lose your share of the ten thousand livres if you shoot the woman and fail to capture the Scarlet Pimpernel.'

'Bah! He'll not come now,' Boyer riposted. 'It is too late. He is looking after his own skin, pardi!'

'He will come, I swear!' Chauvelin said firmly.

Inside the room, Marguerite had heard every word of this colloquy. Its meaning is clear enough. Clear, and horrible! Death awaits her at the hands of those abominable ruffians – here – within half an hour – unless. . . . Her thoughts are becoming confused; she cannot concentrate. Frightened? No, she is not frightened. She has looked death in the face before now. That time in Boulogne. And there are worse things than death. . . . There is, for instance, the fear that she might never see her husband again . . . in this life. . . . There is only half an hour or less than that . . . and . . . and he might not come. . . . She prays that he might not come. But, if he does, then what chance has he? My God, what chance?

A distant church clock strikes the half-hour . . . a short half-hour now. . . .

The evening is sultry. Another storm is threatening, and the sun has tinged the heat-mist with red. The air smells foul, as in the midst of a huge, perspiring crowd. And through the heat, the lull, above the hideous sounds of those ruffians outside her door, there is a rumbling noise as of distant, unceasing thunder. The city is in travail.

Then suddenly Boyer, the Captain of the ruffians, exclaims loudly:

'Let me finish with the aristo, citizen Chauvelin! I want to join in the fun.'

And the door of her room is torn open by a savage, violent hand.

The window behind Marguerite is open, and she, facing

the door, clings with both hands to the sill. Her cheeks bloodless, her eyes glowing, her head erect, she waits, praying with all her might for courage . . . only courage.

The ruffianly captain, in his tattered, mud-stained uniform, stands in the doorway – for one moment only. The next, Chauvelin has elbowed him out of the way, and in his turn faces the prisoner – the innocent woman whom he has pursued with such relentless hatred. Marguerite prays with all her might, and does not flinch. Not for one second. Death stands there before her in the guise of this man's vengeful lust, which gleams in his pale eyes. Death is there waiting for her, under the guise of those ignoble soldiers in the scrubby rags, with their muskets held in stained, filthy hands.

Courage – only courage! The power to die as *he* would wish her to . . . could he but know!

Chauvelin speaks to her; she does not hear. There is a mighty buzzing in her ears as of men shouting – shouting what, she does not know, for she is still praying for courage. Chauvelin has ceased talking. Then it must be the end. Thank God! she has had the courage not to speak and not to flinch. Now she closes her eyes, for there is a red mist before her and she feels that she might fall into it – straight into that mist.

VI

With closed eyes, Marguerite suddenly seems able to hear. She hears shouts which come from below – quite close, and coming nearer every moment. Shouts, and the tramp, the scurry of many feet; and now and then that wheezing, asthmatic cough, that strange, strange cough, and the click of wooden shoes. Then a voice, harsh and peremptory:

'Citizen soldiers, your country needs you! Rebels have defied her laws! To arms! Every man who hangs back is a deserter and a traitor!'

After this, Chauvelin's sharp, dictatorial voice raised in protest:

'In the name of the Republic, citizen Barras!—'

But the other breaks in more peremptorily still:

'Ah, ça, citizen Chauvelin! Do you presume to stand between me and my duty? By order of the Convention now assembled, every soldier must report at once at his section. Are you perchance on the side of the rebels?'

At this point, Marguerite opens her eyes. Through the widely open door she sees the small, sable-clad figure of Chauvelin, his pale face distorted with rage to which he obviously dare not give rein; and beside him a short, stoutish man in cloth coat and cord breeches, and with the tricolour scarf around his waist. His round face appears crimson with choler and in his right hand he grasps a heavy malacca stick, with a grip that proclaims the desire to strike. The two men appear to be defying one another; and all around them are the vague forms of soldiers silhouetted against a distant window, through which the crimson afternoon glow comes peeping in on a cloud of flickering dust.

'Now then, citizen soldiers!' Barras resumes, and incontinently turns his back on Chauvelin, who, white to the lips, raises a final and menacing word of warning.

'I warn you, citizen Barras,' he says firmly, 'that, by taking these men away from their post, you place yourself in league with the enemy of your country, and will have to answer to her for this crime.'

His accent is so convinced, so firm, and fraught with such dire menace, that for one instant Barras hesitates.

'Eh bien!' he exclaims. 'I will humour you thus far, citizen Chauvelin. I will leave you a couple of men to wait on your pleasure until sundown. But, after that. . . .'

For a second or two there is silence. Chauvelin stands there, with his thin lips pressed tightly together. Then Barras adds, with a shrug of his wide shoulders:

'I am contravening my duty in doing even so much; and the responsibility must rest with you, citizen Chauvelin. Allons, my men!' he says once more; and without another glance on his discomfited colleague, he strides down the stairs, followed by Captain Boyer and the soldiers.

For a while the house is still filled with confusion and sounds: men tramping down the stone stairs, words of command, click of sabres and muskets, opening and slamming of doors. Then the sounds slowly die away, out in the street in the direction of the Porte St Antoine. After which, there is silence.

Chauvelin stands in the doorway with his back to the room and to Marguerite, his claw-like hands intertwined convulsively behind him. The silhouettes of the two remaining soldiers are still visible; they stand silently and at attention with their muskets in their hands. Between them and Chauvelin hovers the tall, ungainly figure of a man, clothed in rags and covered in soot and coal-dust. His feet are thrust into wooden shoes, his grimy hands are stretched out each side of him; and on his left arm, just above the wrist, there is an ugly mark like the brand seared into the flesh of a convict.

Just now he looks terribly distressed with a tearing fit of coughing. Chauvelin curtly bids him stand aside; and at the same moment the church clock of St Louis, close by, strikes seven.

'Now then, citizen soldiers!' Chauvelin commands.

The soldiers grasp their muskets more firmly, and Chauvelin

raises his hand. The next instant he is thrust violently back into the room, loses his balance, and falls backward against a table, whilst the door is slammed to between him and the soldiers. From the other side of the door comes the sound of a short, sharp scuffle.

Marguerite, holding her breath, hardly realised that she lived. A second ago she was facing death; and now. . . .

Chauvelin struggled painfully to his feet. With a mighty effort and a hoarse cry of rage, he threw himself against the door. The impetus carried him further than he intended, no doubt; for at that same moment the door was opened, and he fell up against the massive form of the grimy coal-heaver, whose long arms closed round him, lifted him off the floor, and carried him like a bundle of straw to the nearest chair.

'There, my dear Mr Chambertin!' the coal-heaver said, in exceedingly light and pleasant tones. 'Let me make you quite comfortable!'

Marguerite watched – dumb and fascinated – the dexterous hands that twined a length of rope round the arms and legs of her helpless enemy, and wound his own tricolour scarf around that snarling mouth.

She scarcely dared trust her eyes and ears.

There was the hideous, dust-covered mudlark with bare feet thrust into sabots, with ragged breeches and tattered shirt; there was the cruel, mud-stained face, the purple lips, the toothless mouth; and those huge muscular arms, one of them branded like the arm of a convict, the flesh still swollen with the searing of the iron.

'I must indeed crave your ladyship's forgiveness. In very truth I am a disgusting object!'

Ah, there was the voice! – the dear, dear, merry voice! A little weary perhaps, but oh! so full of laughter and of boyish shamefacedness! To Marguerite it seemed as if God's own angels had opened to her the gates of Paradise. She did not speak; she scarce could move. All that she could do was to put out her arms.

He did not approach her, for in truth he looked a dusty object; but he dragged his ugly cap off his head, then slowly, and keeping his eyes fixed upon her, he put one knee to the ground.

'Will you ever forgive me?' he continued.

'Forgive? What?' she murmured.

'These last few days. I could not come before. You were safe for the time being. . . . That fiend was waiting for me. . . .'

She gave a shudder and closed her eyes.

'Where is he?'

He laughed his gay, irresponsible laugh, and with a slender hand, still covered with coal-dust, he pointed to the helpless figure of Chauvelin.

'Look at him!' he said. 'Doth he not look a picture?'

Marguerite ventured to look. Even at sight of her enemy bound tightly with ropes to a chair, his own tricolour scarf wound loosely round his mouth, she could not altogether suppress a cry of horror.

'What is to become of him?'

He shrugged his broad shoulders.

'I wonder!' he said lightly.

Then he rose to his feet, and went on with quaint bashfulness:

'I wonder,' he said, 'how I dare stand thus before your ladyship!'

And in a moment she was in his arms, laughing, crying, covered herself now with coal-dust and with grime.

'My beloved!' she exclaimed with a shudder of horror. 'What you must have gone through!'

'Very little, I swear!' he asserted gaily. 'But for thoughts of you, I have never enjoyed anything so much as this last phase of a glorious adventure. After our clever friend here ordered the real Rateau to be branded, so that he might know him again wherever he saw him, I had to bribe the veterinary who had done the deed, to do the same thing for me. It was not difficult. For a thousand livres the man would have branded his own mother on the nose; and I appeared before him as a man of science, eager for an experiment. He asked no questions. And, since then, whenever Chauvelin gazed contentedly on my arm, I could have screamed for joy!

'For the love of Heaven, my lady!' he added quickly, for he felt her soft, warm lips against his branded flesh; 'don't shame me over such a trifle! I shall always love that scar, for the exciting time it recalls and because it happens to be the initial of your dear name.'

He stooped down to the ground and kissed the hem of her gown.

After which he had to tell her as quickly and as briefly as he could, all that had happened in the past few days.

'It was only by risking the fair Theresia's life,' he said, 'that I could save your own. No other spur would have goaded Tallien into open revolt.'

He turned and looked down for a moment on his enemy, who lay pinioned and helpless, with hatred and baffled revenge writ plainly on the contorted face and pale, rolling eyes.

And Sir Percy Blakeney sighed, a quaint sigh of regret.

'I only regret one thing, my dear M. Chambertin,' he said after a while. 'And that is, that you and I will never measure wits again after this. Your damnable revolution is dead . . . your unsavoury occupation gone. . . . I am glad I was never tempted to kill you. I might have succumbed, and in very truth robbed the guillotine of an interesting prey. Without any doubt, they will guillotine the lot of you, my good M.

Chambertin, Robespierre tomorrow; then his friends, his sycophants, his imitators – you amongst the rest. . . . 'Tis a pity! You have so often amused me. Especially after you had put a brand on Rateau's arm, and thought you would always know him after that. Think it all out, my dear sir! Remember our happy conversation in the warehouse down below, and my denunciation of citoyenne Cabarrus. . . . You gazed upon my branded arm then and were quite satisfied. My denunciation was a false one, of course! 'Tis I who put the letters and the rags in the beautiful Theresia's apartments. But she will bear me no malice, I dare swear; for I shall have redeemed my promise. Tomorrow, after Robespierre's head has fallen, Tallien will be the greatest man in France and his Theresia a virtual queen. Think it all out, my dear Monsieur Chambertin! You have plenty of time. Some one is sure to drift up here presently, and will free you and the two soldiers, whom I left out on the landing. But no one will free you from the guillotine, when the time comes, unless I myself. . . .'

He did not finish; the rest of the sentence was merged in a merry laugh.

'A pleasant conceit – what?' he said lightly. 'I'll think on it, I promise you!'

VII

And the next day Paris went crazy with joy. Never had the streets looked more gay, more crowded. The windows were filled with spectators; the very roofs were crowded with an eager, shouting throng.

The seventeen hours of agony were ended. The tyrant

was a fallen, broken man, maimed, dumb, bullied and insulted. Aye! He, who yesterday was the Chosen of the People, the Messenger of the Most High, now sat, or rather lay, in the tumbril, with broken jaw, eyes closed, spirit already wandering on the shores of the Styx; insulted, railed at, cursed – aye, cursed! – by every woman, reviled by every child.

The end came at four in the afternoon, in the midst of acclamations, from a populace drunk with gladness – acclamations which found their echo in the whole of France, and have never ceased to re-echo to this day.

But of all that tumult, Marguerite and her husband heard but little. They lay snugly concealed the whole of that day in the quiet lodgings in the Rue de l'Anier, which Sir Percy occupied during these terribly anxious times. Here they were waited on by that asthmatic reprobate Rateau and his mother, both of whom were now rich for the rest of their days.

When the shades of evening gathered in over the jubilant city, whilst the church bells were ringing and the cannons booming, a market gardener's cart, driven by a worthy farmer and his wife, rattled out of the Porte St Antoine. It created no excitement, and suspicion was far from everybody's mind. The passports appeared in order; but even if they were not, who cared, on this day of all days, when tyranny was crushed and men dared to be men again?